ANIMAL ARK

Special three-in-one
Hardback Gift Edition
for W H Smith

Lamb in the Laundry
Bunnies in the Bathroom
Donkey on the Doorstep

LUCY DANIELS

Lamb
—in the—
Laundry

Illustrations by Shelagh McNicholas

Hodder
Children's
Books

a division of Hodder Headline plc

This edition of Lamb in the Laundry, Bunnies in the Bathroom and Donkey on the Doorstep first published in 1996

ISBN 0 340 69341 X

**Special thanks to C. J. Hall, B.Vet.Med., M.R.C.V.S.,
for reviewing the veterinary material contained in this book.**

Lamb in the Laundry
Special thanks to Helen Magee

Text copyright © Ben M. Baglio 1995
Created by Ben M. Baglio, London W6 0HE
Illustrations copyright © Shelagh McNicholas 1995

First published as a single volume in Great Britain in 1996
by Hodder Children's Books

The right of Lucy Daniels to be identified as the Author of the Work
has been asserted by her in accordance with the Copyright, Designs
and Patents Act 1988.

10 9 8 7 6 5 4 3 2 1

A Catalogue record for this book is available from the British Library

Typeset by Avon Dataset Ltd, Bidford-on-Avon, Warks

Printed and bound in Great Britain by
Mackays of Chatham PLC.

Hodder Children's Books
a division of Hodder Headline plc
338 Euston Road
London NW1 3BH

One

'Ready?' said Mr Hope.

'Just coming,' Mandy replied, smiling at her dad. 'Blackie wants to carry the picnic basket.'

Mr Hope grinned. 'So long as he doesn't eat all the food,' he said.

'Even Blackie couldn't manage all that,' said James. He pushed his glasses up his nose and bent down to Blackie. Blackie was James's Labrador. 'Put it down, Blackie,' he said.

Blackie looked up at him and wagged his tail – but he held on to the handle of the basket.

Mandy laughed. 'He isn't getting any more obedient,' she said.

James shoved his hair out of his eyes. 'Down, Blackie!' he said.

Blackie looked up at James sorrowfully and barked. The basket tumbled to the ground.

'Got it,' Mandy said, snatching it up. She looked at Blackie. 'You'll get your share of the picnic, Blackie,' she said.

'Lucky there isn't anything breakable in there,' said Mrs Hope.

Mandy looked at her mum, leaning through the kitchen window of the cottage.

'It's a wonder he could pick it up,' she said. 'What have you put in here, Mum?'

Emily Hope laughed and her green eyes danced. Her red hair shone in the sun. 'Oh, this and that,' she said. 'Enough to keep three hungry people happy.'

'And a hungry dog,' James said, grabbing Blackie's collar before he could get to the basket again.

'Enough for a siege,' said Mr Hope as he got into the car. 'Come on then. We haven't got all day.'

Mrs Hope laughed. 'But that's exactly what you have got,' she said. 'A whole day to ramble on the moors and have a picnic.'

Mandy turned to her mother. 'It's a pity you can't come, Mum,' she said.

Emily Hope shook her head. 'Somebody has to mind the surgery,' she said. 'And it's ages since your dad had a day off.'

'And I'm going to make the most of it,' Adam Hope said. 'Get in, you two – three,' he added, looking at Blackie.

Mandy and James got into the car. Blackie bounded after them.

'Have a good time,' Mrs Hope called.

Jean Knox, the surgery receptionist, appeared at the window beside her. 'Enjoy yourselves,' she said.

Mandy looked back as the car drove out of Animal Ark's driveway. Mrs Hope and Jean waved from the kitchen window. It was a lovely sunny morning and Mandy wished her mum could have come with them. She sighed.

Mr Hope turned his head. 'Someone has to look after the animals,' he said.

Mandy nodded. Animal Ark was a busy veterinary practice and both her parents were vets. They didn't have much free time. And Mum was right: it had been ages since Mr Hope had had a day off.

'It's going to be wonderful,' Mandy said.

Mr Hope laughed. 'That's the spirit!' he said. 'I'm looking forward to this picnic.'

'So is Blackie,' James said.

Mandy gave the Labrador a hug. 'First you have to do a bit of walking,' Mandy said. 'Then we eat.'

Blackie wagged his tail and knocked James's glasses off.

'Blackie!' said James, laughing.

Blackie wasn't the most obedient dog in the world – or the best behaved – but he was great fun.

'Where are we going?' James said as he settled his glasses back on his nose.

Mandy turned round to point out of the car window to the moor above Welford village. 'Up there,' she said. 'Black Tor.'

'Terrific,' said James. 'It's ages since I've been up to Black Tor.'

The car swung round the crossroads by the Fox and Goose pub and Mandy and James waved to Mr Hardy, the publican, as they passed. He looked up from rolling a barrel into the pub and waved back.

Then they were out of the village and climbing towards the moor. Mandy loved the moor. It could be wild and windy in winter and the snow could pile itself into drifts two metres deep. But today, in the spring sunshine, it looked perfect.

The car climbed higher and Mandy and James looked back. Welford lay spread out below them. They could see Animal Ark, the old stone cottage at the front and the modern extension that housed the surgery at the back. They spotted James's house at the other end of the village and Mandy's grandparents' cottage with their camper van sitting outside. And behind the Fox and Goose was the lane where Walter Pickard and Ernie Bell lived, both church bell-ringers like Grandad. Then there was the church and the post office and the village hall.

'It looks like a toy village,' James said.

'Look,' said Mandy. 'You can see Walton. There's the school.' Walton was the neighbouring town, two miles from Welford.

'Ugh!' groaned James. 'Don't mention school. Not when the holidays have just begun!'

'And there's the cottage hospital,' Mandy said, pointing to a long, low building on the outskirts of Walton. It was the little local hospital for Walton and Welford. 'Gran says there's a new matron there now.'

James nodded. 'I know,' he said. 'Johnny Pearson broke his leg playing football. He's in the cottage hospital. Mark says he's scared stiff of Matron.' Mark was Johnny's older brother. He was in Mandy's class at school.

Mandy pulled a face. 'She must be bad if Johnny's scared of her,' she said. 'Johnny's a holy terror.'

James grinned. 'Mark says it's time somebody kept Johnny in line.'

Mandy turned to face the way they were going. 'Look, Dad,' she said. 'There are lambs in the fields already.'

Mr Hope's beard twitched as he smiled. 'As if I didn't know it,' he said. 'How many call-outs did I have last week?'

'Ooops, sorry!' Mandy said. The Hopes were always very busy at lambing time.

James was looking out of the side window. 'Mrs McFarlane was saying that somebody has moved into Fordbeck Farm,' he said.

The McFarlanes ran the Welford post office. Mrs McFarlane knew everything that was going on almost before it happened.

Mr Hope nodded. 'The Spillers,' he said. 'I've been in to see them a couple of times.'

'The people with the little girl?' said Mandy.

Her dad nodded. 'Jenny. She's six. And Mrs Spiller is expecting another baby any day now.'

'Have they got lambs?' Mandy said.

Mr Hope nodded again. 'This is their first lambing season. The Spillers aren't country folk. Mr Spiller lost his job and they bought that old farm. I have to hand it to Jack Spiller. He's making a good job of it. Only thing is, they can't afford to pay anybody to help them so he's having to do it all himself.'

Mandy opened her mouth to ask why Mrs Spiller didn't help. She was so used to her mum and dad working together, sharing the load. Then she remembered about the new baby.

'That must be hard at lambing time,' James said.

Mr Hope gave him a smile. 'That's why I thought you wouldn't mind if we popped in on the way to Black Tor. Just to see how they're getting on.'

Mandy grinned. Typical. If her dad thought someone needed a hand he would be there – day off or no day off.

'I'd love to see some lambs,' Mandy said.

Mr Hope glanced at Blackie but James said 'No need to worry. Blackie's no bother around sheep. He's as gentle as . . .'

'A lamb,' Mandy finished and they laughed.

'In here then,' Mr Hope said and he swung the car down a dirt track off the road.

The track was bumpy – as if it hadn't been used in a long time.

'How long have they been here?' James asked.

Mr Hope shrugged. 'About eight months,' he said. 'Jack Spiller has worked his socks off on that farm, trying to make a go of it.'

'It was pretty run down, wasn't it?' James said.

Mr Hope nodded. 'That's the only reason he could afford it. He's put every penny he has into it. And done the work on the farm buildings himself. But you don't get too much done in winter. Let's hope things start looking up for them soon.'

Mandy looked at her dad thoughtfully. It sounded as if the Spillers were having a hard time.

The car bumped and jolted its way along the track and turned in at the farmyard.

Mandy looked round. The farmhouse was the long, low, old-fashioned kind. But it had been freshly whitewashed and there were daffodils growing in half barrels at the door and pots of geraniums on the window ledge. The curtains at the windows were blue gingham and the whole place looked neat and clean.

'Needs some work doing on that barn,' Mr Hope said as he stopped the car.

Mandy looked at the barn. It was true. It did look a bit run down, but there was fresh wood showing here and there where it had been mended. It was clear Mr Spiller was working on the place.

'He's started mending it,' she said. Then she saw an old shed in the far corner of the farmyard. 'Look at that,' she said.

Mr Hope looked. 'That's beyond mending,' he said. 'That needs to be knocked down.'

Mr Hope tooted the horn. Nothing. No sign of life.

Mandy looked at the blue curtains blowing at the windows of the house. Where were the Spillers?

'Jack Spiller is probably out lambing,' said Mr Hope.

'What about Mrs Spiller and the little girl?' Mandy said.

Mr Hope shook his head. He looked worried.

'Maybe you should go inside,' James said to him. 'The door is open.'

Mr Hope hesitated. He wasn't the type to go barging into people's houses without asking. But

Mandy could see he was concerned.

Just then a little girl emerged from the house. Her dark hair was tied in bunches with bright red ribbons. The ribbons matched her red jumper and red gumboots. She stood on the doorstep looking at them.

'Look,' said Mandy.

'That's Jenny,' Mr Hope said.

Mandy scrambled out of the car and walked slowly across the farmyard. The little girl looked scared to death. Mandy didn't want to frighten her any more.

'Hello,' she said as she got nearer. 'You're Jenny, aren't you?'

The child nodded, but didn't say a word.

Mandy smiled encouragingly. 'Where's your mum?' she said.

Jenny turned her face up to Mandy and her eyes filled with tears. She raised a hand and pointed into the house. 'In there,' she said. 'She's sick. She's got a sore tummy – and Daddy isn't here.'

James and Mr Hope were out of the car now.

'Dad?' said Mandy.

Mr Hope's face looked worried. 'I heard,' he said quietly. 'Keep Jenny out here while I go and see what's wrong.'

And he strode into the house.

Mandy and James looked at each other. Jenny's face was streaming with tears now. Mandy reached an arm out to give her a hug but then Blackie bounded up and began to lick the little girl's face.

It was like magic. At once the tears disappeared.

'Oh!' said Jenny. 'Is he yours?'

'He's mine,' James said. 'His name is Blackie.'

Jenny put her hand out to stroke the Labrador. 'He's lovely,' she said. 'Can I play with him? Daddy doesn't let me play with Jess.'

'Of course you can play with him,' James said. Then he turned to Mandy. 'Who's Jess?' he said.

Mandy shrugged her shoulders. Things at Fordbeck Farm were getting stranger and stranger.

It seemed like ages but it could only have been minutes before Mr Hope came out of the house. His face looked very serious.

He drew Mandy away from Jenny and spoke in a low voice.

'Mrs Spiller's baby is on the way, Mandy,' he said. 'I don't think we have much time.'

'She isn't going to have it here, is she?' said Mandy.

Mr Hope shook his head. 'I don't think that would be a good idea,' he said. 'Lambing is one thing but human babies are another.'

Mandy looked at Jenny playing happily with Blackie and James. James was doing a great job keeping the little girl's mind off her mother.

'Is there anything I can do?' Mandy said.

Mr Hope nodded. 'I can't leave Mrs Spiller – just in case,' he said. 'Jack Spiller is in the top field, lambing. Go and fetch him.'

Mandy's mind teemed with questions but one look at her dad's face told her there was no time.

'Tell him to get back here right now,' said Mr Hope. 'He's got to get his wife to the cottage hospital.'

Mandy stood stock-still for a moment, looking at her dad. It wasn't often he was so abrupt. He looked really worried.

'Run!' her dad said.

Mandy turned on her heels and ran for the top field.

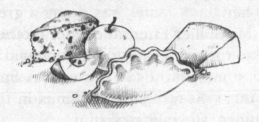

Two

Mandy ran like she had never run before. It *would* be the top field, she thought. The one furthest away from the farmhouse. Her breath rasping in her throat, she scrambled over a dry-stone wall and raced over the field. She looked up. There, outlined against the sky, she could see the figure of a man. He was bending over a sheep. It had to be Jack Spiller.

'Mr Spiller!' she shouted.

But the wind whipped her voice away. Panting, Mandy raced on. 'Mr Spiller!' she called again as she drew nearer.

The tall, dark-haired figure straightened up

and turned round. A flowing black and white shape rose up from the grass and streaked towards her.

'Jess!' Mr Spiller cried and at once the shape halted and turned. Jess was a sheepdog.

Mandy stumbled the last few metres and stood looking up at the farmer, out of breath.

'Mr Spiller,' she said again.

He was a tall man with a kind face and worried eyes. He looked down at her, puzzled.

'That's me,' he said. 'Who are you?'

'Mandy Hope,' Mandy said.

The man's face cleared. 'The vet's daughter?' he said and smiled.

Mandy nodded. Her breath was coming back now. She reached out a hand and tugged at Jack Spiller's sleeve.

'You've got to come,' she said. 'Back to the farm. It's your wife . . .'

At once his smile disappeared. 'Maggie?' he said. 'What's wrong? Has she had an accident?'

Mandy shook her head. 'No,' she said. 'But the baby is coming. Dad says she needs to go to the cottage hospital – right away.'

The words were hardly out of her mouth before Jack Spiller was off, racing down the field, leaping

the dry-stone wall as if it was nothing, running for home with Jess beside him.

Mandy watched as he crossed the bottom field. She hoped Mrs Spiller would be all right – and the baby.

She felt something soft and warm nudge her leg and looked down. A lamb, hardly a day old, blundered into her. Mandy smiled in spite of her worry. It looked so small and fluffy. A ewe, its mother, bleated to it and the lamb turned and trotted towards her. The ewe gave it a gentle butt with its head and the lamb drew close to its mother's side, nuzzling for milk.

Mandy gave herself a shake. The lamb was beautiful but this was no time to stand there admiring it. She turned and ran back down the hill towards the farm.

Mr Hope was helping a young woman into a dilapidated old van when Mandy arrived at the farmyard. Jess, the sheepdog, crouched watchfully beside the farmhouse door.

'Well done, Mandy,' her dad said.

Mandy glowed with pleasure and looked at the woman. She had short dark hair and cheeks that should have been rosy. But now she looked pale and drawn. She turned a worried face to Mandy.

'Thank you so much,' she said. Then she looked at Mr Hope as she eased herself into the van. 'But what about Jenny?'

Mr Hope looked at Mandy and James. Jenny was absorbed in talking to Blackie, kneeling beside him.

'We'll look after her,' Mandy said. 'Won't we, James?'

James smiled. 'Of course we will,' he said. 'Blackie will help.'

Mandy saw some of the worry fade from Mrs Spiller's face.

Then Jack Spiller came hurtling out of the house with a bag overflowing with clothes.

Mrs Spiller smiled. 'I wasn't quite packed,' she said. 'The baby is a bit early.'

Mr Spiller threw the bag into the back of the van. Then he turned to look at Jenny.

'Don't worry about her,' Mr Hope said. 'We'll look after Jenny.'

Mr Spiller ran a hand through his hair. 'I don't like asking favours,' he said.

Mr Hope smiled. 'It isn't a favour,' he said. 'It's a pleasure. Anyway, we have to give one another a hand here in the country.'

Mr Spiller looked at him gratefully. 'I'll be back

as soon as I can,' he said. He looked at his wife and she smiled at him.

'I'll be all right,' she said. 'Just drop me at the hospital.' She turned to Mr Hope. 'It's the lambing, you see,' she said. 'We can't afford to get anybody to help us and I haven't been able to do much to help Jack recently. He just can't be away from the farm for very long.'

Jack Spiller's mouth looked grim. 'You've probably helped too much,' he said to his wife. 'I shouldn't have let you.'

'Don't be daft,' Mrs Spiller said. 'You can't manage it all on your own.'

'I'll have to,' said Jack Spiller. He turned and looked towards the top field. 'There are one or two ewes I'm not happy about up there,' he said. Then he gave Jess the order to stay and got into the van beside his wife.

James came and stood beside Mandy. 'He can't do all that lambing on his own,' he said softly.

Mandy nodded thoughtfully. 'And he really should be with Mrs Spiller at the hospital.'

'What do you think?' said James.

Mandy looked at him. 'No picnic?' she said.

James shrugged. 'I don't mind. There are plenty of days for a picnic.'

'Not for Dad,' Mandy said. 'He hasn't had a day off in ages.'

'He wouldn't mind,' said James.

Mandy grinned. 'No, I don't suppose he would,' she said.

The van engine was revving up. Jenny looked up and ran to the passenger side.

'Will you bring a baby home, Mummy?' she said.

Mrs Spiller smiled but Mandy saw a spasm of pain cross her face. 'In a few days,' she said. 'Be a good girl for Daddy while I'm away.'

The little girl nodded. 'I'll help him,' she said. 'With the lambs.'

'So will we,' Mandy said impulsively. She turned to her father. 'Won't we, Dad?'

Mr Hope smiled. 'Of course we will,' he said. 'I've got gumboots in the car for everybody.'

Jack Spiller's face lit up. 'Really?' he said. 'You'll stay?'

'Take your time,' Mr Hope said. 'We'll look after the lambing for you – Mandy and James and I.'

'And me!' said little Jenny.

Mr Hope laughed. 'And you,' he said.

'I don't know what to say,' Jack Spiller said. 'I never expected kindness like this. You'll find the lambing bag in the top field – I hope the ewes haven't got at it.'

Mr Hope looked at Mrs Spiller. Her face was very pale. 'Don't worry about that,' he said. 'Just get going!'

The engine revved again. Mr Spiller waved and the van was off.

'What's a lambing bag?' said James.

Mr Hope laughed. 'It's the most important thing a shepherd or a sheep farmer has at lambing time,' he said. 'I'll show it to you when we find it.'

'Right,' said Mandy as they watched the van disappear round a bend in the track. 'Let's get to work then.'

'The top field, Jack said,' Mr Hope said. 'I think we'd better take a look up there first.'

'Shall we take Jess?' Mandy said.

Mr Hope nodded. 'We'll need her,' he said. 'Sometimes ewes can bolt and you need a sheepdog to catch them.'

Mr Hope whistled to the black and white collie which came running to his heels. 'Lucky Jess and I have met before,' he said. 'She's a good sheepdog.'

'What about Blackie?' James said.

Mr Hope looked at the Labrador. 'Better put

him on the lead,' he said. 'I know he wouldn't harm the sheep but the sheep don't know that. A ewe panics easily at this time of year.'

Jenny looked up from where she was cuddling Blackie. 'Can I take him?' she said.

James smiled. 'Of course you can,' he said as he clipped on Blackie's lead.

They got gumboots and Mr Hope's bag from the car, then the procession started up towards the top field. Mr Hope with Jess, Mandy and James and Jenny with Blackie.

So much for Dad's day off, Mandy thought.

As they went Mr Hope explained what needed to be done.

'We spread out,' he said. 'We have to check on as many ewes as possible, looking for signs of distress.'

'What signs?' James said.

Mr Hope thought for a moment. 'If you see a ewe lying down, she's probably lambing. But ewes are strange creatures. They're just as likely to give birth standing up as lying down. In any case, you must keep watch to see that the lamb is born safely. Once the birth process starts it doesn't take too long.'

'How do you know everything is OK?' Mandy said.

Mr Hope smiled. 'You'll see the lamb born, then the ewe will get to her feet and start licking the lamb. Once that happens you can be sure everything will be all right.'

'What if the ewe doesn't lick the lamb?' James said.

Mr Hope frowned. 'That can be difficult,' he said. 'You see, if the bond between mother and child isn't formed at once, you can find yourself with a rejected lamb on your hands – and a lot more work. Either you have to bring the rejected lambs into the house and hand rear them or you have to set them on to another ewe.'

'Huh?' said James.

Mr Hope smiled. 'Setting on is when you take the skin of a dead lamb, maybe one that was stillborn, and put it on a rejected lamb. Then, if you're lucky, the mother will think it's her own lamb and feed it.'

'I suppose that's better than having to hand rear a whole lot of lambs,' James said, but he didn't sound too keen on the idea of setting on.

'It's certainly less work,' said Mr Hope.

'And Mr Spiller is so busy already,' James said.

'He wouldn't have time for hand rearing. Lambs have to be fed so often when they're really young.'

Mr Hope smiled at him. 'Sheep farmers don't get much time to rest during lambing. Ask any of them. And besides, it's the farmers' wives that usually do the hand rearing – in the kitchen. Now spread out,' he said. 'The first thing we have to do is find the lambing bag.'

They spread out. Mandy was so enchanted with the little woolly lambs that skipped and hopped beside their mothers that she almost forgot what she was supposed to be looking for. It was James who shouted 'Is this it?'

Mandy looked round. James was holding up a dun-coloured bag with a cord attached.

'That's it,' said Mr Hope, coming over to him. 'Now you can see what's in a lambing bag.'

Mr Hope took the bag and opened it. Mandy and James and Jenny looked on as he emptied it.

'It's a sort of survival kit for sheep farmers,' he said as he laid the various things out on the grass. 'You see, there's string and marking fluid for identifying lambs. Then there's penicillin for giving before a difficult birth. There's lambing oil for when the farmer has to help the birth along and protein drinks for exhaustion, calcium and a

mixture for enteritis. Then the whole bag is lined with sheep's-wool so that if you have to bring a lamb home it'll be cosy and warm in there.'

'That's marvellous,' said Mandy.

Mr Hope nodded. 'Oh, lambing bags are great things,' he said. 'Now, let's get to work.'

They worked hard until midday, when Mr Hope said they could stop and eat their picnic.

'No problems to report?' Mr Hope said as they settled themselves behind a dry-stone wall.

Mandy shook her head, her cheeks aglow as she spread the picnic on the grass beside them. There were pasties and crusty rolls and shiny red apples and wedges of cheese. And there were slabs of fruit cake and tubs of yoghurt to finish with.

'Oh, Dad, I saw a lamb being born! And it was just like you said,' Mandy said.

'I saw one as well,' James said. 'It was tiny. It got up right away and its mother did just what you said – started licking it. Then it began to feed.'

Mr Hope laughed. 'I'm glad you're enjoying it,' he said.

Mandy munched on a vegetable pasty. 'This is good,' she said.

'Hard work makes for good appetites,' Mr Hope said.

James nodded. 'It's good to sit down,' he said.

Jenny looked up, her mouth full of crusty roll and cheese. 'Can I give some to Blackie?' she said.

James nodded and the little girl smiled.

'You really like Blackie, don't you?' he said.

Jenny nodded. 'Dad won't let me play with Jess,' she said. 'I like playing with Blackie. I'd like my own Blackie.'

'Work dogs aren't for playing with,' said Mr Hope. He looked round. 'Where is Jess, anyway?'

Just at that moment a black and white shape raced over the hill and stood a few metres away, looking at them.

'Here, girl,' said Mandy but the dog stood its ground. Her head moved slightly back and forth.

At once Mr Hope was on the alert. He stood up and the sheepdog started to move away.

'What is it, Dad?' Mandy said.

Mr Hope took a step forward. Jess looked back towards him and moved a further few metres.

'I think Jess is trying to tell us something,' Mr Hope said.

Mandy scrambled to her feet. 'What?' she said.

Mr Hope shook his head. 'I don't know,' he said, 'but I think we'd better find out!'

Three

Jess loped in front of them, looking back now and then to see that they were following.

'She's trying to tell us something,' Mandy said.

James nodded. 'It looks like it.'

Mr Hope pointed. 'There,' he said. 'Just under the dry-stone wall.'

Mandy and James looked. A ewe lay stretched out on the ground. As they got closer Mandy could see more clearly. The ewe wasn't moving. She was lying flat on her side, her legs stiff, her body arched.

'Is she dead?' Mandy said.

Mr Hope was already opening the lambing bag.

'No,' he said, 'but there isn't much time.'

'She isn't moving,' said James, 'and her eyes are closed.'

As if the ewe had heard, she opened her eyes and gave a weak bleat.

'Careful now,' said Mr Hope. 'We don't want to alarm her.'

'What's wrong, Dad?' said Mandy.

Mr Hope bent to the ewe and ran his hands over her stiff body.

'Hypocalcaemia,' he said shortly.

'What's that?' said Mandy, kneeling beside him. 'Can you do something for her?'

Mr Hope searched in the lambing bag. 'It's a deficiency of calcium,' he said. 'It sometimes happens with pregnant ewes.'

'Can you cure it?' James asked.

Mr Hope nodded. 'I hope so,' he said. 'If it isn't too late.'

Mandy saw her dad take a syringe out of the bag and a plastic bottle filled with some kind of solution.

'I have to give her an injection,' he said. 'We must just hope it's in time. Mandy, hold her head while I do it.'

Mandy put her arms round the ewe's head. It

felt heavy and the ewe was hardly breathing. 'Quick, Dad,' she said. 'I think she's in real trouble!'

Swiftly, Mr Hope filled the syringe and injected the ewe.

'What now?' said James.

'Now we wait,' said Mr Hope.

'How long?' said Mandy.

Mr Hope smiled. 'Not long,' he said. 'If it works.'

They stood there watching the ewe as the minutes ticked by. Mandy held her breath. She thought she saw the ewe's eyes flicker. Then a tremor ran through the ewe's body and her eyes opened. The frightened animal looked up at Mandy and bleated pitifully.

'Dad?' Mandy said.

Her dad nodded. 'I felt it,' he said. He turned to James. 'Help Mandy hold her head,' he said, 'and get ready to hold the ewe in case she bolts. I rather think I'm going to be busy at this end.'

'Bolts?' said James as he went to help Mandy.

Mr Hope nodded. 'Ewes in trouble often bolt. And with this one so close to giving birth that wouldn't be a good idea.'

Mandy's eyes opened wide. 'Is the lamb coming?' she said.

Mr Hope nodded. 'Soon,' he said. 'But I think she'll need some help.'

Mandy opened her mouth to ask more questions but at that moment the ewe gave a shudder and began to struggle to her feet.

Mandy and James locked their arms round the ewe's neck as she stood shaking her head and pawing at the short grass. Then she gave a long bleat and strained against them.

'Hold her,' Mr Hope said urgently.

Mandy tightened her grip, talking to the frightened animal, soothing her. The ewe began to calm down.

Mandy looked at her father. He rolled his sleeves up and quickly rubbed some lambing oil on his hands and forearms. He looked up briefly.

'Hold tight,' he said. 'Here we go.'

Mandy watched as her father felt for the little creature. She saw him frown.

'What is it, Dad?'

'Twins,' he said. 'And they're a bit mixed up in there.'

Mandy bit her lip. The poor ewe's body heaved with effort and her eyes rolled upwards.

'It'll all be over soon,' Mandy said to her.

Another long shudder passed through the ewe's

body. Mandy looked at her dad's face. He was intent on what he was doing. Then she saw him grin.

'Come on, little fellow,' he said. 'There's another one behind you.'

And suddenly her dad's hands were full of newborn lamb as it slipped and slid on the grass. Swiftly he guided the shaking little creature round to its mother's side.

'For goodness sake, don't let her go now,' he said to Mandy and James. 'There's another lamb to come and if she doesn't start licking them right away, we'll have two rejected lambs.'

Mandy shifted her grasp so that the ewe could get to her lamb. She watched, breathless, as the ewe started licking the little creature clean.

'It's so tiny,' she said, looking at the lamb as its mother cleaned it up.

'And here's another,' Mr Hope said, coming to stand beside her.

Mandy looked up. She had been so busy watching the first lamb she had missed the birth of the second.

'Oh, Dad,' she said as Mr Hope put the second lamb down and the ewe began to clean that one too. 'Two lambs – and the poor ewe looked so sick!'

James grinned. 'Your dad can cure anything,' he said.

Mr Hope laughed. 'Hypocalcaemia isn't hard to cure if you have the right treatment. But it's Jess we have to thank. If she hadn't come to fetch us the ewe would never have made it.'

'And those two little lambs would have died too,' Mandy said. 'What a good dog you are, Jess!'

She turned to give Jess a hug but Jess was looking away down the hill. Her ears were cocked. She was on the alert.

'What is it, girl?' said Mandy. 'Another ewe in trouble?'

But Jess was off, running down the hill towards the farm, long strides covering the distance fast.

Jenny jumped up and down. 'It's Daddy!' she said. 'Jess always does that when Daddy comes home.'

And Jenny was off after Jess.

'Mrs Spiller and the baby,' Mandy said. 'I'd almost forgotten about them.'

'Look!' said James.

He was pointing to a tall figure striding up the hill from the farm. Jack Spiller. As they watched, they saw Jess reach him. Mr Spiller bent down and gave her a pat. Then he saw Jenny running towards him.

Her voice carried on the wind. 'Daddy, Daddy, have we got a baby?'

Jack Spiller broke into a run and gathered his daughter up in his arms, lifting her high over his head.

Mandy felt herself smiling as he swung the little girl up on his shoulders and walked towards them, the dog at his heels.

'A boy!' he shouted as he drew near. 'A beautiful baby boy and Maggie is just fine. Exhausted but fine.'

Mandy grinned and looked at the twin lambs, now busy suckling. Their white woolly coats had dried in the breeze. They looked as if they were made out of fluffy cotton wool. Their little tails wagged madly as they fed.

'I'll bet the new baby is just as beautiful as you,' Mandy said softly to the lambs.

Four

'Home!' said Mandy as the car turned down the track to Animal Ark.

'I'm exhausted,' said James.

Mr Hope laughed. 'Lambing is hard work,' he said.

Mandy frowned. 'Too hard for one person. Too hard for Mr Spiller all on his own – especially with Jenny to look after while Mrs Spiller is in hospital.'

Mr Hope drove through the gate of Animal Ark, past the wooden sign swinging gently in the breeze. Mr Hope drew the car to a standstill and turned to them. 'You know, you could help him,' he said. 'You were a terrific help to me today.'

Mandy shook her short, fair hair out of her eyes. 'Us?' she said. 'But we don't know the first thing about lambing.'

'We might do something wrong,' said James.

Mr Hope shrugged. 'Just a thought,' he said. 'But Jack can't be everywhere at once and he certainly can't afford to lose too many lambs. It's a matter of having somebody there to deal with trouble before it happens – like you were doing for me today.'

'You mean like Jess and that ewe?' said James.

Mr Hope nodded. 'That's what I mean. That ewe was ready to bolt. If it hadn't been for you two holding on to her we might have lost the lambs.' He smiled. 'Think about it,' he said.

Mandy's eyes were shining. 'We don't have to think about it, do we, James?' she said. 'Of course we'll help Mr Spiller – if he'll let us!'

Mr Hope laughed. 'Oh, I think he'll let you all right. Jack Spiller's got too much on his plate to refuse an offer of help right now.'

Mandy smiled up at her dad. He really was kind. If Mr Spiller needed help, then Mr Spiller would get help.

'The only thing is . . .' said Mr Hope.

James and Mandy looked at him. Mr Hope scratched his ear uncomfortably.

'What is it?' said Mandy.

'Jack Spiller came here knowing hardly anything about sheep,' Mr Hope said. 'And he's made a good job of things so far – without asking for help.'

Mandy began to see what her dad was driving at.

'Oh, Dad, we won't go charging in saying that you've been telling us he's in trouble.'

'No, I know you won't,' said Mr Hope. 'It's just that he has his pride and he's done a good job already.'

'I know,' said James. 'We'll ask him if he'd take us on for training, sort of – if it wouldn't be too much trouble. How about that?'

'Then we can help him while he thinks he's helping us,' said Mandy. 'Brilliant! James, you're a genius.'

James flushed with pleasure and shoved his glasses up his nose.

Mr Hope looked at them both. 'James might be a genius,' he said, 'but I'm starving. How about you?'

'Tea,' said Mandy. 'My stomach feels like a great big empty cave.'

'Come on, James,' said Mr Hope. 'Ring your mum and tell her you're eating with us tonight.'

Blackie gave a bark. 'And you too, Blackie.' Mr Hope laughed. 'Would I forget you?'

Mrs Hope and Gran were sitting in the sunny kitchen of Animal Ark. A pot of tea stood on the table between them.

Emily Hope put down her teacup and looked at them in amazement. 'Where on earth have you three been?' she said.

'Had a good picnic?' said Gran at the same time.

Mandy looked down at her muddy clothes and even muddier gumboots. Then she looked at Mr Hope and James. They weren't any better.

Mr Hope ran a hand through his hair. 'You don't stay clean chasing sheep,' he said.

'Sheep?' said Emily Hope.

'On a picnic?' Gran said to her son. Adam Hope might be a grown-up vet to the rest of Welford but to Gran he was still her boy – and a very muddy one at the moment.

'Tell you what,' said Mr Hope, sidling out of the kitchen. 'Why don't we get cleaned up, then we can tell you all about it over tea.'

Gran looked at her watch. 'Goodness! Is that the time already?' she said. 'I must get home.' She bustled about, picking up her coat and giving Emily Hope a hug.

She turned to Mandy and stopped. Mandy grinned. 'It's all right, Gran,' she said. 'I'm much to muddy to hug. I'll save it for next time.'

'Mmm,' said Gran. 'Maybe you're right.' She put on her coat. 'Tell you what,' she said. 'Come round tomorrow, you and James. There's something I want you to help me with.'

'What?' said Mandy.

Gran's eyes twinkled. 'I'm on the campaigning trail again,' she said.

'Not the post office,' said Mandy. 'You won that campaign.'

Gran had organised a campaign to save the McFarlanes' little office in the village when it had been threatened with closure.

'No,' said Gran. 'They're leaving the post office alone. It's the cottage hospital they want to close now.'

Mandy's jaw dropped. 'What?' she said. 'But they can't do that!'

Gran nodded grimly. 'They can if they want,' she said. 'But I intend to make them change their minds.'

'How?' said Mandy.

Gran thought for a moment. 'I don't know exactly,' she admitted. 'We'll need a plan. But one thing's for sure, by the time we're finished, I want them to regret the day they ever thought of closing the cottage hospital! So, can I count you in?' She looked from Mandy to James.

'Of course you can,' said James. 'I remember having my tonsils out there. It's a great place. They gave me ice-cream. And it's so close to school that everybody could come to visit me on their way home. I really enjoyed it.'

Mandy thought of the little cottage hospital near their school in Walton. It was as pretty as a picture with a flower garden in front and green painted shutters on the windows. 'What does Matron say?' she asked.

Gran's eyes twinkled even more as she buttoned up her coat. 'Matron,' she said, 'is on the warpath.'

Mandy felt herself grinning. 'Johnny Pearson is terrified of her,' she said.

Gran laughed. 'Matron's bark is a lot worse that her bite,' she said.

'Even when she's on the warpath?' said James.

Gran laughed again. 'Don't worry, James,' she said. 'I'm the one you'll be helping.' She picked

up her bag. 'Right,' she said. 'I'm off. I'll see you two tomorrow morning.'

'Bye, Gran,' said Mandy and turned to her mother, full of news of Mrs Spiller's baby and questions about the hospital.

Mrs Hope shook her head. 'Oh, no,' she said. 'Not until you clean yourselves up. Wash first, talk later!'

Mandy, James and Mr Hope filed out. Blackie tried to follow them but Mrs Hope stopped him. 'Oh, no, you don't,' she said. 'I'm going to give you a good brushing, Blackie.'

Blackie looked resigned. With Emily Hope in

this mood it was no good anyone arguing with her.

'That was wonderful,' James sighed, leaning back in his chair. 'Thanks, Mrs Hope.'

Mrs Hope smiled at him. 'Glad you enjoyed it, James,' she said, looking at the empty plates on the table.

Mandy followed her eyes and laughed. 'We were hungry, Mum,' she said. 'Besides, it really was an excellent tea.'

They'd eaten quiche and salad and baked potatoes with cheese and coleslaw fillings, followed by the big floury scones Gran had brought, topped with butter and Mrs Hope's home-made strawberry jam. Mandy felt as if she would never move again – and said so.

Mr Hope laughed. 'And who's going to help your poor old father with the animals tonight?' he said.

'You know I wouldn't miss that, Dad,' Mandy said. 'I love helping in the surgery – but maybe not straight away.'

'I should think not,' said Mrs Hope. 'You ate like a horse, Mandy.' She looked at her daughter, slim and long-legged. 'I honestly don't know where you put it!' she said. She leaned her elbows on the table. 'It will really please Gran if you help her with this campaign.'

Mandy looked indignant. 'Of course we'll help her. I mean, how can they think of closing the cottage hospital?'

'To save money,' Mr Hope said.

Mandy shook her head. 'And what about the people who live here – what about Mrs Spiller?' she said.

'That's true,' said Mrs Hope. 'From what your dad says, Mrs Spiller got to the hospital just in time. That little baby was in quite a hurry to be born.'

Adam Hope nodded in agreement. 'And there's the visiting,' he said. 'Jack Spiller would never manage to visit every day if they were much further away – not at lambing time.'

Emily Hope nodded. 'That's a good angle to take for your campaign, Mandy,' she said. 'It isn't just a hospital – it's a life-line in a place like this.'

James grinned. 'And that's a good slogan,' he said. '"It isn't just a hospital – it's a life-line." Do you think your Gran will want to do posters?' he said.

Mandy laughed. 'You know Gran, she'll want to

do everything,' she said. 'Come on, let's take care of the animals and talk about it.'

'OK,' said James, getting up from the table.

'We'll make a start on the cages, Dad,' said Mandy.

'All right,' said Mr Hope. 'I'll be there in a few minutes to do the dressings and medications.'

'Oh,' said Mrs Hope, 'that reminds me. Tom is in again. And he isn't too happy about the dressing I put on him this afternoon.'

'Tom?' said Mandy. 'Again? What happened this time?'

Mrs Hope smiled. 'He took on a terrier twice his size – and he got the worst of it. Five stitches. And stitching Tom up is not my favourite job.'

Mandy shook her head. Tom was Walter Pickard's big black and white cat. He was a real gangster of the cat world, always in trouble.

'So what's the plan?' said James as they made their way into the residential unit.

Mandy looked around the unit. There weren't too many animals in at the moment. A puppy with an infected ear, a gerbil with an eye infection, a tortoise with a rather serious cyst, and Tom. Mandy looked at him, crouched like a sleeping lion in his cage.

'I reckon we should do a poster campaign. Then maybe a petition.'

'And try to get the *Walton Gazette* involved,' said James.

'Good idea,' Mandy said. 'We might even try to get one of the big papers in York interested.'

'Steady,' Mandy said as James approached Tom's cage. 'You undo the latch while I try to charm him out of there.'

Tom lifted his great black and white head and regarded them lazily. The black patch over one eye made him look like a pirate.

'OK, then, Tom,' James said to him. 'No need to get annoyed. We just want to clean your cage out, that's all.'

Tom's massive head swung to look at James and his yellow eyes focused. Then, very slowly, he gathered himself up on to his haunches and spat.

'Oh, Tom,' said Mandy. 'We're only trying to help.' She looked at the dressing on the back of his neck. It was pretty thickly wadded. He must have got a bad bite from that dog. 'Oh, Tom,' she said again, 'why do you get yourself into trouble all the time?'

'That's a question we all ask ourselves,' said Mr Hope, coming into the residential unit. He smiled at Mandy and James. 'That cage looks pretty clean to me,' he said. 'Why don't you leave it until tomorrow? Maybe Tom will be feeling a bit better by then.'

Mandy grinned. 'You think so?' she said.

Mr Hope laughed. 'No, I don't,' he said. 'But you look dead on your feet. Time you were off to bed. And James's mum will think he's lost.'

'I'm pretty tired too,' said James. 'An early night isn't a bad idea.'

Mandy gave an enormous yawn. Tom opened his huge jaws and did the same.

'Good night, Tom,' Mandy said. 'Sleep well.'

Tom gave her a dismissive look and, turning his back on all of them, curled up and went to sleep.

Five

For the next week Mandy didn't know whether she was on her head or her heels. When they weren't at Lilac Cottage doing posters and leaflets for Gran, they were at Fordbeck Farm helping Mr Spiller.

By the end of the week Mandy had designed a dozen posters with the life-line slogan and she also felt she knew nearly everything there was to know about lambing. The weather had been really good and Jack Spiller was pleased with the crop of little lambs. None of the new lambs had to be brought into the kitchen and the ones that Mrs Spiller had been hand rearing were almost ready to be put out in the field.

'I really appreciate your help,' Mr Spiller said to Mandy and James as they stood in the top field watching several woolly lambs frisking round their mothers.

'We haven't done much,' said James.

Jack Spiller laughed. 'You've done enough,' he said. 'Keeping an eye out and letting me know at any sign of trouble, catching the ewes when they bolt, fetching the extra feed. Even helping with the hand rearing. It all helps.'

Mandy and James flushed with pleasure.

'We've enjoyed it,' Mandy said.

'Especially chasing the bolting ewes,' James said. 'Why do they do that?'

Jack Spiller shook his head. 'I think they get frightened,' he said. 'But one thing is sure, it's a lot harder to catch a bolting ewe on your own!'

They all laughed. It was a wonderful spring morning. A light breeze stirred Mandy's hair against her cheek. The sky was blue and the sun shone.

'It's a lovely day for Mrs Spiller coming home,' she said.

Jack Spiller's face split into a wide grin. 'It certainly is,' he said. 'And I'll be glad to have them back – both of them.' His grin got even wider.

'Have you decided what to call the baby?' Mandy said.

Mr Spiller looked a bit shy all of a sudden. 'We thought Adam,' he said. 'After your dad. If it hadn't been for him arriving to see if he could help that day . . .' He didn't finish.

Mandy tried to imagine what would have happened if they hadn't stopped by on their way to their picnic. Would Mrs Spiller have been all right?

'I think that's wonderful,' Mandy said. 'Dad will be so pleased.'

Jack Spiller's face looked relieved. 'You don't think he'll mind?'

'Mind?' said Mandy. 'He'll be like a dog with two tails. Just you wait and see.'

Jack Spiller grinned again. He looked quite young when he wasn't looking worried. 'If it had been a girl we'd have called her Mandy,' he said.

Mandy felt herself flush with pleasure. 'A boy is nice,' she said, embarrassed. 'You've got a girl already.'

At that Jack Spiller looked down towards the farmyard where Jenny was playing with Blackie. 'She just loves that dog,' he said.

'And Blackie has a great time with her,' said James. 'She really looks after him well and it means we don't have to tie him up.'

Mandy looked at her watch. 'Mr Spiller,' she said, 'what time did you say you were collecting Mrs Spiller and the baby?'

Jack Spiller looked at his own watch. 'Oh, Lord,' he said. 'I'll have to run. You're sure you'll be all right while I'm gone?'

Mandy smiled. 'Of course we will,' she said. 'We'll have the kettle on for a cup of tea for Mrs Spiller when you get back.'

They watched as Jack Spiller strode off down the field and into the farmyard. He scooped up his daughter and they saw him get into the van and start off down the track.

'Adam,' Mandy said. 'Isn't that nice?'

James grinned. 'Come on,' he said. 'We've got work to do!' And he whistled to Jess to come to heel.

'Over here,' Mandy said worriedly.

James came and crouched beside her where she was stationed, keeping an eye on one of the ewes a short distance away.

'What is it?' he said.

Mandy frowned. 'That ewe,' she said. 'She's had twins but she only licked one of them. The other one is just lying there.'

James looked at her and Mandy felt her heart sink. 'No, James. It isn't dead. I'm sure it isn't.'

She looked across at the little bundle of wool lying on the short turf, neglected by its mother. It was a tiny black lamb, only minutes old. She had watched it being born.

'So what do we do?' said James.

Mandy shrugged. 'Dad said we mustn't frighten the ewe in a situation like this.'

James nodded. 'She would only bolt. We can't risk going near her, can we?'

Mandy considered. 'Maybe we can,' she said. 'After all, she's looking after the first lamb.'

'Maybe the other one just has to wait its turn,' said James.

Mandy shook her head. 'I've been watching,' she said. 'The poor little thing struggled all the way round to its mother's side but she just pushed it away. She's only interested in the first one.'

'So what can we do?' said James.

Mandy looked at him. 'You know what Dad said,' she said. 'If the lamb doesn't bond with the mother straight away then she won't feed it or look after it.'

James frowned. 'So we've got to try to get them together, one way or another,' he said. 'There isn't anything else for it.'

Mandy nodded. 'I think you're right,' she said. 'We have to risk it. But I wish Mr Spiller or Dad was here.'

James looked at his watch. 'Mr Spiller shouldn't be too long,' he said. 'Do you want to wait?'

But Mandy shook her head. The little black lamb was lying very still now. She didn't want to risk its life. 'I don't think we can afford to wait,' she said.

'OK,' said James.

'Quietly, James,' Mandy said. 'We don't want to scare the ewe.'

Softly, Mandy whistled for Jess. There was a swift flowing movement as the black and white dog came over the grass towards them, looking at Mandy with intelligent eyes.

'Hold her, Jess,' Mandy whispered to Jess.

Jess turned at once and went to the ewe, standing silently at her head, ready to stop her if she should bolt. But the ewe was too busy with the other lamb. She hardly took any notice of the sheepdog.

Quietly, Mandy and James approaching the ewe over the grass. Mandy kneeled beside the wet, little, black bundle on the ground. Gently she lifted the lamb closer to its mother. The lamb stirred in her arms as she did so and Mandy's heart fluttered. It was so small, so delicate.

The ewe took no notice. Mandy tried everything. She almost pushed the poor little lamb under the ewe's nose but it was no good. The ewe had time for only one lamb and it wasn't this little one.

It was when the ewe raised her head and gave an unmistakably angry bleat that Mandy knew it was useless.

'She's rejected it,' said James.

Mandy looked down at the little lamb. 'Poor little thing,' she said. 'What shall we do?'

James was brisk. 'First we get it cleaned up,' he said. 'Then we try and feed it.'

Mandy smiled. 'Of course,' she said. But she looked down again at the poor little thing. 'Poor lamb,' she said. 'We'll take care of you.'

James rummaged in the lambing bag for a rough towel. He handed it to Mandy and she wrapped it round the lamb, drying it, warming it. Although the day was mild, there was still a stiff breeze and

this little thing was only just born.

As they carried the lamb to the shelter of the dry-stone wall Mandy looked back. The ewe was looking as proud as could be, suckling her other lamb. Mandy shook her head. Sometimes she just didn't understand nature.

But one thing was sure. They had to get some food into this lamb – and quickly. Carefully she put the lamb inside the lambing bag. It would be cosy there, lying on the fleecy lining. They started off down towards the farm.

Mandy had been in many a sheep farmer's kitchen at lambing time. It wasn't unusual to see three or four lambs tucked up in cardboard boxes and set close to the stove or the fire for warmth. The Spillers' kitchen was no different. There were three other little lambs being hand reared, Mandy and James were helping with that.

She settled the little lamb on its towel in front of the fire, then took the feeding bottle out of the lambing bag.

'I'll get some milk,' James said.

'Not straight from the fridge,' Mandy said. 'We should warm it a little.'

James nodded. 'I'll do that,' he said. 'You stay with the lamb.'

Mandy looked at the little creature lying in front of the fire. Even for a newborn lamb it was tiny. It was hard to believe that such a little thing could survive.

At last James came back with a saucepan of warm milk. Carefully, Mandy poured it into the feeding bottle and fixed the teat on. Then she sat down on the floor beside the lamb and lifted its little head.

'Here you are,' she said gently. 'It's milk. You'll like it.'

The lamb's eyes flickered. Then its nose twitched. Mandy rubbed the bottle against his lips and the lamb's tongue came out. Then his mouth fastened on the teat and he started to suck hungrily.

Mandy raised her face to James. 'Look,' she said. 'He's feeding.'

James grinned. 'Looks as if he's going to be all right,' he said.

Mandy looked at the stumpy little tail beginning to wag. 'He'll need lots of care though,' she said. 'He's so small. Smaller than any of the others.'

Mandy had just finished feeding the lamb when they heard the sound of an engine.

'That must be the Spillers,' said Mandy.

She laid the lamb gently down on the towel and followed James out into the farmyard.

Jenny was out of the van and across the yard like a whirlwind. 'We've got a baby!' she cried excitedly.

Mandy looked beyond her to Mrs Spiller. She was just getting out of the car with a white woolly bundle in her arms.

'It looks like another lamb,' James said and Mandy gave him a nudge.

'Oh, he's beautiful,' she said as Maggie Spiller proudly came to show the baby off.

Jack Spiller grinned. 'We're going to have our hands full now,' he said.

Jenny had run into the house to find Blackie and tell him the news.

Mandy looked at the proud father and mother. 'Oh,' she said, 'you have two new lambs as well.'

Jack Spiller's face beamed. 'That's good news,' he said. 'Just as long as they're healthy.' He turned to his wife. 'I'll just go and get those lambs from the kitchen. They're fit to go out in the field now. And you won't have time for that sort of thing, not now that you've got the baby to look after.'

Jenny ran out of the house. 'Daddy, Daddy,' she called. 'We've got a lamb.'

Jack Spiller grinned. 'We've got boxes full in there,' he said. 'But I'm just going to put them out. We won't have time to look after them.'

Jenny's face looked stricken. 'But it's so little, Daddy,' she said.

Jack grinned. 'They've been there a week and more,' he said. 'And we have to get rid of them. Your mum has the baby to look after now.'

Mandy looked at Jack Spiller. He didn't understand. Of course he didn't know about the new little lamb.

Jenny looked up at her father. 'Get rid of them? Even the little one?' she said. Her face was stricken.

Mandy turned quickly to Jack Spiller, but he was

taking his wife's things from the van, helping her into the house.

'All of them,' he said.

He'll understand, Mandy thought. *When he sees the lamb he'll understand.*

She looked round to explain to Jenny that her dad had made a mistake. But Jenny had gone.

Six

'We'll find someone to take care of it,' Mandy said. 'Won't we, James?'

They were standing in the Spillers' kitchen looking at the new lamb. James looked at Mandy's face. For a moment Mandy thought he was going to raise some difficulty. Then he nodded. 'Of course we will,' he said. 'Just give us a day or two.'

Jack Spiller shook his head. 'I can't ask Maggie to look after lambs just now – not with a new baby in the house. She's been doing enough of that recently. She's going to have her hands full as it is with me out all hours amongst the sheep.'

Mandy bit her lip. 'Today then,' she said. 'If we

haven't found anyone by this evening . . .' She stopped.

Jack Spiller nodded. 'OK,' he said. 'I'll give you till tonight. But I don't see how you're going to get anybody to take in a sickly little thing like that. Lambing is bad enough without having to look after anybody else's lambs.'

Mandy's mouth set in a determined line. She *would* find somebody to look after the lamb. After all, she had been an orphan and Adam and Emily Hope had looked after her. Her parents had been killed in a car crash when she was a baby and the Hopes had taken her in. She was adopted. Not that it felt like that. To her, Adam and Emily Hope were the best parents anyone could have.

'Till tonight,' she said to Jack Spiller. 'Don't forget – you promised.'

Mandy and James got their bikes from the old, tumbledown shed in the corner of the farmyard where they had left them. Mandy looked round. There was an old stone water trough in the far corner which looked solid enough. But the rest of the place was falling to bits.

'This place looks ready to fall down,' she said.

Mr Spiller came out of the house and called out to them. 'Don't leave your bikes in there. It's dangerous. I don't let anybody go in there.'

'Sorry, Mr Spiller,' Mandy said. 'We didn't know.'

Jack Spiller ran a hand through his hair. 'I forgot to mention it,' he said. 'I've had so much on my mind.' He looked at the old, tumbledown shed. 'First thing I do after the lambing is over is knock that old shed down.'

Mandy smiled. 'It won't be long now,' she said.

Jack Spiller grinned back. 'Nobody ever tells you what things are really like,' he said. 'Lambing looks easy enough but it's far from it.'

Mandy laughed. 'Animals are always a lot of work, Mr Spiller,' she said. 'But they're worth it.'

Jack Spiller smiled. 'You'll make a great vet some day, Mandy, if you've a mind to it.'

Mandy flushed with pleasure. 'I hope so,' she said. 'But right now it's finding a home for that little lamb that's worrying me.'

A shadow passed over Mr Spiller's face. 'It isn't that I'm being cruel,' he said. 'But that little lamb is a weakling. It would need a lot of attention – feeding every two hours or less – and even then it might not survive. Maggie just hasn't got the time or the energy for it just now – no more have I.'

Mandy nodded. 'I understand, Mr Spiller,' she

said. 'But we'll find somebody who has got the time and the energy. All we need is a few hours.'

Jack Spiller shook his head. 'You sound really confident,' he said.

James laughed. 'We haven't failed yet,' he said.

They waved as they pedalled down the track to the main road.

'Who on earth are we going to ask to take in a weakling lamb?' said James.

Mandy shrugged. 'I don't know,' she said. She looked hopeful. 'You don't think Mum and Dad—'

'No, I don't,' James interrupted her. 'You know your parents' rules about that.'

Mandy sighed. Her parents were quite strict about her bringing orphaned animals home. She knew they were right. Unless you said no to all of them you ended up taking all of them in. And then there would be no room for the animals that people brought to Animal Ark.

'It's a vet's practice,' Mrs Hope would say to Mandy, 'not a zoo.'

'What about Walter Pickard?' Mandy said.

James shook his head. 'Tom will be going home soon and he wouldn't be safe around a little lamb like that.'

Mandy sighed. 'I suppose that rules out a whole lot of people,' she said. 'Most people have a dog or a cat.'

'And Mr Spiller is right about the farmers,' said James. 'They're all too busy themselves at the moment to take on a sickly lamb.'

'It isn't really sickly,' said Mandy. 'Just extra small.'

James nodded. 'So it needs extra feeding – every two hours, was it?' he said. 'It wouldn't be so bad if it were sick – then we might be able to take it to Animal Ark.'

'Or the cottage hospital,' said Mandy, laughing. 'Matron could look after it along with the new babies. I've heard Matron never gets tired.'

Then she stopped talking.

James looked across at her. 'What is it?' he said. 'Have you thought of something.'

Mandy turned a shining face to him. 'I've had a brilliant idea,' she said. 'I don't know why I didn't think of it before. We'll take him to Gran! Gran and Grandad can look after him for a week or so – just until he's strong enough to be set on to another ewe.'

James's face lit up. 'Of course!' he said. 'That

would be perfect. Your Gran will love him.'

'I hope so,' Mandy said. 'I've a feeling it's our only chance.'

They found Grandad in the back garden, hoeing his vegetables.

'Hi, Grandad,' Mandy said as they parked the bikes in the back lane.

'Mandy!' said Grandad, his eyes lighting up with pleasure. 'And James. Just give me a minute and I'll put the kettle on.'

'No, no,' Mandy said quickly. 'Let me.'

Grandad's eyes twinkled. 'Uh-oh,' he said. 'Do I see somebody who wants a favour?'

Mandy laughed. 'Am I really that bad?' she said.

Grandad stuck his hoe in the ground beside him. 'You're not bad at all,' he said. 'It's just that your face gives you away. What is it you want?'

Mandy bit her lip. 'I would have to ask both of you,' she said. 'You and Gran.'

Grandad shook his head. 'Your Gran is off organising half the village over this hospital closure,' he said. 'She's called a meeting of the WI in the church hall.' Gran was chairperson of the Welford Women's Institute.

Mandy bit her lip.

'Can it wait?' Grandad said.

Mandy looked at James.

'Well,' said James, 'the sooner we find somebody to take it in the better.' Then he stopped.

Grandad laughed. 'I guess the secret is out now,' he said. 'Let me try and guess. You're looking for a home for some poor old animal you've found.'

'Not old, Grandad,' Mandy said. 'Actually it's young – very young.'

Grandad looked seriously at her. 'You know we can't take on an animal full time,' he said. 'Not the way we are with the camper van.'

Gran and Grandad had bought a camper van when Grandad retired. They were forever taking off on holiday in it. Gran said it made her feel like an explorer.

Mandy shook her head. 'It would only be for a week or so,' she said. 'Then it would be able to fend for itself – or not exactly fend for itself.'

'But it could go out in the top field,' said James.

'If we could set it on to another ewe,' Mandy finished.

Grandad looked from one to the other. Then his face cleared.

'You've been up at Fordbeck Farm helping Jack Spiller out,' he said.

Mandy nodded. 'It's a lamb, Grandad,' she said. 'A poor little lamb that has been rejected by its mother. It needs hand rearing for a week or so – just to get it started.'

'And we thought you and Mrs Hope would take it in,' said James.

'A lamb?' said Grandad.

Mandy looked at him. 'Of course,' she said. 'What did you think it was?'

Grandad chuckled. 'I was beginning to wonder,' he said. He pushed his cap to the back of his head and looked at them. 'Always up to something, you two,' he said. 'And there's always an animal there somewhere.'

'Will you do it, Grandad?' Mandy said eagerly. 'Do you think Gran will agree? It'll be an awful lot of work.'

Grandad's eyes twinkled. 'Tell you what,' he said. 'Let's go inside and get the kettle on and cut a bit of that freshly-baked fruit cake. We can have it ready for her when she comes back. Then, when she's had a nice cup of tea, we'll ask her.'

Mandy looked at her Grandad in mock outrage. 'And you say *I'm* bad?' she said.

Grandad laughed and tucked her arm into his as they walked down the path to the house. 'Can't think where you get it from,' he said, winking at James.

Seven

Mandy and James hurtled down the track to
Fordbeck Farm, feet pedalling madly, bicycle
wheels whizzing.

'It's all right!' Mandy called as they swept into
the yard in front of the farmhouse.

James came to a skidding halt beside her and
looked up at Jack Spiller. 'Mandy's Gran and
Grandad are going to take the lamb,' he said.
'We've found a home for it. I told you we would.'

Jack Spiller didn't smile.

'What's wrong?' Mandy said.

Suddenly her heart felt heavy as lead. Surely the
little animal hadn't died. It had been weak, yes,

but not so weak as to die in a couple of hours. And Jack Spiller had promised to look after it until they came back.

Mandy stood there watching him as he shook his head.

'I don't understand it,' he said. 'It was there in front of the fire.'

'What do you mean, *was?*' said James, puzzled.

Jack Spiller spread his hands. 'Come and see,' he said.

Mandy and James followed him into the kitchen. Mrs Spiller was sitting in front of the fire, the baby cradled in her arms.

At her feet was a box with a clean piece of wadded sacking in it.

'There,' said Jack Spiller. 'That's where I left it. And when I came back half an hour later it had gone.'

Mrs Spiller shook her head. 'Poor little thing,' she said. 'It didn't look to me as if it could get very far on its own. Still, it's amazing how tough these hill sheep can be. Maybe the little thing wandered off.'

Mr Spiller looked completely puzzled. 'I don't see what else could have happened,' he said. 'But I would have sworn that little fellow wasn't strong enough.'

Mandy was worried. 'But if he's gone off, what will happen to him? Who will feed him?'

Mr Spiller shook his head. 'Even if he manages to find his way back to the other sheep, none of them will feed him,' he said.

'But haven't you looked for him?' said James.

Jack Spiller turned to him and Mandy saw how tired he looked.

'There have been a couple of ewes in a bad way up in the top field,' he said. 'I've been up there this last hour. But I didn't see the little fellow.'

Mandy turned to Mrs Spiller. But she shook her head.

'I was having a very welcome lie down,' she said. 'And now I have to feed the baby – if I can find that bottle.' She turned to her husband. 'Jack, I made up a feed and put it in the fridge. You haven't seen it, have you?'

Mrs Spiller stood up and went out of the room with the baby. 'I must have left it down somewhere,' she said. 'I'll lose my head next.'

Mr Spiller pursed his mouth. 'Look, you two,' he said. 'I'm really sorry about this. I left that lamb there and now he's gone.' He smiled. 'At least he was strong enough to get up and go,' he said.

Mandy felt troubled. 'Maybe he was,' she said. 'But he can't feed himself, not yet. And none of those other ewes will feed him.' She felt tears prick at the back of her eyes and blinked them back as she looked out of the window.

It was evening. The sky was darkening. And out on the hill was the little lamb she and James had saved, had found a home for.

'It won't last the night,' James said, putting all her fears into words. 'Not if it's out there on the hill with no mother to shelter it or feed it.'

All of a sudden Mandy made up her mind. 'Come on, James,' she said. 'We'll look for it.' She turned to Jack Spiller. 'Is that all right with you, Mr Spiller?'

Jack Spiller looked out of the window to where the light was waning. 'It'll be dark soon,' he said. Then he saw Mandy's face. 'But of course you can try. Take a torch.'

Gratefully, Mandy and James went with him while he looked for a powerful torch. Then they were running uphill towards the top field, searching the ditches on the way, looking behind dry-stone walls, into hedges. And all the time it was getting darker.

Neither of them said how hard it would be to find a tiny black lamb in the dark. Neither of them wanted to think about that. The wind blew chill and Mandy turned her collar up. *Poor little thing,* she thought. They had to find it.

'It's no good,' James said at last. 'We're only scaring the sheep. And that can't be good for the ones that are still to lamb.'

Mandy started to argue, then thought better of it. James was right. For nearly an hour they had searched the field, burrowed in ditches, torn their clothes and hands on thorn bushes. And now it was almost dark. But she didn't want to give up.

'Just one more look around, James,' she said.

But it was no good. Wearily they trudged downhill – empty handed.

Jack Spiller met them at the farmyard. He didn't
have to ask. He could see by the look on their
faces that they hadn't found the lamb.

'He might not have survived anyway,' the farmer
said, and Mandy nearly burst into tears.

Oh, yes, he would, she thought. *If he'd had a nice
cosy place by the fire at Lilac Cottage and Gran and
Grandad to fuss over him and look after him – he would
have survived.*

But it was no good trying to say that to Mr
Spiller. He was only trying to comfort them in his
own way. And farmers had to be tough to survive.
They couldn't become sentimental about losing
lambs. It happened too often.

'Come in and have some milk and a biscuit
before you go,' Jack Spiller said. 'And tell Maggie
and Jenny I'll be in directly. I have to go and have
a quick look at that old bulldozer in the far field
before it gets too dark.'

Mandy and James walked into the warm and
welcoming front kitchen. Maggie Spiller looked
up at them and smiled. The baby was lying asleep
in her arms.

'Isn't he lovely?' said Mandy.

Mrs Spiller smiled proudly and touched the baby's cheek gently with her fingertip. 'He is now,' she said. 'But he'll probably grow up just as wild as Jenny!' She looked up, still smiling. 'Where is Jenny?' she said.

Mandy looked round. 'Isn't she here?' she said.

Maggie Spiller's eyes looked at her sharply. 'I thought she had gone with you,' she said.

Mandy and James shook their heads. 'We haven't seen her,' Mandy said.

'But she was here in the kitchen just before you arrived,' Mrs Spiller said. She was looking distraught. Then her face cleared. 'Of course, she must be with her dad.'

She looked at Mandy and James and the smile died on her lips.

Mandy bit her lip. 'We met him outside, Mrs Spiller,' Mandy said. 'He said he was going over to have a look at the old bulldozer. He said we were to tell you and Jenny he wouldn't be long.'

Maggie Spiller's face was paper white. 'Me and Jenny?' she said. 'But Jenny isn't here. Jenny hasn't been in the house for the last hour or so.' Mandy and James looked at her as she sat, her face pale and drawn, holding the new baby closely to her.

'Where is Jenny?' Mrs Spiller said for the second time.

It was at that moment that they heard a crash. It came from outside in the yard. Mrs Spiller turned towards the sound.

'What was that?' she said.

Eight

The sound seemed to echo around them. Mandy stood, rooted to the spot, her eyes still fixed on Mrs Spiller and the baby.

'What was that?' Mrs Spiller said again.

Her hand went to her mouth. Then she stood up quickly and tucked the sleeping baby into his carrycot. Her face was grim as she turned to them.

Mandy rushed to the window and looked out. Blackie went with her. He jumped up, resting his front paws on the window ledge. Then he was down again and running out into the yard.

'Blackie!' James called after him. But the Labrador took no notice.

There was dust still settling in the far corner of the farmyard.

'What is it?' said James.

'It's the old shed,' Mandy said, turning back into the room. 'The one Mr Spiller said was dangerous. It's collapsed.'

'That shed,' Mrs Spiller said. 'I've been telling Jack. Something needs to be done about it.' Her breath caught in her throat. 'You don't think . . . not Jenny . . . she can't be . . .' Then she was running for the door and out into the yard.

'Come on,' Mandy said to James. 'It might still be dangerous!'

They raced out into the yard and stood looking at the far corner where a heap of rubble lay. One side of the shed had collapsed entirely while the other side looked ready to collapse at any moment. Blackie prowled round the edges of the rubble.

'You don't think Jenny is in there, do you?' James said.

'Why should she be?' Mandy said. 'She was told to keep away from it. Mr Spiller said nobody was allowed to go near it.'

James nodded. 'You're right,' he said. 'But what about Mrs Spiller?'

Mrs Spiller was standing by the ruins of the

shed. She was calling Jenny's name.

Mandy went to stand beside her.

'It's all right, Mrs Spiller,' Mandy started to say.

'But where is Jenny?' Mrs Spiller said. She turned, distraught, looking for her daughter. She was more anxious than ever now.

'Look,' said Mandy. 'There's Mr Spiller coming.' She pointed towards the far field.

At once Mrs Spiller began to run towards her husband.

Mandy bit her lip. 'The poor Spillers,' she said. 'They aren't having much luck.'

James wasn't listening.

'James?' Mandy said. 'What is it?'

James shook his head. 'Nothing,' he said. 'I thought I heard something.'

Mandy looked at the ruins of the shed where Blackie was sniffing around. 'Blackie,' she called. 'Here, boy.'

The black Labrador took no notice.

'Call him, James,' Mandy said. 'The rest of that roof looks as if it's going to go any minute.'

James was watching Blackie intently.

'Look, Mandy,' he said. 'Look at the way Blackie's behaving. Sniffing, searching.'

Just then Blackie gave a short, sharp bark and

looked towards them. Then he began sniffing at a torn off sheet of corrugated iron.

'Come out of there, Blackie!' James said.

But the dog stayed firm where he was and barked again.

'What do you think he's found?' Mandy said.

James licked his lips and looked towards the far field. Jack Spiller had started running now. He was shouting something but he was still too far away for them to hear what it was. One thing was certain: Jenny wasn't with him.

'Do you think it's Jenny?' Mandy said.

'It might be,' James said. He looked at the sagging remains of the roof. The whole structure groaned and there was a sharp crack somewhere amongst the timbers.

'It's going to go any minute,' said Mandy. 'The whole thing is going to collapse!'

Blackie looked at them urgently, pawing the corrugated iron and barking.

Mandy and James looked at the remains of the overhanging roof, then at each other. The roof swayed.

'Come on,' said Mandy, 'We take an end each and heave. We'll be out of there in no time.'

Without giving themselves too much time to

think they scrambled over the collapsed wall into the shed. The roof creaked and groaned.

'Heave,' said Mandy as she grasped an end of the corrugated iron sheet.

James heaved. Blackie whimpered and began scrabbling at the edges of the sheet. Nothing happened.

'It's stuck,' said James, his face grim with effort.

Mandy nodded. 'It's wedged under that,' she said, pointing to a big stone that had fallen out of the wall. 'You shift the stone. I'll lift a corner of the sheet. We don't even know if Jenny is here.'

But, Mandy thought, *where else could she be?* The noise of the shed collapsing would have brought her running to see what had happened. The roof creaked again as James heaved on the stone and rolled it out of the way. Mandy bent and eased the corrugated iron sheet up a little. Then she gasped. A bright red gumboot lay at an awkward angle under the edge of the sheet.

Her face white, Mandy turned to James.

'I saw,' he said.

Then he was bending, straining to lift. Above them the roof swayed dangerously. Blackie whined and barked in warning.

'Again,' Mandy said through gritted teeth.

Slowly the corrugated iron sheet lifted. Mandy felt a sharp edge scrape along her forearm. With an almighty effort they pushed it to one side and looked down.

'Is she . . .' James didn't finish the sentence.

Mandy looked at Jenny. The little girl lay at an odd angle, her head twisted to one side. Blood flowed freely from a gash in her forehead and another in her leg. She looked very pale.

'Maybe we shouldn't move her,' Mandy said.

James looked up. Above them the roof beams cracked. A great cloud of dust fell and a stone dislodged itself from the wall, hit Mandy's knee and rolled, banging, on the corrugated iron. The roof creaked and groaned.

'It's going!' James said urgently. 'We've got to move her. We can't leave her.'

Grimly, Mandy nodded and together they bent and lifted the little girl's body. She was very light.

As they carried her through the door of the shed into the yard Jack Spiller came racing up, his face a mask of horror.

Grasping hold of Jenny, he took her from them, then urged Mandy and James in front of him across the yard.

Behind them the crash resounded, louder,

longer than before as the remains of the roof fell inwards.

Mandy and James stood there covered in dust, looking at the shed. Only one corner was intact now. The rest was hanging precariously in ruins.

'Is she hurt?' Mrs Spiller came running up, face white with strain.

Mr Spiller shook his head. 'She's bleeding badly,' he said. 'And she's unconscious. We have to get her to hospital as quickly as possible.'

At once everything was happening. Mandy rushed inside for fresh towels to wrap round Jenny's head and leg. Mrs Spiller collected the baby in his carrycot. Gently, Mr Spiller laid Jenny in the back of the van, wrapped in a rug, then jumped in and started to rev the engine.

Mrs Spiller leapt into the van beside Jenny, the baby on the floor beside her. She looked at Mandy and James. 'If you hadn't got her out . . .' she began.

'Go!' said Mandy as Mr Spiller revved the engine and put the car in gear. 'We'll follow on our bikes.'

The van leapt into life and surged off down the driveway.

Mandy and James looked at each other. They were filthy, and Mandy saw a long scratch on

James's cheek. She looked at herself. There was a graze on her arm.

'Come on,' said James. 'Let's go to the hospital. It's better than waiting here for news.'

The cottage hospital was warm and welcoming, its lights shining out through the gathering darkness. Mandy and James parked their bikes and ran up the steps into the hall.

A young nurse smiled at them, 'You two have been in the wars,' she said. 'Have you come to get yourselves patched up?'

Mandy frowned. 'No,' she said. 'It's Jenny, Jenny Spiller. Her mum and dad just brought her in.'

The smile disappeared from the nurse's face and Mandy felt her heart grow chilled.

'She's all right, isn't she?' said James.

The nurse pursed her lips. 'The doctor is with her now,' she said. 'And Matron.'

'Matron?' Mandy said. If Matron was there it must be serious.

'What's happening?' said James.

The nurse looked as if she wasn't going to tell them, then a voice said from the other end of the corridor, 'It's all right, Nurse Williams. I'll deal with this.'

Mandy and James looked up as the tall, straight figure of Matron came quietly down the corridor. Mandy gulped; Johnny Pearson was right. Matron was looking at them with a severe expression. She had neat, grey hair and piercing blue eyes. She was looking very serious indeed.

'Mr and Mrs Spiller told me how you rescued Jenny,' she said as she reached them.

'Is she going to be all right?' said Mandy.

Matron pursed her lips. 'We'll know very soon,' she said. 'Jenny has concussion and she's lost a lot of blood. She also has a broken leg. She's having a transfusion at the moment.'

'A blood transfusion?' Mandy said and gulped.

Matron's expression softened a little.

'Her parents are in my office with the baby,' she said. 'I don't think they should be disturbed just at the moment. Why don't you go into the waiting-room if you want to wait and see how she is?'

Mandy and James nodded. 'Yes, we'd like to wait,' said Mandy.

Matron nodded understandingly. 'Of course you would,' she said.

The waiting-room was tiny. It was brightly-painted and there was a pile of magazines and a box of children's toys in the corner. Mandy didn't feel like reading.

She and James sat there in silence. There didn't seem anything to say. It was just a matter of waiting.

Nurse Williams looked in on them after half an hour.

'There you are,' she said. 'Now I hope you two aren't worrying too much.'

Mandy looked at her hopefully. 'Any news?' she asked.

Nurse Williams pursed her lips. 'No news is good news,' she said. 'But it's lucky her mum and dad got her here so quickly. If they'd been much later that little girl would have lost too much blood. As it is, they got that transfusion started just in time.'

Mandy's mouth went dry with fright. It had been much worse than they'd thought.

'Nurse Williams,' said a voice from the door, 'I wonder if you would look in on the children's ward. Mary Anne Malloy wants to show you her new nightie.' It was Matron, looking disapproving.

Nurse Williams flushed to the roots of her hair. 'Another new nightie?' she said. 'She must have dozens of them.' And she bustled off.

'Little Jenny is going to be fine,' Matron said

firmly. 'You are not to worry about her.' She looked at Mandy. 'I've telephoned your grandmother, Mandy. She is going to let your parents and James's know where you are.'

'Oh, thank you, Matron,' Mandy said. 'I didn't think.'

Matron smiled. 'I know you're worried,' she said, 'but that doesn't mean we should worry your parents too.'

'No, Matron,' Mandy said meekly. She felt quite sorry for young Nurse Williams.

Then she looked at Matron. Matron's face softened. She turned in the doorway as she was leaving. 'I'll put some antiseptic on those cuts before you go,' she said.

'Oh,' said Mandy. 'It's nothing. They don't hurt.'

Matron merely smiled. Then she was gone.

'They always say that, don't they?' James said gloomily when Matron had gone.

'What?' asked Mandy.

'That people will be fine,' James said.

Mandy nodded. 'But she will be. I know she will.'

At last there was the sound of voices in the corridor and the whimper of a very young baby crying.

'The Spillers!' Mandy and James said together and shot out of the waiting-room.

Mandy looked at Maggie Spiller. She was crying. Mandy's heart lurched. Then she realised she was smiling as well.

Mrs Spiller saw Mandy and came over and put her arms round her.

'She's going to be all right, thanks to you two,' Mrs Spiller said. 'She needed some blood really quickly but she'll be OK now.'

Mandy smiled up at her, then she looked at Mr Spiller. But he wasn't smiling. His face was grim.

He came and stood in front of them. 'I can't thank you two enough,' he said. 'But right now I'm going home to get that bulldozer fixed, and as soon as it's fixed I'm going to knock down the rest of that shed.'

Mrs Spiller looked at the baby. 'This little one needs feeding,' she said. 'Jenny is asleep and she isn't to be disturbed tonight. Come on, you two. Put your bikes in the back of the van and we'll take you home.'

Mandy and James looked at her gratefully. Suddenly they were both quite tired.

'One moment,' said Matron. She eyed them up

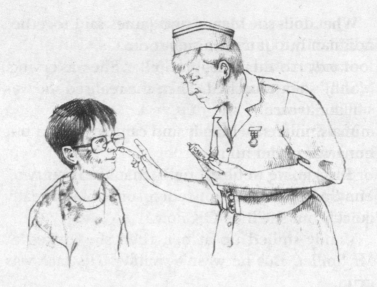

and down. 'I wanted to put some antiseptic on those cuts.'

'Oh, don't bother,' James said at once. 'They don't hurt at all.'

'Anyway Mum will do it,' Mandy said, rolling down her sleeve to hide the graze on her arm.

'Mandy's mum is a vet,' James said.

Matron smiled thinly. 'I should hope you appreciate the difference between people and mere animals,' she said.

Mere animals! Mandy thought, outraged. She opened her mouth to protest but the Spillers were leaving.

'What does she mean "mere animals"?' she said indignantly to James as he bundled her out of the door towards the van.

'Shh!' said James. 'She'll hear you.'

'I don't care if she does,' said Mandy. 'Mere animals, indeed. Huh! It was Blackie who knew Jenny was under all that rubble. If it hadn't been for Blackie, we wouldn't have been able to rescue Jenny. Mere animals! *Wonderful* animals is more like it!'

Nine

'So that's why I was so late home,' Mandy finished. 'And that's why you won't have that little lamb to look after.' She looked round the faces at the table.

Gran and Grandad had come for supper at the Hopes' cottage.

'We'd have been happy to look after the little fellow,' said Grandad, 'but I must say we were more worried about you.'

'Matron didn't go into details when she phoned,' Gran said.

'With all that going on, I don't think being late home is very important,' Emily Hope said smiling.

Mandy noticed she didn't say anything about

the lost lamb. There was no point. A lamb as small as that could never survive on its own.

'Poor Mrs Spiller,' Gran said. 'What a worry for her!'

'Farms can be dangerous places for children,' Grandad said. 'Especially children not brought up on a farm.'

'Mr Spiller had told Jenny never to go into that shed,' Mandy said.

Mr Hope shook his head. 'I'm sure he did,' he said. 'But I must say I can't blame him for wanting to bulldoze it as soon as possible.' He looked at Mandy. 'And as for you and James rushing in there . . .'

Mandy looked guilty. She wished James was still here but he had gone home. 'There was nothing else to do,' she said.

Her dad smiled but she could see the worry behind his eyes. 'Of course not,' he said. 'And it all turned out for the best. I just wish you wouldn't get yourselves into these scrapes.'

Mandy bit her lip but didn't say anything. She had tried to make as little as possible of the danger but Jack Spiller had praised her and James to the skies when he had brought her and James back to Animal Ark.

'Time enough for all that tomorrow,' Mrs Hope said. 'Mandy, your eyes are almost closing, you're so tired.'

Mandy yawned. 'What about the animals?' she said.

'The medications are all done,' Mrs Hope said. 'Don't worry about that.' She looked at her daughter. 'I think you should have a bath to ease those bruises and I'll come up later and put some cream on your cuts.'

Mandy pulled a face. 'Matron wanted to put antiseptic on them,' she said.

Mum laughed. 'I'll bet she did,' she said. 'Don't worry, this cream won't sting.'

Mandy yawned again as she got up from the table.

'Good night, Gran,' she said but Gran didn't answer. She was staring into space.

'Gran?' Mandy said.

'Oh, yes, sorry,' Gran said. 'I was miles away.'

Grandad laughed. 'Maybe you need an early night as well,' he said.

But Gran was as bright as a button. 'No,' she said. 'It's just that something occurred to me.' She turned to Mandy. 'You said that Matron told you Jenny got her blood transfusion just in time?' she said.

Mandy shook her head. 'It wasn't Matron, it was the nurse who said that.'

Gran nodded. 'That sounds more like it,' she said. 'Matron would be far too discreet to say a thing like that.'

'What are you getting at?' said Grandad.

Gran turned to him. 'I was wondering what would have happened if Jenny hadn't been able to have that blood transfusion when she did.'

Mandy shivered. 'But she did, Gran. That's all that matters,' she said.

Grandad laid a hand on Gran's arm. 'I know you feel really sorry for the Spillers and the trouble they've had lately, but the little girl is on the mend now.'

'Only because she got that blood transfusion,' said Gran.

Grandad looked puzzled. 'Of course,' he said.

'But don't you see?' said Gran. 'If Jenny hadn't got that transfusion so quickly she might have died. What I'm getting at is, if the accident had happened after they closed the cottage hospital, Jenny wouldn't have got that transfusion so quickly. What happens if there is another accident like this – after the hospital is closed?'

Mandy looked at her. 'Of course,' she said. 'I didn't think of that.'

Gran nodded. Her face was very serious. 'As your Grandad says, farms can be dangerous places and accidents can easily happen.' She looked round the table. 'We need that hospital,' she said. 'It really is a life-line for us. And I'm going to make sure that we keep it.'

Mandy threw her arms round Gran's neck and hugged her. 'And I'll help you,' she said. 'What do you want me to do?'

Gran squeezed Mandy's hands. 'Tomorrow I'll go and see Marion Timpson,' she said.

'Who?' said Mandy.

Gran's eyes twinkled. 'Matron,' she said. 'She isn't happy about this closure business. In fact she's hopping mad about it.'

Mandy blinked. She couldn't imagine the cool and frosty Matron hopping mad about anything.

'The campaign is all very well as it is,' Gran said, 'but we aren't making an impression on people. We've got to get the message across. That hospital is important. It isn't like other things. Keeping it open could make the difference between life and death. And if it takes a fight to keep it open then I'm ready to fight.

And so will a whole lot of other people in Welford and Walton.'

Gran paused, then her eyes lit up. 'In fact,' she went on, 'if they're trying to close one cottage hospital, you can bet your boots they're trying to close others. I wouldn't be surprised if there are a whole lot of communities facing this at the moment.' Her head came up. 'What we need,' she said, 'is a national campaign. We need to get the media on to this. Press coverage, TV. You wait and see. Once I'm finished we'll have a whole lot of support from all over the country, you see if we don't. Close our cottage hospital? Over my dead body!' Gran finished triumphantly.

Mandy gave Gran an extra hug. Adam Hope began to clap and Emily Hope and Grandad joined in.

'What a speech!' Mr Hope said. 'One thing's for sure, we're all behind you.'

'Just let us know,' Mrs Hope said. 'Fund-raising, posters, you name it – we'll help.'

Grandad didn't say anything. Mandy looked at him, puzzled. Then she saw the pride in his eyes as he looked at his feisty little wife. 'Come on, Dorothy,' he said to Gran. 'Time we were off.' He turned to Mrs Hope. 'I'll take this firebrand out of your kitchen, Emily, before she sets the whole place alight!'

Emily Hope laughed. 'You don't fool us,' she said. 'You're as proud as Punch of your firebrand. And she can set our kitchen alight any time she likes.'

'Ouch!' said Mandy as she emerged from sleep next morning. She looked round her, puzzled for a moment. Why did she feel stiff and sore? Then she remembered the events of the day before and sighed in relief. Jenny was all right. James and she were going to the hospital today to check up on her.

It was a moment before Mandy remembered the little black lamb. Her mouth turned down. There was no way the little fellow could have survived a night outside with no mother to protect him. Mandy would just have to put him out of her mind. There was nothing else for it.

Mandy threw back her duvet and swung her legs out of bed. She winced again as she did so. There was an ugly looking bruise on her knee.

'At least Matron won't see it,' she said to herself as she crossed the room towards the window.

Leaning across the pine table in the window,

Mandy drew the flowery curtains aside and looked down into the garden.

A whole family of rabbits scuttled around, tearing up mouthfuls of grass, chasing each other in and out of bushes. Mandy laughed at their antics and turned back to her room. With its old pine furniture and posters of animals it was her haven.

'Mandy,' a voice called from downstairs.

Mandy threw open her bedroom door and leaned over the banister to look down the twisty stair. 'Good morning,' she called back to her mother.

'James has just phoned,' her mum called back. 'He'll be over in half an hour.'

'Good,' said Mandy. 'We're going to the hospital to see Jenny.'

'You might see Gran,' Mrs Hope called back. 'She's going over to see Matron this morning. She's fizzing with energy over this campaign. Scrambled eggs for breakfast?'

Mandy laughed at the change of subject. 'Yummy!' she said. 'I'll be there in five minutes.'

A quick shower, a clean shirt and a fresh pair of jeans and Mandy was running downstairs, her hair still damp.

Mr Hope emerged from the door that led to the surgery. 'You've done the morning medications,' Mandy said. 'Did I oversleep?'

Her dad grinned and ruffled her hair. 'Don't you think you deserved an extra half hour after yesterday?' he said.

Mandy frowned. 'I like helping you,' she said.

'I know you do,' said Mr Hope. 'And you can give your mum a hand with the evening medications. I'm going to be out until quite late doing tuberculin injections.'

'Hard work,' Mandy said. 'But worth it.' She knew the injections helped to stop cows from passing on tuberculosis. 'How is Tom?'

Mr Hope grinned. 'Back to his old anti-social ways. Honestly, they might talk about a cat having nine lives but that animal has twice that at least.'

'I'll just pop in and see him before breakfast,' Mandy said.

A bright red head peeked round the door, 'Oh, no you won't,' said Emily Hope. 'Breakfast is on the table. You can go and see Tom afterwards – and add a few scratches to the ones you've already got.' She looked worriedly at her daughter, then her face cleared. 'You look completely recovered,' she said.

Mandy grinned. 'Oh, I'm fine,' she said, 'But I'm starving.'

Mrs Hope laughed. 'That's a good sign at least,' she said. 'Come on, before the eggs get cold.'

Mandy followed her mum into the kitchen. The sun shone through the windows, making the copper pans sparkle where they hung on the oak beams. The table was laid with a fresh, red-checked cloth and on it stood a plate mounded with honey coloured toast, a dish of pancakes and a great heap of butter-yellow scrambled eggs in a blue bowl.

'Terrific!' Mandy said with feeling.

Mandy was just polishing off the last pancake when she heard the sound of a bike scattering the gravel in the drive.

'It's James,' said Mrs Hope, looking out of the window. 'And Blackie.'

'I'm off,' said Mr Hope. 'And don't you two get up to any mischief today. Your mum and I have had enough excitement for one week.

Mandy grinned. 'Don't worry,' she said. 'James and I have had enough as well.'

'Enough what?' said a voice and James appeared round the kitchen door, shoving his brown, floppy hair out of his eyes.

'Excitement,' said Mandy.

'Too right,' James said. 'I had to promise Mum I would behave before she would let me out. Behave? We didn't do anything wrong.'

Mr Hope laughed as he gathered up his vet's bag and passed James on the way to the door. 'Parents always blame you when they're worried about you,' he said. 'You just have to put up with it.'

James grinned back. 'I suppose so,' he said. His eyes went to the table. 'Did you have pancakes?' he said.

Emily Hope looked at Mandy and James and shook her head. 'I don't know where you two put all the food you eat,' she said. 'There isn't an ounce of fat on either of you.'

'I'll just be going,' Mr Hope said, sidling out of the door.

Mandy laughed. Mrs Hope was always getting at him about his weight. It wasn't that he was fat – just not thin. And he did jog to try and keep his weight down.

'Bye, Dad,' she called after him.

Mrs Hope looked at her watch.

'Surgery in half an hour,' she said. 'Tell you what. You two go and look in on Tom and I'll make another batch of pancakes. I'll call you when they're ready.'

'Great,' said James. 'You make the best pancakes, Mrs Hope.'

Mrs Hope grinned. 'Flattery will get you everywhere, James,' she said. She looked at Blackie. 'I suppose you want some too?' she said.

Blackie wagged his tail and Mandy just managed to catch the butter dish before it was swept off the table.

Tom was, as Mr Hope had said, on the mend.

'Ow!' said James as he lifted the cat out of the cage.

'His claws are really sharp,' Mandy said.

James sucked his hand. 'Don't I know it,' he said. 'What a monster!'

Mandy looked at the old cat. 'He isn't a monster,' she said. 'Just a bit grumpy.'

'Grumpy is pretty normal for Tom,' James said.

Mandy frowned. 'I hope Jenny is back to normal today,' she said. 'Poor little girl. She must have got a terrible shock.'

James put Tom back in his cage. 'Let's go this morning,' he said. 'As soon as we've had the pancakes. Matron must let us see her today.'

Mandy nodded. Surely Jenny would be well enough to have visitors today.

Mrs Hope called them back just as they were leaving. 'Take this to Jenny,' she said, holding out a prettily-wrapped parcel.

'Thanks, Mum,' said Mandy. 'What is it?'

'Soaps,' said Mrs Hope, 'shaped like flowers. I thought she would like them.'

'She will,' said Mandy.

'Mum sent some fruit,' said James.

'And I've got a card and a little game here for her,' Jean Knox said. 'Just hold on while I write the card.'

Mandy looked at the receptionist with affection as Jean caught the glasses swinging from their chain round her neck, put them on, and wrote a message on the card.

'Thanks, Jean,' she said. 'It'll be like Christmas.'

James called to Blackie and they were off down the track from Animal Ark and heading for the Walton Road.

They passed Walter Pickard on his way to the church for the bell-ringing practice. He was carrying a big bunch of flowers from his garden. 'Your grandad tells me you've been in the wars, young miss,' he called to Mandy.

Mandy grinned and stopped her bike. 'So has Tom,' she said.

Walter scratched his head. 'You'd think he'd be old enough to know better, wouldn't you?' he said. 'Your mum says I can have him back tomorrow – if I can keep him out of trouble.'

Mandy laughed at the idea of keeping Tom out of trouble.

'We've been told to stay out of trouble as well,' James said gloomily.

Walter laughed. 'Where are you two young ones off to?'

'The cottage hospital,' Mandy said. 'To see Jenny Spiller.'

Walter grinned. 'At least you can't get into any trouble in a hospital,' he said. Then he shook his head. 'Bad business, that,' he said. 'But you two did well from what I hear. You tell the little lass I'm asking for her,' he went on. He looked at the flowers he was carrying. 'I was taking these along to the church for the WI ladies to arrange,' he said. 'But I reckon young Jenny would like them. Here you are, young miss,' And he handed the bunch of flowers to Mandy.

'Oh, Mr Pickard, thank you,' Mandy said as she put the flowers in her bicycle basket. 'They're lovely. Jenny will be so pleased.'

Julian Hardy, who owned the Fox and Goose, stepped out of his pub as he saw them coming. 'How's little Jenny?' he said.

Mandy smiled. News certainly got round fast in Welford. 'We're just going to see her,' she said.

'Wait there, then,' said Mr Hardy and disappeared into the pub. He was out again in a moment carrying a bottle of orange squash. 'Give her this from me,' he said.

It was like that all through the village. Mrs McFarlane from the post office saw them passing and called them in while she made up a pile of comics to take to Jenny. By the time they got to the hospital their arms were full of presents. Mandy looked at Blackie trotting along beside them. She smiled. She had the feeling that Blackie might be the best present of all. Jenny was so fond of him.

'And Mr Spiller thought they might not be accepted in these parts,' Mandy said to James.

'What?' said James.

Mandy explained as they rode along. 'One of the reasons they kept themselves to themselves was that he thought they would be looked on as not really country folk. You know, with him losing his job in the town and all. He thought he might be resented.'

Mandy looked at the pile of gifts in her bicycle basket.

'Well,' she said. 'They can't very well think that people don't care about them now!'

Ten

'Where do you think you're going with that dog?' said a voice.

Mandy and James turned.

It was Matron, looking really forbidding.

'What does she mean "that dog"?' James whispered to Mandy. 'Blackie isn't "that dog".'

'Shh,' said Mandy. 'She'll hear you.'

'I certainly did hear you, James Hunter,' said Matron as she strode down the corridor towards them.

'We brought Blackie to see Jenny,' Mandy said.

'Yes,' said James. 'She and Blackie get on really well.'

Matron stopped in front of them and folded her arms. 'No animals are allowed inside the hospital,' she said.

'But why not?' said Mandy.

Matron looked shocked. 'Why not?' she said. 'Because they're unhygienic, that's why not!' she said. 'They'd bring all kinds of nasty germs into the hospital. We've got sick people here, you know.'

Mandy frowned. 'We wouldn't let him jump on the beds or anything,' she said. 'And besides, sick people are supposed to get better quicker if they have pets.'

'That's right,' James said. 'I read that some-where. Pets are good for sick people.'

Matron drew herself up. 'Not in this hospital,' she said. She looked at Mandy. 'I was having a long talk with your grandmother this morning about trying to save the hospital,' she said. 'Your grandmother said you were helping her.'

Mandy nodded. 'James is helping too,' she said. 'We've done lots of posters and leaflets and things.'

Matron sniffed. 'Fine way to help,' she said, 'bringing animals into the hospital. That's just the kind of thing that would do us a lot of harm. If

we're going to run a campaign to save the hospital
we have to be sure everything is run perfectly. We
can't have animals running around everywhere.
Now put that dog outside – and wash your hands
before you go into the ward.' And Matron stomped
off down the corridor.

'Gosh,' said James. 'You'd think we'd brought
in a whole zoo full of animals instead of one
harmless dog.'

Blackie looked up at them with mournful eyes.

'Don't take any notice, Blackie,' Mandy said. 'We
don't think you're full of germs.'

They took Blackie outside and left him tied to a
tree in the garden before they went back into the
hospital to find Jenny.

'Don't stay long,' said Nurse Williams.

Mandy and James looked at her.

'She *is* better, isn't she?' Mandy said.

The nurse smiled. 'She's still very tired,' she said.
'But her broken leg should mend well. It isn't like
poor Johnny Pearson's. That was a really bad
break.' She frowned. 'I think something is
worrying her, though, but she won't say what it
is.' Then she looked at the pile of presents Mandy
and James were carrying. 'I should think that lot
will cheer her up,' she said.

'Have Mr and Mrs Spiller been in today?' Mandy asked.

The nurse nodded. 'They were here first thing,' she said. 'Isn't that baby a darling? They left not long ago. Mr Spiller said he had to get back.' The nurse smiled. 'Funny man – he said he had a bit of bulldozing to do.'

Mandy frowned as they followed the nurse down the corridor. What could be worrying Jenny?

'You go ahead,' said Nurse Williams as she showed them into the bright, sunny ward. She took the bunch of flowers Mandy was carrying. 'Aren't these lovely?' she said. 'I'll just put them in water.' And she walked briskly back down the corridor.

The children's ward was quite small – only six beds, and three of them were occupied.

Poor Johnny had his leg in traction. His curly, red head turned as they came in and he gave them an impish grin. Mandy and James grinned back.

'How are you, Johnny?' Mandy said as they passed his bed.

'Bored,' said Johnny. 'There's nothing to do.'

'You could read,' said Mandy.

'I've read all my comics twice,' Johnny said. His eye fell on the bundle of things in Mandy's hands. 'Is that this week's comics?' he said.

Mandy nodded, grinning. 'Maybe Jenny will let you read them when she's finished with them,' she said.

Johnny looked at Jenny over the sling his leg was caught up in. 'I bet she won't even read them,' he said. 'She just lies there and cries.'

Mandy opened her mouth to say something but a voice piped up from the next bed.

'There's somebody she wants to see but when you ask her who it is she won't tell you.'

Mandy looked at the next bed. A plump little fair-haired girl was perched on the end of it, brushing the hair of a fair-haired doll. Mandy didn't recognise her.

'Hi,' she said. 'I'm Mary Anne Malloy. I've had my appendix out. I've seen it. They showed it to me after the operation. It was disgusting!'

Mandy blinked and heard James laugh beside her.

'You didn't want to take it home in a jar or anything?' he said.

Mary Anne carried on brushing her doll's hair. The doll had a pink nightie on, just like Mary Anne's.

'No way,' she said She looked up at them. 'I wish Jenny felt a bit better. I offered to let her play with Gilda,' she held up the doll, 'but she didn't want to.' Mary Anne sighed.

'That was kind of you,' said Mandy. 'But maybe she isn't well enough yet.'

Mary Anne smiled. 'That's probably it,' she said. 'I felt awful for the first couple of days after I had my appendix out. I was an emergency case.'

'What, with an ambulance and everything?' James said.

Mary Anne nodded proudly. 'Daddy says they stopped all the traffic on the Walton roundabout.' She gave them a huge smile. 'Fancy that,' she said.

Mandy couldn't help laughing. 'Fancy,' she said. 'Look, Mary Anne, we're going to see Jenny now.'

'Tell her she can play with Gilda any time she likes,' said Mary Anne.

'We shall,' said Mandy.

'She's a riot,' James said as they made their way across to Jenny's bed. It was set next to the french windows that opened up into the garden at the back of the cottage hospital. The sun came streaming through the light, flowered curtains on to the neat bed where Jenny lay. Her face was turned away from them.

'Maybe she's asleep,' said Mandy.

But at the sound of her voice the head on the

pillow turned and Jenny gave them a weak smile.

'Hello,' said Mandy. 'We've brought you some presents. Everybody is asking about you.'

Jenny didn't say anything.

James looked uncomfortable. 'Is there anything you want?' he said. 'Anything we can do for you?'

Jenny shook her head and a big fat tear ran down her cheek. She moved her lips and said something but so low that they couldn't hear what it was.

'What?' said Mandy.

Jenny turned to her. 'Blackie,' she said.

Mandy bit her lip. 'We brought him,' she said. 'But Matron wouldn't let us bring him in. She won't allow animals into the hospital.'

Jenny's face had brightened but now with Mandy's last words she looked sad again.

'He's dead, isn't he?' she said.

Mandy was shocked. 'Dead?' she said. 'Of course he isn't dead. He's outside, tied to a tree.'

Jenny shook her head. 'You're just saying that,' she said and another big tear ran down her cheek.

Mandy and James looked at each other as Jenny turned her face away.

'Why on earth does she think he's dead?' said James.

Mandy shrugged. 'I don't know,' she said. 'But she's obviously worried about it. She won't get better if she goes on worrying like this.'

'But we can't bring Blackie in,' said James. 'You heard Matron. She'd kill us.'

Mandy nodded, trying to think. Her eyes rested on the french windows beside Jenny's bed.

'We don't have to bring him in,' she said. 'We just have to bring him round to the french windows. Then Jenny can see he isn't dead.'

'Brilliant,' said James. 'You wait here with Jenny. I'll go and fetch Blackie.'

Mandy nodded and James went quickly out of the ward.

'James has gone to get Blackie,' Mandy said to the little girl. 'You wait and see. He'll be here in a minute.'

Jenny's eyes looked bright with tears. 'Are you sure?' she said.

Mandy nodded. 'I promise,' she said.

There was a tap on the french windows. Mandy went over and unlatched them.

'Look, Jenny,' she said. 'Here's Blackie come to see you.'

Eagerly the little girl sat up in bed and leaned forward to see. Then her face crumpled. Her mouth drooped and she said, 'Not that Blackie. I want *my* Blackie.'

Mandy looked at her in astonishment.

'Your Blackie?' she said. 'What do you mean?'

Jenny shook her head, the tears running down her cheeks. 'My Blackie,' she repeated. 'My little black lamb.'

Light began to dawn on Mandy.

'What's going on?' said James from beyond the window. 'Is she pleased?'

Mandy shook her head. 'There's a problem,' she said. 'It seems we've got the wrong Blackie.'

'What?' said James. In his surprise he stepped over the sill into the ward. Blackie came with him.

'Oh!' said Mary Anne from her bed. 'What a lovely dog. Can I pet him?'

James nodded absently and Mary Anne trotted over to pet Blackie.

Mandy turned to Jenny. 'Your lamb,' she said. 'Is that the one that went missing, the one we left in the kitchen? The tiny one?'

Jenny nodded. 'Daddy said we couldn't have it. He said it was too much trouble – it would have to go.' She looked up, her little face fixed. 'I took him away,' she said. 'I hid him. Then I took one of the baby's bottles and some milk to feed him – just the way you said you did. Just the way Mum did with those other lambs. I know how. Mum showed me.'

James started to speak but Mandy shook her head. Very gently she sat down on Jenny's bed and put her arm round her.

'Jenny,' she said, 'where did you hide the lamb?'

Jenny's eyes filled with tears again. 'If I tell you then Daddy will get rid of him,' she said.

Mandy hesitated. There was no easy way of putting this. 'But, Jenny,' she said, 'if your Blackie is all alone then he'll get sick. Lambs as small as that need someone to take care of them.'

Again Jenny shook her head. 'Daddy would be angry,' she said.

Mandy sighed. 'But how can we find Blackie and bring him to see you if we don't know where he is?'

Jenny looked up at her. 'You wouldn't tell anybody?' she said. 'You would bring him here so that I could see he was all right?'

'Cross my heart,' said Mandy. 'And I'll look after him until you get out of hospital. I promise.'

Jenny looked at her again. 'I put him in the shed. The old one.'

It took a moment for Mandy to realise what the little girl was saying.

'The old shed?' she said. 'The one you got hurt in?'

Jenny looked puzzled and Mandy realised she didn't remember how she got hurt. She had been unconscious when they had found her.

'You mean the one your dad told you not to go into? The tumbledown shed. That one?'

Jenny nodded. 'He wouldn't let anybody go in there so I knew nobody would find Blackie.'

Mandy and James looked at each other. 'Where did you put him?' Mandy said.

Jenny frowned. 'Right at the back,' she said. 'In the water trough, so that he couldn't run away and get hurt.'

Mandy conjured up a mental picture of the shed as she had last seen it. The water trough was right over at the back. As far as she could remember the roof was still intact at that point.

It was then that James said, 'The bulldozing – remember what Nurse Williams said?'

Mandy turned to him.

'Oh, no,' she said.

'What is it?' said Jenny.

Quickly Mandy smiled. She couldn't very well

tell the little girl that her father was going to bulldoze the shed that very afternoon.

'It's nothing,' Mandy said. 'But we have to go.' She looked at James.

'We have to go and get your Blackie,' James said to Jenny.

Jenny's face lit up. 'And bring him back.'

'If he's well enough,' Mandy said. 'You just get better now, won't you?'

Jenny smiled and snuggled down in bed. 'And don't let Daddy put him out, will you?' she said.

Mandy shook her head. 'He won't do that,' she said. She turned to James. 'We'd better phone – just in case.'

'I don't believe my eyes!' a voice said – a familiar voice.

Mandy and James turned. Matron stood at the door of the ward. 'How dare you disobey my orders?' she said.

'We didn't,' said James. Then he looked at where Mary Anne was playing with Blackie. 'Oh, dear,' he said.

'We have to make a phone call,' Mandy said.

Matron looked outraged. 'Phone call!' she said. 'I've never heard such cheek in my life. Phone call, indeed. You will put that animal outside, then you will report to me in my office.' And she turned on her heel and left the ward.

Matron was obviously not used to being disobeyed.

Mandy looked at James in horror.

'We have to get in touch with the Spillers,' James said.

'She won't let us. She won't listen,' said Mandy. 'You heard her. She's on the warpath.'

'So what do we do?' said James.

Mandy shrugged. 'There's only one thing to do,' she said. 'We make a run for it. We've got to get to Fordbeck Farm before Mr Spiller bulldozes that shed!'

Eleven

Mandy's legs were aching by the time the track to Fordbeck Farm came into view.

'What's that noise?' she said as they rounded the bend in the track, earth spurting beneath their wheels.

'Look!' shouted James as he hurtled down the track towards the farm. Mandy followed his gaze.

'Oh, no!' she gasped. 'Hurry!'

Jack Spiller was driving the bulldozer through the gate at the back of the farm into the farmyard. He was making straight for the shed.

'Too late!' James yelled over the increasing roar of the bulldozer.

Mandy thought of Jenny. 'We can't be too late,' she said.

Together they hurtled through the farm gates right in front of the bulldozer.

'Stop,' they yelled. 'Stop!'

Mandy saw Jack Spiller's face look down at them, astonished. He swerved the bulldozer to one side, put on the brakes and leapt down from the cab.

'What the devil do you two think you're doing?' he yelled. 'Have you any idea how dangerous that was?'

Mandy leapt off her bike and ran to him. 'Mr Spiller,' she said. 'You must listen. It's Jenny.'

At once Jack Spiller stopped shouting. His face went white. 'Jenny?' he said. 'Is she all right? What's happened?'

Mandy shook her head. 'Nothing,' she said. 'At least she's so unhappy because of the lamb – the one that disappeared – Jenny took it – she hid it in the shed. It's still there.'

'Say all that again slowly,' said Jack Spiller.

Mandy did, with James's help. Blackie arrived, panting, as they finished talking.

'So you see,' Mandy finished, 'she's so worried about that little lamb, she isn't getting better. We promised her that we'd bring the lamb to see her.

It's in that shed, Mr Spiller. We told Jenny we'd look after it – and we will, if it's still alive.'

Jack Spiller looked undecided. 'That place is dangerous,' he said.

Mandy nodded. 'I know,' she said. 'But the lamb is hidden in the old water trough.'

'At the back of the shed?' Mr Spiller said.

'Yes, the roof hasn't fallen in back there,' said James.

Mandy watched as Mr Spiller weighed up the chances of finding the lamb alive.

'It's just that she wanted that little lamb so much,' said Mandy.

Jack Spiller made up his mind. 'Wait here,' he said. 'And don't move.'

Mandy, James and Blackie stood watching as Mr Spiller moved cautiously round to the back of the shed. Part of the wall had given way. They saw him step carefully over the rubble. As he did so his foot scraped on stone and Mandy thought she heard the wall creak. She held her breath. It seemed ages before he came out again. Mandy looked. Was he carrying something? Yes – something black and woolly.

She looked at Mr Spiller's face. He was smiling.

'He's alive?' she said.

Jack Spiller shook his head in wonder. 'I wouldn't have given tuppence for this little thing when I first saw him,' he said. 'But he's alive all right. He must be a real fighter. And look at this.'

Mandy looked at what he was holding.

'A baby's bottle,' she said.

Jack Spiller grinned. 'I reckon we've found the one that Maggie lost,' he said. 'Take this little chap into her and see if you can get some fresh milk into him. He was licking the teat of this bottle when I found him in the water trough. Lucky for him he was there and the bottle beside him. He was protected from the worst of the damage.'

'Oh!' said Mandy, taking the little creature. 'He's so frail.'

Mr Spiller scratched his head. 'I reckon he'll survive,' he said. 'After what he's been through I wouldn't put anything past him.'

James grinned. 'This is going to make Jenny get better in a hurry,' he said.

Mr Spiller grinned back. 'In that case I'd better get that shed knocked down good and proper,' he said. 'Before she gets back and starts hiding more animals in there.'

Mandy and James took the lamb into the house.

'Good heavens!' said Maggie Spiller when she

saw what they were carrying.

Once more, Mandy explained, while Mrs Spiller got some milk ready for the lamb.

'If you have any protein supplement . . .' Mandy began.

Mrs Spiller nodded. 'Your dad left some with us the other day,' she said. 'I'll get it.'

Mandy and James watched as Mrs Spiller mixed the protein supplement with the milk. Then she handed the bottle to Mandy.

'Here,' she said. 'See how much of this he'll take.'

The lamb was hungry. He sucked eagerly at the mixture in the baby's bottle and after a while his little tail began to wag.

'I really think he's going to be all right,' said Mandy.

Mrs Spiller laughed. 'Who would have thought it?' she said. 'Our Jenny will be pleased.'

Mandy smiled. Oh, yes, Jenny would be pleased.

'But I want to see him!' Jenny said.

'Just as soon as you get out of hospital,' Mandy said to her.

It was the day after the bulldozing of the shed and they were visiting Jenny.

Jenny shook her head. 'You're only saying he's

well so that I won't worry,' she said.

'No, we're not,' James said. 'He's fine, really. Your mum is feeding him and he's amazingly strong. He'll soon be able to be set on to another ewe.'

Jenny looked mutinous. 'You're just saying that,' she said again.

'Here comes Matron,' Mary Anne said from the door where she was keeping lookout. Mandy and James had sneaked past Matron's office. She hadn't seen them come in.

'Quick,' said James. 'We'll go out by the french windows.' Jenny clutched Mandy's arm. 'When will you bring Blackie?' she said.

'Hurry!' said Mary Anne.

Mandy looked at the little girl desperately. 'You know Matron won't have animals in the hospital,' she said.

'Run!' Mary Anne called.

Jenny looked at Mandy.

'Tomorrow!' Mandy said, then she leapt for the french windows.

Any moment she expected to hear a shout behind her but there was nothing.

'That was close,' said James, as they made their way round to the front of the hospital. 'How on earth are we going to get the lamb in to see Jenny?'

Mandy shrugged. 'Through the french windows, I suppose,' she said.

James looked doubtful. 'We were lucky that time,' he said. 'But I don't fancy trying to escape Matron's eagle eye very often. And what about Nurse Williams? She's always around.'

'We'll manage,' said Mandy. 'It's obvious Jenny isn't going to get better until she's seen that lamb.'

James nodded. 'At least you sound confident,' he said. 'It's more than I feel.'

But Mandy didn't feel half as confident as she sounded.

Her confidence didn't improve when she got home either.

'Gran rang,' Mrs Hope said to her.

'Oh, yes,' said Mandy.

'She wanted to know what you've been doing to upset Matron,' Mrs Hope said.

'What?' said Mandy. 'What did Gran say exactly?'

'So you *have* been up to something!' Mrs Hope said.

Mandy sighed. 'Not exactly,' she said. 'It was a mistake.'

'Hmm,' said Mrs Hope. 'I expect I should leave well enough alone and not ask difficult questions,' she said.

Mandy looked at her mum gratefully. Mrs Hope knew that if Mandy was in real trouble she would tell her.

'Anyway,' Mrs Hope went on, 'Gran says she's got a TV crew coming tomorrow to cover the story about the hospital closure. So Matron will have other things on her mind.' Mrs Hope grinned. 'She said to let you know you could relax tomorrow at least but Matron still wanted to see you and James.'

Mandy sighed. Life was just too complicated sometimes.

'But we promised to take the lamb to see Jenny tomorrow,' James said when she told him.

Mandy nodded. 'I know,' she said. 'But how can we? If the TV crew are going to be there . . .' Then she stopped.

'What is it?' said James.

'That's just it,' said Mandy. 'The TV crew are going to be there. If we find out when they're coming then we can be sure Matron will be busy with them.'

'And we take the chance to sneak Jenny's lamb into the ward,' James said.

Mandy nodded. 'I know we aren't supposed to,' she said. 'But Matron would never listen and Jenny will go on pining until she sees her lamb.'

'So we'll just have to go for it,' said James. 'We don't have any choice, really.'

Mandy nodded in agreement.

'So how are we going to find out when the TV crew is coming?' James said.

Mandy frowned. 'I'll ask Gran. She'll be there for the filming. After all, she was the one who organised it.'

'Right,' said James. 'You go and see your Gran and I'll go up to Fordbeck Farm to see if the lamb is going to be strong enough to take tomorrow.'

Mandy nodded. 'OK,' she said. 'Let's meet at Animal Ark after tea!'

'Eleven o'clock,' Mandy said as she and James did the rounds of the animal cages in the residential unit. 'First they want an interview with Gran and Matron, then they want to film the wards and talk to the patients.'

James grinned. 'Can you imagine how pleased Mary Anne will be?' he said. 'Does she know?'

Mandy laughed. 'Of course she knows,' she said. 'Can you imagine trying to keep anything secret from Mary Anne? She was supposed to go home this morning but she asked if she could stay just one more day.'

'And Matron let her?' said James.

Mandy grinned. 'Gran pointed out to Matron that the more patients they had the better it would look.'

'Your gran is amazing,' James said.

'Gran also says that Mary Anne's mother brought her in another new nightie and a matching one for Gilda.'

James shook his head. 'She'll be a riot on TV,' he said.

'Who? Gran or Mary Anne?' said Mandy.

'Both!' James said.

'What about Blackie?' Mandy said.

'Oh, I don't think we'll take him,' said James. 'That's asking for trouble.'

'Not your Blackie, Jenny's Blackie,' Mandy said.

'Sorry,' said James. 'That lamb is amazing. He's as fit as a flea, jumping all over the place. Mr Spiller says he should have him set on in no time.'

'So he's fit to go to the hospital tomorrow?' Mandy said.

'No problem,' said James.

Not for the lamb, Mandy thought. But getting in and out of the hospital unseen by Matron could be a big problem for them!

Twelve

Mary Anne's new nightie was bright yellow with blue polka dots.

'Do you like it?' she said to Mandy and James.

'It'll make the cameras go funny,' James said.

Mary Anne's mouth turned down.

'James is only joking,' Mandy said. 'It's lovely, Mary Anne.'

'Well, it makes my eyes go funny looking at it,' James said.

'Shh,' said Mandy. 'We're depending on Mary Anne to let us in.' She stood on tiptoe again to talk to the little girl through the open window of the children's ward.

'Remember, Mary Anne,' she said. 'Just as soon as the coast is clear, come round and open the french windows, then we can bring Jenny's lamb in to see her.'

Mary Anne nodded. 'Jenny doesn't think you're telling the truth. Is he really in there?' she said looking at the cat basket Mandy was carrying.

Mandy nodded. 'You'll see him when we bring him in,' she said.

'OK,' Mary Anne said in a whisper. She turned back into the room. 'Somebody is coming,' she said.

'You get back into bed,' said Mandy. 'We'll wait here.' She indicated a bush out of sight of the ward windows.

'I feel like a criminal,' James said.

Mandy sighed. 'Never mind,' she said. 'All we have to do is slip in, show the lamb to Jenny and slip out again. It won't take long.'

'It certainly won't,' said James. 'Not if Matron catches us. It'll be over in minutes – painfully.'

'Matron won't catch us,' said Mandy. 'She and Gran are having their interview just now. It's just a matter of waiting until Nurse Williams is out of the way.'

'*Psst!*' came a voice from the window.

Mandy and James looked up.

'Nurse Williams is in the storeroom,' Mary Anne called softly.

'OK then, open the french windows,' Mandy said.

Quickly she and James ran round to the french windows. There was the sound of a latch being lifted from inside and then Mary Anne was standing there.

'You're terrific, Mary Anne,' Mandy said as she and James stepped into the ward.

Mandy turned to Jenny's bed. A tousled head turned towards her.

'Jenny,' said Mandy. 'Look who we've brought to see you.' She opened the lid of the cat basket.

Jenny sat up, her eyes wide. 'Blackie?' she said. 'My very own Blackie?'

Mandy put the basket down on top of Jenny's bed.

'Let me see,' said Mary Anne, wriggling in front of Mandy.

'Careful,' said Mandy. 'Don't frighten him.'

'Oh, look,' said Jenny, and she lifted the little woolly lamb out of the basket.

'Hi,' said a voice from the other end of the room, 'Don't forget me.'

'I'll let Mary Anne bring him over to see you, Johnny,' Jenny said.

Mandy opened her mouth to say no, but when she looked at Jenny's face she couldn't bear to. Instead of the white face and big sad eyes, Jenny looked the picture of happiness.

'Be quick then,' said Mandy. 'We can't stay long.'

Jenny handed the little lamb to Mary Anne and Mary Anne scurried across the ward with him.

'There,' said Mary Anne and she plonked the lamb down on Johnny's bed. Its black woolly legs splayed out on either side as the lamb tried to stand up.

'He's terrific,' Johnny was saying when there was a sound in the corridor.

'Who's that?' said Mandy.

Mary Anne rushed to the door.

'Matron!' she said. 'And another lady and a man with a camera!'

'What?' said James. 'Where are they going?'

Mary Anne darted back into the room. 'I think they're coming here,' she said.

Mandy dashed across the ward, grabbed the lamb and thrust him into the cat basket. The footsteps were getting nearer. She looked across the ward. They would never get out without being seen. She backed towards the wall and found a door behind her.

'What's this?' she said.

'I don't know,' said Mary Anne.

Mandy pushed the door open. 'Come on, James,' she said. 'Get back into bed, you two, and don't say a word!'

James got the door shut just in time.

They heard voices and Nurse Williams said 'Look who's here to see you, children. Matron. And this is Mr Peters, who is going to take some pictures for the television.'

'Phew!' said James. 'That was close!'

Mandy looked round. What they needed was a way out.

'What is this place?' James whispered.

Mandy looked at the machines. 'It's the hospital laundry,' she said. 'Look, those are washing machines and dryers.'

'They're a lot bigger than ours at home,' said James.

'They would have to be,' Mandy said. 'And look at the big buckets of soap flakes.'

'Like snow,' James laughed.

Mandy frowned. There were windows in the

room but they were high up, right next to the ceiling.

'It's OK,' said James. 'They won't come in here. Why on earth would they want to come into the laundry?'

At that, the door opened and Matron's voice said, 'And this is the laundry!'

There was a scuffling sound inside the cat basket and the little black lamb leapt nimbly out.

'What on earth are you doing here, Mandy?' Gran asked. Mandy whirled round to catch the lamb, missed, and gasped in horror as it skipped into one of the buckets of soap flakes.

Scrabbling for a foothold the lamb kicked up clouds of soft white flakes which floated in the air before coming to rest all over the laundry room.

'A lamb?' said Mr Peters. 'In the laundry?'

Then Blackie got a grip on the side of the bucket and, with a kick of his heels, he was free and scampering between Matron's feet and into the ward.

'Catch him!' said James.

'Is that an animal in my hospital?' cried Matron. 'Another one?'

'Oh, Mandy,' said Gran.

In the background Jenny's voice could be heard calling to the lamb and Mary Anne was squealing with delight.

'Oh, Lord,' said James. 'We're really for it now!'

Thirteen

Matron drew herself up and looked at Mandy and James.

'You can't be cross with them,' said a small figure in a blue and yellow polka dot nightie.

Matron looked down. 'Mary Anne,' she said. 'Get back into bed at once!'

'But they only did it to make Jenny better,' said Mary Anne. 'She wasn't getting better because she was worried about her little lamb. She's much better now. It isn't fair to blame Mandy and James. They rescued her and now they've made her better.'

Mandy and James looked at her, aghast. They

would never dare to speak to Matron like that.

Mr Peters cut in before Matron could speak.

'What's this about a rescue?' he said.

Mary Anne launched into her story. There was no stopping her once she got going. Not only that, but the story was growing as she told it. Mary Anne obviously had a terrific imagination.

'She's making half of it up,' James said to Mandy. 'Sounds good though, doesn't it?'

But Mandy was listening to Mary Anne and watching Mr Peters. He had signalled to another man standing behind him, the man with the camera, and Mary Anne was being filmed while she spoke.

'This is a great story,' Mr Peters said.

At last Mary Anne ran out of steam and Mr Peters looked beyond her at the ward.

'Hey, Phil,' he said to the man with the camera, 'get a shot of the little girl with the lamb, will you?'

Mandy looked. There was Jenny with Blackie in her arms. Only he wasn't totally black any longer. He was still covered in white soap flakes. Jenny was rubbing him down with a towel.

'Hey, Matron, this is a great idea,' said Mr Peters. 'Just what we need – human interest. Pets in hospital and all that.' He turned to Matron. 'You

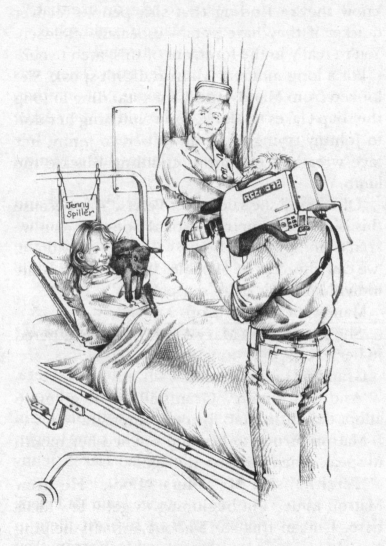

know they're finding that sick people recover quicker if they have pets – especially children. You're really in the forefront of this, aren't you?'

For a long moment Matron didn't speak. She looked from Mandy and James standing among the soap flakes to Mary Anne clutching her doll to Johnny trying to sit up in bed to Jenny, her face wreathed in smiles, cuddling Blackie the lamb.

'Of course,' she said to Mr Peters. 'Just because this is a small country hospital doesn't mean we aren't modern. And being so small,' she added, 'we can afford to be flexible. We can cater to the individual needs of all our patients.'

Mandy felt her jaw drop.

'She's worse than Mary Anne!' James whispered in her ear.

Gran was smiling broadly.

'And what's more,' Gran said, 'we're going to adopt that little lamb for our campaign.'

Matron turned to her and opened her mouth to speak. Then she closed it again.

'Terrific,' said Mr Peters. 'Look.' He drew Matron aside. 'I'm beginning to get a few ideas here. I mean this stuff about animals helping people recover is pretty interesting. Say we combine your closure campaign with a story on how pets can aid recovery? I reckon we could get you pretty wide coverage.' He scratched his chin. 'Have you ever thought of having a pets, corner in the hospital?'

'Of course we have,' said Gran, winking at Mandy and James. 'Matron and I were just talking about that, weren't we, Matron?'

Matron looked at Gran, then she coughed. She looked across at Jenny, her head to one side. Mandy held her breath.

'You know,' Matron said, 'it's only when you see the difference this kind of thing can make to a child's recovery that you realise how important pets are to people.' She turned to Mandy and James and smiled. 'Some of us take longer to learn that than others,' she said. 'But it's a lesson not easily forgotten.'

She turned back to the television crew. 'Why don't you come to my office and we'll discuss your film? I think I can assure you that we are very seriously considering having a pets' corner at the hospital and I can think of two young people who would be ideal for running it.' She turned back and looked at Mandy and James. 'If they would take the job on,' she said.

'Would we?' said Mandy.

'You bet!' said James.

'It's like a little coat,' Jenny said.

Mr Hope and Mandy looked at each other.

'That's just what it is,' Mr Hope said.

Mandy smiled at Jenny's description. No point in telling the little girl it was the skin of a dead lamb they were putting on Blackie. Instead she said, 'It's called setting on. If we put this coat on Blackie, the ewe will think it's her own lamb and then she'll feed him.'

'But I'll still be able to come up to the field to see him,' Jenny said.

'Of course you will,' said Mr Spiller. 'He's your lamb, isn't he?'

It was two weeks after the scene at the hospital and Jenny was her old self again. She had looked after Blackie well when she had come home from hospital but now it was time for the little lamb to be put with the others in the field – if they could find a substitute mother for him.

Jenny smiled happily as they watched the ewe nuzzle Blackie and sniff suspiciously. Mandy held her breath. If the ewe wasn't fooled by the smell of her own dead lamb's coat she would reject

Blackie. The ewe sniffed again. Then she nudged Blackie towards her and the little lamb started to suckle.

Mandy breathed a sigh of relief.

'It worked!' said James.

'Like a dream,' said Mr Hope. 'I reckon that's the last of your lambing problems, Jack.'

Jack Spiller turned to him. 'The end of my first lambing season. I couldn't have done it without your help,' he said. 'Not to mention these two and the people from Welford. They've been so good to us.'

'Why wouldn't they be?' said Mr Hope. 'They're neighbours, aren't they?'

Jack Spiller smiled. 'The best,' he said. 'I really feel as if I belong here now.'

Mr Hope laughed. 'That's just as well,' he said. 'Because I had it in mind to ask you to lend a hand at this year's Welford Show. And I thought you might enter Jess in the sheepdog trials.'

'I'd be delighted,' said Jack Spiller.

There was a shout from down the hill. Maggie Spiller was waving a newspaper and running up the hill towards them.

'What is it?' Jack Spiller said as she reached them.

'Look!' his wife said. 'We're famous! At least Jenny's Blackie is.'

Mandy and James craned to see what was on the front page of the paper.

The headlines stood out:

LAMB SAVES HOSPITAL

'What?' said Mandy.

Maggie Spiller laughed. 'Yes,' she said. 'It's Blackie. The cottage hospital has had a reprieve. After that TV programme went out they had hundreds of letters and phone calls. Blackie is to be the logo for a national campaign to save cottage hospitals.'

'Gosh,' said James. 'Your gran will be pleased.'

Mrs Spiller nodded. 'It says here that Mrs Dorothy Hope is to be on the national committee.'

'Good for Gran,' Mandy said. 'Isn't that terrific, Dad?'

Mr Hope ran a hand through his hair. 'I only hope Grandad can stand the pace,' he said. Then he laughed. 'Of course it's terrific. And I hope she saves lots more cottage hospitals!'

'Oh, she will,' said Mandy. 'With a logo like that, how could she fail?'

She looked at the national campaign's logo. It showed a little black lamb clutched in the arms of a child. Then she looked at Jenny, who was absorbed in watching Blackie and his new mother.

The little girl looked up. 'Blackie will always be my lamb really, won't he?' she said.

Mandy knelt down beside her. 'Of course he will, Jenny,' she said. 'Nobody loves him like you do.'

LUCY DANIELS

Bunnies
—*in the*—
Bathroom

Illustrations by Shelagh McNicholas

Hodder
Children's
Books

a division of Hodder Headline plc

Bunnies in the Bathroom

Special thanks to Jenny Oldfield

Text copyright © Ben M. Baglio 1995
Created by Ben M. Baglio, London W6 0HE
Illustrations copyright © Shelagh McNicholas 1995

First published as a single volume in Great Britain in 1996
by Hodder Children's Books

One

'James, come and look at these!' Mandy Hope hovered over a counter full of chocolate bunnies, all wrapped in cellophane and tied up with pink, yellow and blue ribbons. Rows of little rabbits crouched, looking up at her with their enormous almond-shaped eyes. Their ears seemed to twitch. 'They're so lifelike!' she whispered.

James Hunter sighed. 'Uh-oh, I can see this is going to be your newest craze. Rabbits!'

'What's wrong with that?' Mandy knew he was teasing. 'It's nearly Easter, isn't it? Easter bunnies!'

'Yes, well, they're better than boring old eggs, I

suppose,' James grumbled. He joined Mandy at the counter. There were rows of fat chocolate pigs beside the shy bunnies, and some cheerful frogs squatting, dark brown and shiny, along the back of the counter.

'Yes, please?' Mr Cecil said, coming out from the back room. He brought with him the delicious bittersweet smell of melted chocolate. He wore a spotless white coat and sparkling, silver-rimmed spectacles. His head was round and bald and shiny. 'Can I help?'

Mandy took ages to decide. She wanted a small gift for each of her friends in Welford village: for Jean Knox who worked as the receptionist at Animal Ark; for Simon, their nurse; for Lydia Fawcett on the goat farm up at High Cross; and for Ernie Bell in the cottages behind the Fox and Goose pub.

'Do you do squirrels?' she asked Mr Cecil. A squirrel would be ideal for Ernie, who had his own pet squirrel in a run in his back garden.

'Squirrels? Certainly.' The old man spread his hands to display the bushy-tailed creatures. Each clutched a hazelnut in its front paws. 'In dark chocolate, milk chocolate, or white chocolate?' he asked.

Mandy hesitated again. 'Oh!' she sighed. 'They're all so . . . perfect!'

'Frogs for me,' James decided in an instant. He pointed to the comical shapes, all squatting on their haunches, their mouths stretched wide. He ordered six in milk chocolate and waited for Mr Cecil to pack them into a white cardboard box with 'Cecil's Confectionery' printed in elegant silver letters on the top and sides.

'Of course, they'd be too good to eat.' Mandy switched her gaze back to the baby rabbits. She peered once more through the glass counter and took a deep breath. 'I'll take a squirrel for Ernie, please, a pig for Simon, a frog for Jean, oh – and a bunny for Lydia!' She'd made up her mind at last.

'She'll love you for that!' James warned with a wry grin.

'Why?'

'Her fields are overrun with them. She's always going on about it. Rabbits make such a mess of the land.'

'But Lydia likes them all the same.' Mandy smiled across at her best friend. He looked so serious sometimes, with his glasses and his floppy fringe of dark brown hair. She turned to the shopkeeper. 'I don't suppose you do goats, by any chance?' she said suddenly.

Mr Cecil smiled and his eyes twinkled. 'No, I'm sorry. Their legs are too thin; they'd break. The same with horses, I'm afraid. Now, did you want this little chap in dark, milk, or white?' He pointed to the row of enchanting bunnies.

At last, the big decisions were made and all Mandy's little chocolate animals were safely packed inside a second cardboard box. Then the kind old man smiled and gestured for them to wait. 'I think you'd like to take a peek at something I've just finished,' he whispered. 'And I must say I'm rather pleased with it myself!'

Mandy balanced her light box with both hands and waited for him to return. He came back through the swing-doors, proudly displaying his latest masterpiece. It sat on an icing-sugar nest on a silver cardboard disc about thirty centimetres wide; a huge, glossy, chocolate hen, perfect in every detail, down to her beady eye and last wing feather. When Mandy looked more closely, she saw tiny white chocolate chicks peering out of the nest, and when Mr Cecil lifted the broody hen, there were the discarded shells and three more chocolate eggs with a pale brown sugar coating,

speckled and looking as though they were about to hatch.

'Wow!' Even James allowed himself to be impressed.

Mandy was speechless. Her eyes darted over the beautiful, delicious object.

'Special order,' Mr Cecil said proudly. 'For Mrs Parker Smythe. It's an Easter gift for her little girl, Imogen.'

'Lucky thing!' Mandy breathed. She secretly thought that spoilt Imogen Parker Smythe, who lived in luxury up at Beacon House, just above Welford village, had done nothing to deserve such a special gift. She was a girl who had everything but seemed pleased with none of it.

Mr Cecil glanced across at Mandy. 'You like animals?' He nodded and smiled as she pored over the hen and her brood.

'Ha!' James laughed. 'You could say that!'

'I live at Animal Ark,' Mandy explained. 'My mum and dad are the Welford vets.'

'Ah!' The old man looked up as the doorbell gave a high, tuneful tinkle. Another customer had come into the shop. 'In that case, you'd be interested in the new pet shop that's just opened down the road.'

No sooner said than Mandy shot out on to the street, ahead of James, gabbling her thanks as she went.

James followed. 'Mandy, we have to catch the bus, remember!' He called after her. 'I promised my mum I'd be back home for tea.'

Mandy ran as fast as the precious box allowed her to, down Walton's main street with its rows of smart shop fronts, its cafés and bookshops. 'Just two minutes!' she shouted. 'I think we can still make it!'

She spotted the new pet shop and dashed over to peer through the window. At first she saw only her own reflection; a tall, slim figure in jeans and a sweater, with shortish blonde hair. Then, she made out racks of dog leads, furry playthings for kittens, imitation bones for dogs to chew, packs of dry rabbit food, budgerigar cages, and, at the back of the dark shop, a big glass aquarium with fish darting back and forth; vivid streaks of silver, blue and fiery red.

'Here comes the bus!' James warned.

'Hang on a sec!' The pet shop owner was carrying a bulky cage towards the window, coming out of the gloom of a back room. Struggling, he reached over a ledge and set it firmly in a space in the crowded window, in full view. The cage was lined with fresh straw. There was a clear drinking bottle tilted towards the floor, and when the cage was firmly settled and the warmth of the late sun struck through the glass of the shop window, Mandy saw a small movement. 'Look!' she whispered.

James instantly forgot all about the approaching bus. 'What is it?' He craned forward to look.

Two noses emerged from the more private wooden section, through a hole in the side. They were small, round and brown, with long whiskers. Then the ears came into view, erect and twitching; listening, listening.

'Baby rabbits!' Mandy breathed.

Two small, furry shapes shyly hopped into view. One sat and scratched his ears with his back leg, the other perched upright, his nose twitching. Then he came to the water bottle and began to drink, ears back, eyes still wide and staring.

'They're so perfect!' James marvelled at the tiny creatures. The second baby came to crouch in the sun, side by side, fawn-coloured and adorable, with great, liquid, dark eyes. 'But you've got three rabbits at home,' he reminded her. 'So don't get any ideas.' He glanced up at the name of the new shop; 'Pets' Parlour', written in bright red and gold letters.

'But *you* haven't!' Mandy turned sideways and widened her blue eyes in his direction. 'James . . .'

'No!' He jumped in quickly. 'Blackie and Eric are already a handful!' But he sighed all the same. The baby rabbits were irresistible. Still, Blackie, his Labrador, needed a lot of walking to keep his weight down, and Eric the kitten was into everything.

'Do you think someone nice will come along and buy them?' she asked with a touch of regret. She yearned to take them home, yet she knew that common sense said no. Animal Ark was always overflowing with visitors and patients; anything from Jack Russells with mites in their ears, to badgers wounded in traps.

'They're bound to,' James reassured her.

'I just hope they buy both of them together. Rabbits like company.' Slowly she stood back from the shop window. She smiled briefly at the owner; a tall young man in a dark blue sweater, with a red checked shirt.

'Mandy!' James reminded her about the time. He heard the bus engine choke and roar at the stop on the other side of the street.

Mandy stepped back again. 'Bye, bunnies!' she said wistfully. The two babies took slow, identical, rocking hops across their cage and sat, ears up, noses twitching.

'Don't worry, they'll find a good home,' James said as they crossed the busy street. They climbed on to the bus just as the driver let off the handbrake and signalled to pull out. He took their money and they sank into a nearby seat.

As the bus drew out of town and set off over the moor road towards Welford, Mandy found herself dreaming. Spring was in the air. The sticky-buds on the horse chestnut trees were beginning to burst open, the hawthorn hedges were tipped with green. In the fields, lambs nibbled at fresh young shoots or skipped up and down the hillside. She would have called those twin rabbits Barney and Button, she decided, and they would have the best food, with carrots and apples as a treat every weekend. She stared up at the drifting clouds as the bus rocked and swayed along the twisting road.

Gently James dug his elbow against her arm. 'Look!' He pointed out of the window.

The sun had sunk low, leaving the crest of the eastern hill bathed in warm, yellow light. Shadows fell long and deep over the rough pasture. In the distance there was a stretch of pale purple heather that ran all along the valley ridge. Nearby, in the soft sunlight, the green field was dotted with wild rabbits.

They sat in twos and threes; small brown shapes with pointed ears. At the sound of the bus they stamped their back legs and sniffed the air for danger. They looked startled, froze for a split second, then bolted. They fanned out across the field, scattering into the brambles and ditch bottoms. Some made for their underground runs. They vanished inside with a flash of white tail and one last kick of their powerful hind legs.

'Brilliant!' Mandy said. Then she turned to James. 'You were right!'

'What?' He blushed under her direct gaze.

'Today *is* the day for rabbits!' She held her box of chocolate animals safely on her knee as the bus jolted and lurched.

Two

The bus dropped them off outside the Fox and Goose. Mandy spotted Ernie Bell and his neighbour, Walter Pickard, sitting outside the pub. The two old men were chatting as usual on the porch by the front door of the low stone building. One either side of the door, they sat and watched whoever came and went.

'There you are!' Mandy went across with a bright smile.

'Where else?' Walter asked.

'Like a pair of bookends, we are,' Ernie agreed. 'You always know where to look for us on a fine night like this, sitting over a good pint, putting

the world to rights. You can't beat it!' He took a
sip from his glass, then pointed to Mandy's box.
'What've you got in there?'

'Aha, close your eyes!' Mandy replied. James
joined her, and together they opened the boxes
and took out one of the chocolate figures.

'Happy Easter!' they cried. Mandy presented a
squirrel to Ernie and James gave a frog to Walter,
who kept his eyes closed, his hands outstretched.

They opened their eyes. 'By gum!' Ernie said
with a look at the squirrel. 'Lord knows what
Sammy will make of this!' He gave Mandy a
crooked, embarrassed smile.

'Well, I'll be . . . !' Walter's frog smiled up at
him. 'He's a funny little fellow!'

'Don't you like them?' James was anxious not
to offend the two old men. Walter was a cat lover;
a steady, reliable friend to Mandy and James. Ernie
seemed grumpier, with his low, growly voice and
short, grey stubble. But adopting Sammy the
squirrel and Tiddles the cat had softened him up,
and ever since he'd always been willing to help
them out of a tight corner.

Ernie sat and studied his cellophane-wrapped
squirrel. 'What do I do with him? Eat him, or stick
him on my mantelpiece?'

'Nay, the poor chap would melt by the fire!' Walter put in. He grinned at James. 'Young sir, you should never have gone to this trouble for old Ernie and me, you know!'

'Hey, hey, I'm not so old!' Ernie grumbled. He winked at Mandy. 'I reckon you've been into Walton and paid a visit to Harry Cecil's posh shop. He's not cheap, I'm told. You shouldn't have, like Walter says.'

His face set in a frown, but Mandy could tell he was pleased. She and James turned to leave, but Walter half stood up from his bench and stopped them.

'Hang on a minute! What's this?'

A low, dark green car sped down the high street, past the post office. It drew into the pub carpark and the engine died.

'It's the boss!' Ernie said, meaning Mr Hardy, the pub landlord. He called a warning to the bar staff inside. 'Look lively! He's back!'

They heard empty glasses clink and rattle as the staff quickly removed them from view.

'Didn't he go over to fetch his boy earlier this afternoon?' Walter asked. He turned to James. 'It seems to me young John Hardy is in for a surprise when he goes inside!'

John had just got out of his father's car. He looked up at the pub, at the room where he lived with his father during the holidays. During term time he lived seventy or eighty kilometres away at Grange School in the Lake District.

James frowned, then turned to Mandy. 'Didn't his dad tell him about Sara?'

'Shh!' Walter warned.

Mandy widened her eyes and shook her head. John's dad, Julian, had announced his engagement just a week ago. His fiancée was one of the women who helped behind the bar.

'Just look at that whacking great suitcase,' Ernie pointed out. 'What's he got in there, the kitchen sink?'

Mandy saw Mr Hardy lift a case out of the boot. He let it thump heavily to the ground.

It was all too easy to forget about John Hardy when he was away at school. Mandy had known him all her life, yet never known him. That was the peculiar thing. He was eleven, the same age as James, and he was even born in the same week at Walton Maternity Hospital. He was a small, neat, ordinary-looking boy, with dark, wavy hair that seemed to make his face rounder and a bit too goody-goody. It was the sort of hair that always stayed in place. He was never untidy, never hot, never running; always walking in his cool, collected manner. He looked more grown-up than eleven, but Mandy never thought he looked very happy.

'Come on, John,' his father said, leaving the suitcase where it was. He headed for the front door with eager steps. 'Leave that. I've got some news for you, and there's someone inside I want you to meet.' He smiled and went on ahead.

Mandy saw John hesitate. He was wearing a light Aran sweater and jeans. His white sports shoes looked brand-new, but somehow he looked as if he was in his Sunday best. Then Sara came to the door to greet them both. She looked nervous as she stood there waiting.

Ernie grunted, but Walter leaned across and jabbed him with his elbow. 'I'm saying nothing!' Ernie protested. But Mandy thought his sour look said plenty.

They watched uneasily as Sara clasped her hands in front of her.

'John, this is Sara,' Mr Hardy said, his voice tinged with pride and affection. There was a broad smile on his face as he leaned over and gave the woman a reassuring peck on the cheek.

John stood stock-still. He frowned at his father.

'Didn't I say he should have told the boy beforehand?' Ernie mumbled.

'Shh!' Walter warned again. He took a long sip from his glass.

But Mandy agreed with Ernie. If your father suddenly got engaged, you'd want to be the first to know. 'This isn't the kind of Easter surprise I'd like!' she whispered to James. She felt sorry for John, standing there by his suitcase.

'John, this isn't like you,' Mr Hardy said. The smile had vanished from his face.

Instead of saying hello to the fair-haired woman, as his father wanted, John deliberately turned aside and made a great show of having spotted Mandy and James. He greeted them like long-lost friends. 'Hey!' He waved, and strode across. 'Just the people I wanted to see!'

'I don't think!' Ernie muttered.

'John!' Julian Hardy called, obviously annoyed.

'Hello, John,' Mandy stammered. 'How was school?'

'Fine, thanks. I wanted to talk to you about a project I have to do this holiday.' Still he ignored his father and poor Sara, who between them came out and struggled towards the door with the

outsize suitcase. 'This project has to do with animals,' John explained. But his warm tone seemed forced. 'I have to choose an animal and study it in its natural habitat. You know all about animals, don't you, Mandy? You must do; you live at the vets' place.'

Mandy swallowed hard and glanced at James. John Hardy seemed to have the habit of coolly ignoring everyone except the person he wanted to speak to. For the moment, that was her. 'What kind of animal?' she said, blushing at his rudeness.

'That's what I want to talk to you about,' John began. But before he could get any further, his

father reached the door. Mr Hardy had to stoop
to enter the porch. Mandy noticed that he had
the same wavy hair as his son, but a thinner face,
and there was a scattering of grey at the temples.
He turned to whisper a word to Sara, who nodded,
smiled emptily, then went inside once more.

'John!' Mr Hardy said in a stern voice. 'Come
here!'

His son pursed his lips. 'I'll come and see you
at Animal Ark soon,' he told Mandy. Then he
obeyed his father.

'I said it meant trouble!' Ernie warned.

Mandy saw Walter lean over and carefully,
deliberately, step on his toe.

'Ouch!' Ernie yelled.

Julian Hardy took John off to a far corner of
the carpark to give him a good dressing-down for
his rudeness to Sara.

Mandy heard his raised voice. She saw John
duck his head and take a step back.

'Well, I'm off home now,' James said quickly,
and shot off down the road.

'Bye!' Mandy waved. She didn't like rows either,
but somehow she felt rooted to the spot, there
outside the Fox and Goose. Soon Mr Hardy
lowered his voice and led John out of sight, round

the back of the pub. 'Why did John behave like that?' she asked Walter and Ernie.

'Refuse to say hello to Sara, you mean?' Walter shrugged. 'It looks like it was too much to cope with. The poor lad's had his dad to himself all these years.'

'He's not usually like that,' Mandy agreed. Just the opposite. Whenever she'd seen him before, John was always annoyingly polite. 'But he'll soon find out that Sara's OK. I like her. She calls in at Animal Ark sometimes to chat with my mum. She's just moved up to Welford from Sheffield.'

'OK or not, John doesn't want to know,' Ernie pointed out.

'But she even looks great,' Mandy objected. Sara wore fashionable, bright clothes, and looked young for her age. Mandy's mother and Sara had been at school together.

'Give him time!' Walter stood up. 'It'll sort itself out.' He picked up the chocolate frog from the bench beside him and strolled the short distance to his own cottage.

Ernie gave a grimace. 'Maybe.' He followed slowly after Walter. 'Then again, maybe not.'

Mandy stood for a while in the empty porch. *Poor John,* she said to herself. *It can't be easy coming home to find everything has suddenly changed.*

She wasn't surprised when, just seconds later, a side door flew open and John Hardy burst out. His father shouted after him, but the boy took no notice.

He ran through the walled garden at the back of the pub. He flung open the gate and began to leap, then stumble, up the steep hill. He cut across one field, vaulted a low stone wall and kept on running. Mandy had glimpsed his face as he came out. It was crumpled and tear-stained. John looked desperate.

Where can he run to? Mandy wondered. He was bolting, just like a rabbit. She watched him charge wildly up the hill into the middle of nowhere.

Three

'*Run, rabbit, run, rabbit, run, run, run.*
Here comes the farmer with his gun, gun, gun!'

Mr Hope's rich baritone voice rang out through the empty surgery.

'*He'll get by without his rabbit pie,*
So run, rabbit, run, rabbit, run, run, run!'

'Very nice,' Jean Knox commented, peering into the treatment room. She had just arrived at Animal Ark. 'Now, where did I put that appointment book?' She searched high and low behind the reception desk. 'I don't know, I'd forget my head if it were loose!'

Mandy grinned at her dad, then went through and put her hands straight on the big red diary lying on the desk. 'Here it is!'

Their grey-haired receptionist gave a surprised gasp. 'Oh, thank you, Mandy dear. What would I do without you?' Jean, flustered as usual, began the search for her car keys. 'Now *where* did I put those keys?' she muttered.

'In your coat pocket?' Mandy suggested.

'Ah yes, how clever!' She felt in her pocket and gave a relieved sigh.

Jean went back to reception, clutching her keys, searching for her glasses, which hung as usual on a chain round her neck.

Mandy giggled. 'Dad, do you need me?' she asked. It was the first proper day of her school holiday, a Monday morning, and she had great plans. She and James wanted to go bird-watching by the river. He'd recently seen a kingfisher wing its way under the low stone arch of the old bridge, and they wanted to spot it together.

'Twitching, is it?' Dad said, locking the door of the drugs cupboard and looking at his watch. 'Twitching' was his name for crouching in the

undergrowth with a pair of binoculars, waiting
for the kingfisher to show up.

'I've got to feed the rabbits first,' she
announced. 'Then maybe we'll go twitching.
James said he'd ring me.'

She went out into the garden, armed with the
bag of dried oats and other cereal for Flopsy,
Mopsy and Cottontail. She thought of scatter-
brained Jean, whom she often felt like teasing.
'Now, *where* did I put those rabbits?' she said,
teetering on the doorstep.

Dad laughed and wandered out after her. The
grass was dewy in the cool morning air as they
headed for the hutch at the bottom of the
garden.

Mandy greeted her three rabbits and quietly
set about clearing the cage of the old bedding,
while Dad set first Flopsy, then Mopsy, then
Cottontail out in the long wire run where they
exercised. Big, sleek, black and white rabbits, they
sat in the sun and combed their whiskers.

'Dad, I was wondering. How do you think they'd
feel if I changed their names?' she asked. She laid
fresh straw in the clean cage. *You grow out of names,*
she thought. Now she preferred Button and
Barney, and perhaps Benji in honour of James's

cat, who had died. The old names seemed a little childish.

'Hmm,' Dad said thoughtfully. 'On the whole, I think they'd probably prefer to stay the same.'

'You're probably right,' she agreed. 'Flopsy, Mopsy and Cottontail is what they've always been.'

Dad helped Mandy by tying a tight knot in the top of the bag of used straw and droppings. 'Good for you,' he said.

She smiled.

'Mandy, you've got a visitor!' Mrs Hope called from inside the house. Her long, red hair was framed in the doorway, and shone bright in the morning sun. 'It's John Hardy!'

'Uh-oh!' Mandy stood up. She'd managed to forget the uncomfortable scene at the Fox and Goose when John had snubbed his father's new fiancée. Now she remembered that he'd promised to call in at Animal Ark.

'Trouble?' Dad asked.

'Not really. I'd better go in and see, though.' She left her father to finish tidying up in the garden and traipsed indoors. Her mum had vanished somewhere upstairs, so she stood face to face with John in the empty kitchen.

'Hello, Mandy,' he said. He was calm and matter-of-fact again, but she still had a clear memory of his tear-stained face as he ran up the hill. He'd come today equipped with camera, notebook and binoculars, and stood looking annoyingly neat and studious. He forgot to smile when he greeted her.

'Hi.' Her own friendly smile faltered. Why did she feel as if she'd just walked into an exam room? Her stomach knotted as she felt him sum up her and her surroundings. She kicked her dad's scruffy slippers out of sight under the table.

'Animals!' John Hardy announced. 'What sort do you suggest?' He looked round the kitchen as if a suitable specimen might suddenly appear.

'Well, there's a lot to choose from at this time of year. If you just look around for something to study, there's—'

'Before you go on, don't say tadpoles, whatever you do!' John interrupted. 'Everyone suggests tadpoles, and they're so boring!'

'Oh, but they're not!' Mandy began. 'Their life cycle is amazing!' Then she stopped. She saw his mind was set against them.

'Anyway, that's kid's stuff,' John said. 'No, I want

to study something that's nice to look at, not disgusting, like tadpoles. Something I can take good pictures of!' He tapped his camera, slung on a strap round his neck. It had levers and lenses and buttons all over the place. This was no seaside holiday camera. 'Well?' John prompted. He stood with his feet wide apart on the Hopes' flagged kitchen floor.

She looked to the beamed ceiling for inspiration, then her gaze swept round the room. There on a shelf on the pine dresser sat her Easter present for Lydia Fawcett, all done up in its bright yellow bow. 'Rabbits!' she said suddenly.

'Rabbits?' John looked suspicious. 'Don't they just sit there and eat lettuce?'

'No, they're brilliant creatures to study. I've been reading up about them. For instance, their warrens are amazing! They meet in big underground chambers, held up with tree roots, with air-conditioning and everything!'

'Air-conditioning?'

'Yes, they build their runs facing away from the wind for warmth, but they connect them up with small runs that open on to the fresh air. Of course, they sleep close together for warmth.'

'How do you know all this?' John was still frowning, but the bit about air-conditioning seemed to have roused his interest. He strode to the window to look out down the lane.

'You won't see any down there,' Mandy explained. 'There are too many trees. And rabbits like high ground. Hillsides, where the wind can carry sound, the ground is dry, and they can smell danger.'

'How do you *know*?' John insisted.

'Like I said, I just sat down last night and read a book,' she confessed, feeling herself go red. She'd taken it down from the shelf in the surgery. 'It's over there on the dresser. I'll ask my dad if you can borrow it, if you like.'

The idea of a textbook also appealed to John, as Mandy guessed it would. He was a boy who liked to study. '*The Private Life of the Rabbit* by R.M. Lockley,' he read out loud as he picked up the heavy volume. 'Have you read it all?'

'No, but it's best to study the rabbits out in the wild before you go in for too much reading. Your project will be much better if you begin with a kind of diary of their habits.' Actually, Mandy was keen to get John Hardy to make up his mind. Then she thought she could take him up to the Celtic cross on the moorside, to one of the High Cross fields. At the same time she would deliver the chocolate bunny to Lydia. 'You know; begin with a chapter called "Rabbit Habits", or something like that!' she said eagerly.

No smile appeared in response, to crack the earnest expression on John's face. 'I suppose you're right. I've got thirty-six exposures on this film. Colour. Fast speed. High definition.' He paused again. 'You're sure rabbits are interesting enough?'

'If you've got enough patience to study them – yes!' Mandy grabbed the present from the shelf. 'I know just the place!' she insisted. 'Ready?'

He nodded, and Mandy called up to her mum. She was anxious to set off. 'Won't be long! I'm just taking John up to High Cross!'

'OK!' Mrs Hope's voice floated downstairs. 'Oh, Mandy, James Hunter phoned while you were busy in the surgery. I said you'd ring him!'

'Thanks. I'll do it when I get back.' She scrambled into her jacket, which hung from a hook on the wall, and dashed out of the house.

At least she'd got John Hardy sorted out with a school project. She breathed in deeply and marched alongside him up the lane.

They trekked by the public footpath across the
fields beside Brandon Gill's pig farm. Mandy
paused to pick up a stick and give Nelson, the
great black and white boar, a quick backscratch.
Nelson grunted contentedly and trampled the
earth.

John wrinkled his nose. 'I'm glad you suggested
rabbits, not pigs,' he said.

Mandy's eyebrows shot up. John Hardy had
nearly made a joke. In fact, he seemed to be
unwinding as they walked. The wind had even
ruffled his hair. There was colour in his cheeks,
and his dark eyes had come alive. They darted
from hedgerow to bramble thicket, searching for
rabbits.

It must be difficult for him, she thought again,
*trying to settle in at home, with Sara there so much of
the time.* Mandy knew better than to mention
Sara's name outright, or to seem too curious.
Walter Pickard was right; John would need time
to get used to the new situation.

As he relaxed, John began to chat about the
Celtic cross landmark way up on the hill, past
Beacon House. He knew its history and how it

had come to be there. Mandy noticed he didn't vary his pace, but strode on like a man with a mission. Most kids she knew would stop to poke round in ditches or to climb a tempting tree. But John Hardy set his face straight ahead and made it a route march. Soon they'd passed the grand iron gates of Beacon House, the Parker Smythe place, and then the entrance to Upper Welford Hall. Mandy had to drag John to a halt by the old five-barred gate that marked the entrance to High Cross Farm.

'Hang on a sec!' she gasped. 'We're here! Let me just pop in and ask Lydia if we can use her fields to scout around for rabbits. And I want to give her this.' She held up the cellophane package.

'Hmm . . .' John frowned. 'I'll wait here and keep a lookout!' He stood bolt upright, binoculars poised.

Mandy dashed inside. She found Lydia in the barn, tending to her beloved goats. Dressed in her oldest wellingtons and her tattered brown work jacket, she was mucking out the stalls and turning each of her goats out to graze in the spring pasture. Houdini, the most mischievous of all, stood in his stall and snickered at Mandy as she approached.

'Hello, Houdini!' Mandy circled her arms about his neck and hugged him. Houdini bared his teeth. His hooves clattered against the wooden door. 'Steady, boy!' She backed off and greeted Lydia. 'Happy Easter!' she said shyly, handing over the small present.

'What's this?' A smile lit up Lydia's face, so that it wrinkled like a shiny old apple. 'Why it's a little bunny rabbit; how clever!' She unwrapped the chocolate like a child at Christmas, then she perched the rabbit gleefully in the palm of her hand.

In an instant, Houdini's bony head darted forward, and he wrapped his rubbery lips round the too-tempting gift. Gulp! Swallow! Lick! It was gone.

'Oh!' Lydia cried out, her face crumpling. Then she laughed. 'Oh, Houdini!'

Mandy joined in the laughter. 'He must have thought it was for him!'

'Tut!' Lydia clicked her tongue. 'His manners are appalling, and he's old enough to know better!' With a good-natured pat of the goat's neck, she unbolted the door and led him out into the farmyard. 'I bet it tasted first class, didn't it, boy?' she grumbled. 'And I'm sure you'd like to say a big thank you to Mandy here!'

Houdini tossed his head and trotted on.

'Talking of rabbits . . .' Mandy said as she spied John Hardy waiting patiently by the gate.

'Were we?' Lydia shot Mandy a quick glance. 'Oh, yes, rabbits . . . chocolate . . . oh, Houdini . . . oh dear!' She chortled and led him on, out to the near pasture. 'Rabbits, yes. Well, we have plenty of them round here, of course.' She let Houdini loose in the field, closed the gate, and leaned forward against the top bar. She gestured towards the field full of fresh dandelions, willowherb and yellow coltsfoot. 'Not in here, of course. The little nuisances know to keep off when the goats are about. No, the sly things keep their distance. But if you go up to the far pasture, the one beyond the house, that field will be alive with them. You can't move up there without tripping over a rabbit hole!'

As Lydia grumbled on, Mandy lost heart. It really did seem that even gentle Lydia saw rabbits as pests. In that case she might not be keen to let a stranger from the village begin his study on one of her fields.

'Mind you, I have to admit that they're bonny little things.' She leaned both elbows on the gate and clasped her broad hands. 'And friendly, so long as you keep your distance; and who can blame them? Many a time I go up there in the evening and watch them come out to feed. They're quite delightful!' She laughed and brought herself up short. 'We farmers aren't supposed to have a soft spot for rabbits, I suppose!'

'But you wouldn't mind if a friend of mine came up to take pictures and make notes, would you?' Mandy seized her chance. 'He has to do some work on rabbits for a school project. I said I thought it would be OK.'

Lydia stood upright and glanced in John's direction. 'That's not young James Hunter, is it?' She screwed up her eyes and raised one hand to shield them from the sun.

'No, it's John Hardy from the Fox and Goose.'

Lydia nodded, then looked up at the sun. 'Time I was getting on with the cheese-making,' she said. 'You know there's no peace for the wicked!' She glanced again at the lonely figure by the gate. 'Tell your friend he's welcome. And to call in at the house for a cup of tea whenever he has the time!'

Mandy thanked her and ran back to John. Soon they were up on Lydia's far pasture and he was crouched down behind the rain-blackened stone wall, camera at the ready. One or two rabbits roamed the far side of the field. He stood up suddenly. They stood stork-still, then vanished down separate holes as he clicked the shutter.

'Missed!' he muttered.

'See!' Mandy told him. 'Didn't I say they were clever? They have fantastic hearing!'

John nodded, then scanned the rough, empty field. 'I'll wait,' he insisted. This time he put his binoculars to his eyes and trained them on the grass.

'It's probably a bit late for rabbits by now,' Mandy said. 'But they do like the sun, so maybe a few will come back for a snack!'

'I'll wait,' he said again, crouching down still as a statue. 'You know, I think your idea about rabbits was good,' he admitted, giving Mandy a brief smile. 'Thanks.' And he settled down to watch.

It was the start of a long, patient campaign by the boy from the pub.

A short time later, Mandy left John to go home and phone James. Then her day was busy. First she went bird-watching. After lunch she helped in the surgery, then she popped into Lilac Cottage to visit her grandparents. But when she cycled back up to High Cross after tea, John Hardy was still there, crouched behind a wall. He hadn't moved all day. All round him, scattered on the grass, lay white sheets of paper.

Mandy left her bike at the main gate and walked across.

'Hush!' he warned. The rabbits were coming out in their hordes as dusk approached. This was their liveliest time of day.

Quietly Mandy crouched beside him. Many of the sheets were covered in tiny writing; scrawled notes about sightings and the position of rabbit burrows. Sometimes John had stopped to sketch a rabbit in fine pencil. She picked up one of these drawings and found it beautifully done. The rabbit's eyes shone like blackcurrants out of its soft, furry face. The ears stood straight, paler on the inside, with black, pointed tips. 'This is good!' Mandy exclaimed. 'I never knew you could draw!'

'You never asked!' John whispered. 'Art is one of my favourite subjects at school. Now quiet, please, or you'll scare them off.'

They watched as more rabbits popped out of their holes, then stopped and sniffed the air. They rocked forwards on to their short front legs and lazily hopped towards a tender shoot of cowslip or dandelion. Their ears twitched and they sniffed the air, but they grazed happily enough. The large male rabbits stayed at the centre of the warren, pushing the smaller yearlings to the outskirts. The young ones had to look out for foxes, weasels, or even the vicious rooks that sat high in the ash trees and cawed.

After a day on duty, John seemed to have learned a lot about studying rabbits. He'd taken off his white sweater, realising that his dark blue T-shirt made him stand out less. He moved smoothly, and didn't jerk when he raised his head above the wall to take more photographs. This time the rabbits' ears still twitched in response, but they carried on feeding, untroubled.

'Well done!' Mandy whispered.

John crouched back down and nodded. 'Thanks. I've had a great time!' He confessed it awkwardly, blushing. The sun had brought up the freckles in his dark skin. 'Now I'd like to find a field with an old warren in it; one that's not used any more. I want to explore how the rabbits make their burrows.'

'How about tomorrow?' Mandy suggested. 'You must be starving hungry. And doesn't your dad need to know where you are?'

Sharply John shook his head. 'He doesn't care.'
His voice was flat. Carefully he unscrewed the
big lens from his camera and packed it into its
case.

'Oh, I'm sure he does!' Mandy began.

But John ignored her. 'So where can I find an
old warren?' he insisted.

She thought hard. 'Let's go and ask Lydia,' she
suggested. She could see that this would be the
first of many visits this Easter to High Cross and
the rabbit fields. John had taken to her idea better
than she expected. What's more, it would keep
him busy, and well out of the way of Sara and his
dad. No wonder he seemed keen.

'You should be a wildlife artist,' she told him as
she helped pack away the sketches. 'I never
thought you'd be so interested in animals!'

'You never asked!' he said again.

Mandy stared at him. This time she knew it was
a joke. She checked his dark brown eyes; they were
sparkling. 'Come on, let's go,' she said. They ran
down to the farm together, to a cup of hot tea
and Lydia's home-made scones.

Four

'Mandy, James phoned again!' Jean Knox called from the surgery.

Mandy had just got back from High Cross. It was the second week of the Easter holiday; every day the weather grew warmer, the trees greener.

'Or was it John Hardy?' Jean's puzzled voice quavered. 'Oh dear, which one was it?'

Mandy went into reception. She felt flushed from the sun, and tired after the day's explorations. 'It can't have been John,' she exclaimed. 'I just left him outside the Fox and Goose.'

'Oh well, it was James, then,' Jean decided. She

was searching for something in a drawer as usual. 'Now where did I put that—'

'Appointment book?' Mandy broke in.

'Yes, how did you know? . . . Oh, thank you, dear!' Jean smiled brightly. 'Yes, now I come to think of it, it must have been James. He told me he was just back from visiting his aunt and uncle in London, and he wondered if you wanted to play tennis.'

'Great, thanks.' Mandy had dashed back to Animal Ark to do her cleaning chores, but she broke off to pick up the phone and ring her friend. 'Sorry, James, I've just been so busy all day. Did you have a nice couple of days in London?'

'It was OK, thanks. What have you been up to?'

'I've been busy helping on John's school project. We're making a detailed study of the female rabbits now, and their young. John's numbered all the burrows with kittens, and . . .'

'Kittens?'

She heard James's voice sounding confused. 'The baby rabbits. They're called kittens. The females are called does. It says so in this book we've got, *The Private Life of the Rabbit* by R.M. Lockley.'

'Oh.' Now James sounded distant and bored.

'Anyway, we've noticed that most of the litters have five kittens. Some have six. And when the yearlings are strong enough, they move off to form new warrens because the old one gets overcrowded with the new babies. They start all over again on fresh ground.' She rattled on.

'Fancy a game of tennis tonight, then?' James asked in an offhand way.

Mandy thought ahead. She hated to turn him down. After all, he was her best friend, and they always tried to arrange to do things together. 'Oh, James, I'm sorry, I can't! I'm going back over to John's to help him choose some photos for his project. I promised!' Then she hit on an answer. 'How about tomorrow morning?' she asked. 'Meet at my house at about ten? I'll have to dig out my racket from somewhere, and see you then.'

'Fine,' came James's quick reply. 'Bye.' The phone clicked and the line went dead.

Jean nodded her approval. 'Good for you. He rang earlier, but you always seem to be out.'

Mandy sighed. 'I know. Anyway, I must get a move on. I said to John I'd be back at his place by six-thirty!' She swept round the treatment rooms like a whirlwind with her disinfected cloths and hot mop and bucket. In the residential unit at the back of the surgery, she spoke nicely to the Persian cat who'd just been spayed. Then she went out briskly to clean and feed her own rabbits. It was time to go. 'See you later!' she called to whoever was inside the house to hear.

'Don't forget to pop in and see your gran sometime soon,' her dad said. He was sitting with his feet up in the lounge. 'She tells me she hasn't set eyes on you for ages!'

'OK, I'll call in later! Got to dash!' Mandy scrambled free of the house and cycled off up the lane. She was eager to see how John's latest batch of photos had turned out. He'd used his zoom lens to take close-ups of the babies as they emerged from the burrows for the first time. They looked like small fawn balls of spun sugar, with enormous eyes and ears.

She propped her bike against the side wall of the pub and nipped in through the garden. She knocked at the door, then went quickly up the back stairs to John's room. It was a low, old house with thick stone walls and small windows. There was a landing halfway up the stairs with a red and blue stained-glass window which overlooked the garden. The old wooden boards creaked as she went on upstairs, and the dark corridor to John's room sloped at an odd angle, like a gangway on a ferry. She knocked loud and clear on the old panelled door.

'Come in!' John looked up excitedly as Mandy opened it. 'The photos have arrived!'

'I can see that!' she laughed. John sat amongst dozens of colour pictures of the rabbits on the far pasture at High Cross. They were scattered across the red carpet, and some were pinned crookedly to his bedroom walls. More scribbled notes lay across the desk, and his sketches decorated the front of the wardrobe, the door

into his bathroom, and even inside the bathroom itself. 'It's worse than *my* room, and that's saying something!' Mandy liked to stick pictures of all her favourite animals on the walls at home, but at least she put them on straight and arranged them neatly. John had simply slapped these on anyhow, and she was surprised because he seemed so tidy in other ways.

'They're the best yet!' he announced. He held up a large, glossy photo to the light and studied it. 'See, I got the angle just right on this one, and the focus is really sharp. The doe is sitting upright at the entrance to the burrow. See, even her whiskers have come out clearly!'

Mandy admired the photos. 'They're really good, John. It's going to be difficult to choose the best.' She knelt down on the floor beside him, but then she glanced at her hands and saw that they needed a wash. 'Hang on, I'll just have to go and wash my hands,' she told him. She went through into the small white bathroom.

'I'll nip down and get us some juice.' John managed to tear himself away from his precious pictures.

Mandy heard the bedroom door open and close. She took her time running the water, soaping her hands and gazing round at John's beautiful sketches of rabbits. His pictures showed their gracefulness; the thing she most loved about them herself. He really was a good artist, she thought. 'Bunnies in the bathroom!' she said to herself with a funny little smile.

She dried her hands. John was taking a long time fetching the drinks. She crossed the bedroom floor, picking her way between the photos. Then she peered out into the long, crooked corridor.

'Hi!' A bright, pleasant voice caught her by surprise.

'Oh, hi!' Mandy recognised the golden hair and neat, slim figure of Julian Hardy's fiancée, Sara. She was dressed in a loose, silky, white shirt and a long blue skirt, with open sandals and bare legs. She wore her long hair swept up casually on top of her head, but strands had escaped and caught in her dangling gold earrings. Her face had tanned in the sun, emphasising her wide, light grey eyes. 'I'm looking for John,' Mandy explained, feeling out of place.

'I saw him go downstairs not long ago.' Sara smiled. 'I'm Sara Lawson. I'm engaged to John's dad.'

'I know.' Mandy saw the diamond engagement

ring on her left hand. She blushed. John really would have to get used to the new situation, like it or not. She thought again that Sara seemed friendly and pretty.

'I'm afraid John and I haven't hit it off yet,' she confessed. She seemed to want to talk to someone. 'Things have been a bit tense since he came back from school. He's out studying those rabbits all the time, or else he just stays in his room and avoids me.' She gave an embarrassed little laugh. 'I don't think he likes me much!'

'Oh, he's never said that!' Mandy protested. She felt her clean palms go hot and sticky again. She didn't fancy being caught up in this problem; it seemed too big for her to do anything about.

'Why, what has he said?' Sara stood facing Mandy in the corridor, a serious look on her face.

'Nothing. He never mentions you.' Mandy had spent hours with John during this last week, while James had been away. They'd braved the wind, rain and sunshine up on the fields at High Cross. She'd crouched behind thick tree trunks with him in the hour before dawn, and returned at dusk to study the rabbits. But he'd never once talked about his family or home.

Sara nodded. 'Exactly. He treats me as if I'm invisible. He seems to think that I'll just vanish, I'm sure he does!' She glanced into his room at the sketches on the walls. 'He's got talent though. You have to say that for him.'

'Yes!' Glad to change the subject, Mandy agreed. 'I think he should be a wildlife artist, or a photographer!'

Raised voices from the garden filtered through the open window. Mandy paused and checked Sara's worried expression. They both recognised another row brewing between Julian Hardy and his son.

'And another thing; just when are you going to tidy up that room of yours?' Mr Hardy demanded. His voice came from the kitchen downstairs. 'It's a complete mess in there. You can't expect Sara or me to go in and tidy up after you, if you leave it in that sort of state!'

There was no reply. Mandy heard a fridge door slam shut.

'John, I'm talking to you! I said, when are you going to clean up all that mess? Scraps of paper and drawings everywhere!'

'It's for my school project.' John sounded slow and sulky. 'I've got to get it finished.'

'But you don't have to clutter the whole place up!' Mr Hardy's voice faded, then John appeared from the kitchen at the foot of the stairs. He began to trail up them, a glass of orange juice in each hand. 'Are you listening to me, or am I just wasting my breath?' His father pursued him into the hallway.

Sara took a deep breath and leaned over the banister. 'Leave him alone now, Julian,' she called out. 'I'm sure he'll tidy up when he's finished his project!'

Mandy felt she could have heard a pin drop. John looked up at Sara with a blank expression. Julian stood, taken aback, hands on hips, one foot on the bottom step.

'And you should see his sketches of those rabbits! They're brilliant!' Sara tried to smooth things out.

There was another tense silence. Then John snapped. His face crumpled. 'Who asked you?' he demanded. 'Who said you could go in my room and snoop around?'

Suddenly he turned and tripped. Mandy watched as the two full glasses tipped against the white wall. The orange liquid splashed against it and trickled down. John stared at it in dismay.

'John!' His father yelled out a warning, but it was too late.

Sara put one hand over her mouth and stepped quickly back.

But John dived downstairs with a weird cry. He rushed past his father and fled, head down, straight out through the kitchen, across the garden into the main street. Mandy raced after him.

'Nay,' Ernie Bell advised. He stopped her short by putting out a hand from his position on the bench in the front porch. 'Leave him be. There's enough trouble round here as it is. Don't you go adding to it.'

Mandy glanced down at Ernie, her eyes watering, her heart pounding. She saw John disappear over a stile into the fields behind the McFarlanes' post office.

Ernie was right; she was out of her depth. Sadly she went home in the fading light.

John came over to Animal Ark early next morning. He was dressed in a green zip-up jacket, camera at the ready. His face gave nothing away as Mandy went to answer the door. 'Hi, I thought we could get the bus over to Walton today, before we go up to High Cross.' He waited for her to collect her thoughts. 'There's a book I want to get from the library.'

Mandy glanced at her watch. It was half-past nine. Mrs Hope and Simon were busy in the surgery. Her father was out on his rounds. There was no chance of a lift into town, and she knew that John didn't have a bike. 'I'll just ask Jean what time the next bus goes,' she told him. 'Hang on here a minute.'

Though he looked the same as usual, spruced up and calm, Mandy thought he sounded tense, and she spotted a pleading look behind his eyes, as if he needed her company today of all days. She opened the door into reception, to a chorus of growls, barks and miaows. 'Jean, when's the next bus into Walton?' She leaned across the counter and shouted over the noise.

Jean checked her watch. 'In ten minutes. From the post office.'

'We'll just make it. Thanks!' Mandy made as if to sprint off.

'Mandy!' Jean called.

'See you later. Tell Mum I've gone into town, will you, please?' She shot off back into the house, to find John answering the front door to James Hunter.

James stood on the doorstep, tennis bag in one hand. He wore his blue and red track suit and white tennis shoes. He looked up at John. 'Is Mandy in?' he stammered.

'James!' she gasped. She dashed up from behind. 'Oh no, I forgot!' Both boys stared at her. 'I mean, I didn't exactly forget! Anyway, you're early!' She felt her stomach tilt. What should she do now?

'It's all right, never mind.' James stood there, two steps down in the breezy morning air. 'I should have rung you up to check it was still OK.' He stopped, lost for words.

John stood in the hall with a slight frown creasing his smooth forehead. Then he caught sight of Jean Knox, following Mandy through from the surgery.

'James, can we just change our plan a bit?' Mandy asked. She felt flustered. 'Why don't we all slip over to town together, then fit in a game of tennis?'

'No thanks. I'd rather go on down to the tennis-courts by myself,' James said quietly. He turned and wandered off up the drive. 'I'll find someone to play with, no problem. See you later.'

John blinked at Mandy. 'Is it my fault?' he asked.

'No, of course not; it's not your fault.' Mandy's stomach still hadn't regained its balance. She felt churned up inside.

'Mandy?' Jean said quietly. She came up close. 'John, why don't you go ahead to the bus stop?' she suggested in a firm but kindly voice. 'And perhaps Mandy will join you later.'

A blush flooded across John's face, but he nodded and went off nonetheless. Jean closed the door after him and put an arm around Mandy's shoulder. Then she led her into the kitchen.

'I never meant to do that to James!' Mandy said. She felt helpless, and a kind of hot guilt was creeping up her neck. She put up her hand to hide it.

'No, I'm sure you didn't.' Jean put on the kettle. She seemed to know exactly where everything was at this moment; the switch, the tea-bags, her glasses. She sounded calm and looked gently at Mandy. 'But if you were James and thought that someone had come along and stepped into your shoes, how do you think you would feel?'

'Lousy,' Mandy admitted. 'But it won't be for long. John has to go back to school next week, and he has to finish that rabbit project. I'm just lending a hand!'

'Yes.' Jean gazed steadily at her. 'You know, it puts me in mind of something that happened to me when I was eight; and that's well over fifty years ago now!' She settled at the table opposite Mandy and seemed to look down a long corridor into the past. 'It was summer, I remember, and I'd been on holiday to Blackpool. I brought a stick of pink rock back for my best friend. She was called Margaret; Margaret Taylor. We were like two peas in a pod.

'Well, I went up to her back garden with the stick of rock the minute we got home. She was playing there with a girl who lived down the street; Susan Turnbull. A girl with beautiful blonde plaits. Margaret looked at me across her garden fence. Her nose went up in the air. "I don't want your smelly stick of rock!" she told me. And she turned back to play with Susan. Well, sometimes we can all be nasty and spiteful like that, I know, but it was worse than any smack or telling off I'd had in my entire life, I can tell you.'

'And you were best friends?' Mandy asked. Her throat felt dry and narrow. Did it look as if she'd just done something similar to James?

'Yes. That's probably what put me in mind of you and James.' Jean stopped to sip her tea.

'And did you ever play with her again after that?' Mandy hoped the story would have a happy ending.

'I expect so. Yes, of course I did. Next day she was my best friend again, no doubt. And I suppose we were even nasty to Susan Turnbull on occasions. She was a big-headed girl because her father owned a chemists' shop and drove a Morris Oxford; a big black car,' Jean explained. Then she sighed. 'But I never forgot that stick of rock!'

Mandy jumped up from the table, her mind made up. 'Thanks, Jean!' she said.

'Why, where are you going?'

'To find my tennis racket!' Mandy said.

'It's under the counter in the surgery,' Jean told her with a smile. 'I noticed it lurking there yesterday. And there's a new set of balls and your tennis shoes. I expect your track suit's up in your wardrobe drawer!'

Mandy nearly dropped through the floor with shock. She stared at Jean. 'Thanks!' she stammered again.

'Now, *where* did I put my glasses?' Jean

mumbled. She carried the empty mugs to the sink. 'I'm sure I put them somewhere sensible . . .'

'Round your neck!' Mandy yelled. She was through the door, racket in hand, shoes hooked by their laces round her own neck. She dashed up the drive. 'See you later, Jean!'

James beat her seven-five, six-four, even though she was trying really hard to win.

After the game, they went straight back to Mandy's house for a sandwich lunch.

'Sorry about this morning,' Mandy mumbled, her mouth full of crusty french bread. 'It's just that I was pretty worried about John. Things aren't any better for him at home. In fact, I think they're worse. He can't seem to get over the shock of his dad getting engaged.' She told James about her visit the previous evening.

'Maybe he's jealous?' James said thoughtfully. 'Of Sara, I mean.'

'But she's really nice. He hasn't even given her a chance!'

'You don't when you're jealous, do you?'

Mandy stopped chewing and sighed. 'You're right. Anyway, I am sorry!' she repeated.

James grinned and switched the subject back to tennis. 'You lost it in the vital seventh game of the second set!' he reminded her. 'You served those two double faults.'

She nodded. 'I know, I know; I lost concentration.'

The sound of footsteps on the drive interrupted them. Through the window they could see John Hardy come bounding up to the door. They dashed out, glad to see him looking flushed and excited for once.

'What's got into you?' James demanded. He dragged John inside. 'Did you finish your project?'

John sank breathlessly into a chair. He ran a hand through his wavy hair. 'No, it's not that. I've just got back from town, and guess what?'

'What?' Mandy pushed a drink of juice across the table in his direction.

'There's a new pet shop that's just opened up on the High Street!'

'We know. Pets' Parlour,' James cut in.

'That's the one. But guess what, guess what!' John was almost spluttering with excitement. He unzipped his jacket and rested on the two back legs of his chair. 'They've got rabbits! Rabbits in the window! Little brown ones! For sale!

They're selling pet rabbits!'

'That's Button and Barney,' Mandy grinned. 'Anyway, that's what we call them.' She glanced across at James.

'You mean you've already seen them?' He looked astonished that his news wasn't new.

She nodded. 'Last week. I suppose that means that no one's come along and bought them yet.'

'Yes, thank heavens!' John gasped.

'Why, what are you up to now? Don't you want them to go to a good home then?' She glanced across again at James. What was going on in John's mind?

'No, I want them to come to *my* home!' he declared. He laughed out loud at their surprise.

'*You* want them?' she repeated.

'Yes, why not? I know lots of stuff about rabbits now. I can look after them. I went straight in and paid the money and asked the woman in the shop to keep them to one side for me!' John's face had come alive. He leapt up from his chair. 'Come on, you two! Let's go home and tell Dad!'

'But . . . !' Mandy felt a niggling doubt rise to the surface. What would happen to Button and Barney when John was away at school?

'Come on, what are you waiting for? Come and help me explain to my dad!'

Mandy shrugged, James nodded. 'You seem to have made up your own mind already!' he said.

'You bet!' John ran ahead. 'I bought them with my own money! Button and Barney are going to be all mine! I'll build a hutch, they can live in the garden! This is going to be great!'

Mandy and James followed him up the lane. She kept her fingers crossed for John as they headed for the Fox and Goose, but she had a nasty feeling that it wouldn't be quite that simple. Keeping pets when you had to go away to school was complicated. How would John feel when he had to leave them behind and set off for the Lake District? And who would be left to take good care of Button and Barney?

Five

'Don't be daft, John!' Julian Hardy stood in the kitchen at the back of the pub, armed with two massive plates of ham sandwiches. 'How can we keep pet rabbits here? Where on earth would we put them, for a start?' He was on his way back into the bar to cope with the busy lunch-time rush.

'In the garden, in a hutch.' John's eager face began to shut down. He glanced at Mandy and James, who hung back outside. 'They wouldn't be any trouble, honest!'

'And what happens when you're away at school? Who would you get to feed them then?' Mr Hardy pushed open the inner door with his foot. He balanced the plates carefully. '*And* keep them clean? *And* make sure they got some exercise?' He waited a second for John to see sense.

Mandy sighed. She'd feared this was going to happen.

'But, Dad, it doesn't take long. They're dead easy to look after. Aren't they, Mandy?'

She nodded, but she could see they were fighting a losing battle. Button and Barney would have to spend more time in the pet shop until another kindly owner came along.

'See – Mandy knows! And I've already paid for them, Dad. I can't back out now!'

Mandy looked at James. She could tell that his heart had sunk as low as hers. John was in for another big disappointment.

'Look, can we talk about this some other time?' Mr Hardy was beginning to frown. He hopped and wobbled on one foot, struggling to keep his balance. Then Sara opened the door from the far side. She stopped short, immediately sensing that something was wrong.

'I need to know straight away!' John persisted. 'Rabbits are my main project for science this year. I'll be at home for the whole of the summer to look after them. And I can come back for more weekends and half-terms. You'll hardly have to do anything!'

'That's what you say now, and it's all very well. But just you wait; it'd be me looking after them most of the time. I'd bet a lot of money on it!'

'Honestly, Dad! Listen, they're fantastic, aren't they, Mandy? They're brown all over and really friendly. They need a good home; they're getting bored cooped up in the pet shop all day long. I want to look after them!'

Mr Hardy sighed. 'Listen, once and for all, John. I said no! It's not practical. So you'll just have to go straight back to the shop, tell them you changed your mind, and get your money back!' He marched on through the door. It was his final word.

Sara hovered nervously, just inside the kitchen door. She peered into John's face. 'Never mind. Let me have a talk to him for you; see what I can do.'

Mandy noticed that John, who was quite small himself, easily reached Sara's shoulder. She was a shy, bright, bird-like woman.

'If you leave it a day or two, perhaps I can talk him round,' she suggested.

John hung his head. He was silent.

Oh no! Mandy thought. She half expected to see John rush off again.

But he kept his head low and stood there thinking. 'It wouldn't do any good,' he said at last.

'How do you know? You could let me have a go at least.' Sara spoke gently, pushing her loose hair back behind her ears.

'What for?' he demanded. He looked her straight in the eye. 'Do you like rabbits, or something?'

Sara's face broke into a smile. 'As a matter of fact, yes! I had some myself when I was a kid!'

'Hmm,' John scuffed at the table leg. He hung his head again, then sighed. 'No thanks, don't bother.'

Mandy frowned. She wanted to shake some common sense into him, but she knew how upset he must be.

'Why not? Since I'm going to be living here after the wedding, I could easily take care of a couple of little rabbits when you're away. No problem!'

'They won't always be little!' John broke in scornfully. 'They'll grow. And anyway, I said no thanks!'

'OK.' Sara backed off, ready to retreat into the bar.

'Anyway, you'd never be able to persuade him. You don't know my dad like I do. Once he's made up his mind, he never changes it!' He gave her a haughty look, back to his old buttoned-up self. 'Come on, James, you haven't seen the latest photographs. Have you got five minutes to come up and have a look?' He went off, quietly accepting his father's decision.

Mandy shot a wide-eyed look in Sara's direction. 'Time for a juice?' Sara asked.

Mandy nodded. John was hard to work out. What had happened to his bubbly excitement over Button and Barney? He seemed just to have swallowed it as he led James up the narrow stairs.

'I'm not getting any better at it, am I?' Sara sighed and stared out through the back door. Tiny pink and white blossom flowers framed their view of the old-fashioned walled garden. 'Julian and I get married in June, during John's half-term holiday, but I'm beginning to think he'll even refuse to show up for the wedding!'

'I just think it takes a long time to get to know him,' Mandy admitted.

'If ever!' Sara sighed again and shrugged.

'What happened to his real mum?' Mandy asked. As far back as she could remember, there had always been just John and his dad at the Fox and Goose.

'It was very sad. She was badly injured in a motorway crash. She was unconscious in hospital for five months, then she died.'

Mandy greeted the news in silence.

Sara continued in a slow, quiet voice. 'From what your mum has told me about it, Julian and John got quite a lot of money from the insurance firm after the crash. It helps to pay John's school fees and so on. But of course it never made up for losing his mum.'

Mandy nodded. She felt tears come to her eyes, hot and shining. '*My* real mum and dad were killed in a car crash,' she said at last. 'I'm adopted. I was only a baby when it happened, so I don't remember.'

'So was John. In fact the crash happened before he was born. He was lucky to survive.'

Mandy nodded. Now she understood much more about John's moods; his long silences, his serious gaze. 'Does he like his school?' she asked, trying to find something good to say about the whole sad situation.

But Sara shook her head. 'Not much. It's because Julian has to work all hours in the pub;

he feels John gets a better deal away at Grange.
And between you and me, I think poor John feels
a bit guilty about not liking school as much as he
should. After all, it was his mother's death that
paid for it.'

Mandy nodded and sighed. 'Yes, poor John.'

She felt Sara give her a quick hug and saw her
brush a forefinger across her own lashes.

'Never mind, perhaps things will work out in
the end,' Sara said quietly as James and John came
back downstairs.

John gave her a cool stare and walked on out of
the house. 'I'm on my way up to High Cross. Does
anyone feel like coming along?' he said to James
and Mandy in his distant, couldn't-care-less way.

Next day, it was James's idea to head back to the
Fox and Goose after they'd helped Mr Hope on
his afternoon round. 'Let's see how John's getting
on,' he suggested.

Mandy readily agreed.

They found Mr Hardy busy shifting crates and
stacking them by the side door, ready for
collection. John was up at High Cross again, he
told them. 'I don't know what's got into him lately.'
He shook his head, and stared into the distance.

Mandy glanced at James. 'Did he go back to the pet shop to tell them he can't have Button and Barney after all?' she asked.

Mr Hardy shook his head. 'I've been thinking about that, though. Maybe I was a bit harsh,' he confessed.

'Here, here!' Sara popped her head round the door, a smile on her face. She grinned at Mandy and James. 'Hello, you two! That's just what I was thinking!' she told her fiancé. She put a cardboard box full of crisps on a nearby table and came out to join them. 'You could still change your mind, Julian. Give John a chance

to look after those rabbits. It'll do him good.'

'Hmm.' Mr Hardy frowned.

Mandy showed James her fingers crossed behind her back. John's dad seemed to be weakening.

Sara went confidently on. 'He's proved it's not just a whim,' she reminded Julian Hardy. 'Rabbits mean an awful lot to John. He really cares. OK, so he shouldn't have gone ahead and paid for Button and Barney without asking you first. I agree about that. But he was obviously carried away. Poor kid. I can't get his face out of my mind when you told him he couldn't bring them home!' She paused.

Me neither! Mandy thought. There was the hurt look, then the blank expression came down like a shutter. 'Poor John,' she said under her breath.

'OK, OK!' Mr Hardy put up his hands to defend himself. He sighed. 'I was only thinking how hard things had been up till now. I mean, having pets really was out of the question before I met you, Sara. I didn't have time for anything except work!'

Sara went up and put an arm round his waist.

'But now?' James prompted. He stood alongside Mandy with his own fingers crossed.

Mr Hardy's face broke into a smile. 'Now it's

different! Now we can all muck in together. And rabbits are pretty straightforward to look after, aren't they?' He turned to Mandy.

'Nothing to it!' she vowed. 'You just have to keep them clean, warm and well fed!'

'OK, that does it!' He gave Sara a hug. 'I've changed my mind. Button and Barney can come!'

James leapt in the air like a footballer who'd scored a winning goal. Mandy shot straight off across the car park.

'Hang on, where are you going?' James yelled.

'To tell John, of course! I can, can't I?' She checked with his dad.

Everyone grinned. 'Yes, go on! Run up to High Cross and tell him the good news!' Mr Hardy agreed. 'And tell him to get himself back down here. It looks like it's going to rain before too long!'

They ran straight through the village, and up the hill to the remote farm. Then they headed quickly for the far pasture, to John's favourite look-out spot.

There, by the wide bole of an old ash tree, they found his purple and green rucksack propped on top of his green jacket. But there was no sign of John himself.

'He must have gone across to the nursery

warren,' Mandy said. She peeked inside the bag, surprised to see that he'd left his expensive camera unguarded. He was getting careless. She knew that he was determined to study and record each stage of the baby rabbits' progress, but he ought to have taken more care about his belongings.

Mandy and James strode along the wall side, careful to steer clear of the area where the yearlings had set up a new warren. Mandy was bursting to give John the good news about Button and Barney. 'Where's he got to?' she whispered, as they made their way across to the nursery.

They wove their way through five or six low hawthorn trees at the far end of Lydia's pasture. Beyond that, there was a low, rocky ridge running up to the moor top at right angles to it. It made a white ledge that dipped down into rough, unfarmed land. Few people strayed beyond this point, just the odd walker and one or two sheep farmers with their dogs, so the rabbits used it as a safe, quiet place to rear their young. Mandy stood on the ridge and put her hand to her eyes to scan the horizon. She was downwind of the warren, and knew that she was too far away to disturb the rabbits at their evening feed.

Where are you, John? Mandy was starting to feel impatient with him for not being in any of the usual places. Heavy, cold drops of rain began to fall. They made dark blotches on the white rock. She zipped up her jacket against the wind. In the distance she could see a dozen or so adult does hopping uneasily out of their burrows; ears up, back legs kicking. She knew they didn't like the rain, but she guessed there was something extra in the air which made them nervous. None of the babies had followed their mothers into the open. Mandy and James squatted to watch them.

Soon they spotted a few rabbits busily scratching openings in a patch of loose, bare earth, close to a hawthorn tree. They were making new burrows for their litters. But they too kept stopping, sitting up and glancing round, ready to bolt.

'What is it? What's happening?' James whispered. They listened hard for any unusual sound.

Maybe John was hiding upwind of the rabbits by mistake. 'Perhaps they can smell him,' Mandy suggested.

An explosion ripped through the air. High and sharp, it rattled down the hillside from the ridge above. Mandy felt her stomach lurch as she recognised the sound of farmers' guns. The rabbits scattered in an instant. They were gone. The hillside stood eerily empty.

A figure started up from behind a rock. It was John. He began to run up the hill. More gunshots echoed down the valley side.

'John!' Mandy stood and yelled as loud as she could. She and James set off after him.

Another shot cracked through the dull air above. 'John, wait!' she yelled. The wind caught her voice and whipped it back down the hillside into the valley bottom.

He ran, fast as a hare, over the rough ground. The rain had brought down a mist which clung to the ridge and hid the men with the shotguns. Soon John too was a pale figure vanishing into the mist.

'Come back, you'll get shot!' The stuttering guns rattled on. The men were out to get rabbits, to thin down their numbers. Farmers hated rabbits on their land; they ate crops and ruined the soil.

Mandy and James ran and stumbled up the hill. Their breath became short, their legs weakened. They just managed to keep John in view as he leapt over rocks, across rough grass; head back, feet pounding over the distance between him and the sound of guns. He was yelling at them to stop.

Another gust of wind swirled the mist clear of the ground. A dog barked and growled. Mandy saw the black outlines of three men with shotguns to their shoulders, standing on the ridge. Their barrels were tilted down towards the nursery warren. John hurtled straight at them.

Mandy jumped down a drop of about a metre, from a boulder on to a soft bed of couch grass. She stumbled forward, then pushed herself on after John. Nothing would stop him. He seemed to have lost his senses, still running, and only seconds away from the men on the ridge.

'Hold it, there's a kid down there!' the nearest man warned. They let their guns drop to waist height. But they stood, feet planted wide apart, glaring at John. One kept a squat white bulldog close to heel. It growled and bared its teeth as John kept on coming.

'You want to get yourself killed?' the first man yelled in a rough voice. 'Because you're going the right way about it down there!'

John ran at him. 'Don't shoot the rabbits!' He was beside himself with fright.

The man braced himself. He slung his gun over

his shoulder. 'Now, steady on!' he shouted. 'Just
hold it where you are. We've got a job to do here,
and we aim to do it. So just stand out of our way,
sonny, and let us get on with it!'

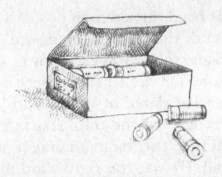

Six

Mandy didn't stop to think. Her long legs carried her swiftly over the last stretch of rough ground. John had got himself into deep trouble with the men with the guns. She went straight at him from behind, flung herself forward and threw her arms round his waist. She tackled him to the ground.

The first man strode down the hill towards them. The bulldog growled and snapped. James caught up with Mandy and began to pull her and John to their feet. Mandy could feel her heart thumping, her knees hurting from the heavy fall. Still she clung on to John, in case he struggled up and kept on charging. But he stood there gasping, his head turned away.

'All right, all right, just calm down!' The man came down and seized John roughly by the elbow. 'Will someone tell me what the heck's going on round here?' He glared at Mandy and James.

Mandy recognised the thin, sharp features of Dennis Saville, the farm manager at Upper Welford Hall. He was the right-hand man of the owner, Sam Western. She knew him as a hard-hearted, no-nonsense sort who simply carried out his boss's orders. No doubt Mr Western had sent Dennis and a couple of lads up on to the ridge with orders to thin down the local rabbit population.

'It's OK, let me talk to John,' she said. She stooped to brush herself down. She and John were covered in dirt. His face was marked and scratched, and he still struggled as Dennis tried to restrain him.

Another figure, one of the two stocky lads in jeans and heavy boots, came lumbering down the hill. He held his gun under his arm and kicked loose stones as he pulled himself up short alongside Mandy's little group. 'What's up?' he demanded. 'Has the kid gone nuts or something?'

'No!' James was stung into a reply. 'Just leave

him alone, will you? He was only doing what he could to save the rabbits!'

'What?' the lad jeered, as if unable to believe his ears. 'Save rabbits? You must be joking!'

'It's their nursery warren down there, full of babies!' Mandy reminded him.

'So?' The lad stood with one hand in the pocket of his denim jacket, letting the shiny steel barrel of his shotgun drop forward. The polished wooden butt rested under his arm.

'They're just a few weeks old. They're still helpless!'

'So?' He stood and sneered. 'All the better for us!'

John shoved his shoulder against Dennis Saville's chest to try and push him off. His face was drained and white, with a bright red graze on one cheek where he'd fallen against a rough stone.

'Steady on!' Dennis insisted. He was wiry and strong, and kept a firm hold of John's arm. John beat at his tight grasp with his spare hand. 'Now if you don't calm down, I'll set the dog on you!' the manager threatened. Above them, the second lad held the bulldog by its steel-studded collar. It crouched low, ready to leap forward.

'John!' Mandy pleaded. She caught hold of his sleeve. 'Wait a minute, let's just try to explain!' She waited for him to stop pushing, and watched, as slowly the older man released him.

John's breath came out in harsh gasps. His chest and shoulders heaved, but he looked stunned now, rather than wild with fear. His hands shook as he tried to brush mud from his sweater.

'Mr Saville, John's doing a study on the rabbits for a school project. He's been hard at work up here for more than a week now.' She tried to sound calm and reasonable.

The man allowed his frown to relax a fraction. 'Has he now? Yes, that'd be right. I've seen him coming by the big house with his camera often enough. Does Miss Fawcett know you're here? You'd need her permission to cross that last field.'

'Yes, she knows.' Mandy could see that John was still too shocked to answer.

The lad laughed out loud. 'Not much use expecting her to take a gun to a few rabbits,' he scoffed. '*She* probably feeds 'em dandelions and invites 'em in the house. She's as daft as a brush, just like him!' He pointed with the gun at John. 'They're both off their heads, if you ask me!'

'Dean, that'll do!' Dennis Saville warned. 'What

Lydia Fawcett gets up to on her own land is her business, and we can't do a thing about it if she chooses not to shoot rabbits. But this is common land, and up here we've every right to try and cut down on this year's young 'uns.'

'But why?' Mandy pleaded. 'What harm are they doing to you if they dig their warren way up here?'

Dennis Saville gave an exasperated sigh. 'They don't stay put here on this stretch, do they now? Soon as they've found their feet these young ones come scampering down to the Hall, looking for whatever they can find. Nice juicy fruit from the currant bushes, anything they can sink their teeth into, little devils. And they dig up the lawn and make a right mess of things. Can you blame Mr Western for wanting to get rid of them?'

Mandy wasn't convinced. She thought a rabbit had as much right to be where he or she wanted as any local landowner. But she bit her tongue. 'Can't you put wire netting round the fruit bushes?' she asked, looking for a logical way out.

Dean snorted and stamped off back up the hill. 'Why are we wasting time with these loonies?' he asked in a loud voice. He released the barrel on his gun, ready to load more shot.

John seemed to come back to life at the sound

of the click of metal. He turned on Dennis Saville. 'You're not going to let them start up again, are you?'

The farm manager shrugged. 'Listen, why don't you three just move off back to High Cross for half an hour? There'll be plenty of rabbits left for you to carry on studying, even after we've finished here.'

Mandy felt her blood run cold. She turned to James. 'Tell them that's not the point!' The mist was lifting and the clouds rolling away. Soon the rabbits would get back their nerve and emerge from the nursery warren.

'It's no use, they won't listen!' James turned and walked three or four paces downhill. 'But it's just like you said,' he told the farm manager. 'This is common ground. We've got as much right to be here as you lot. And we're not shifting! This is where we're staying, right here!' He stood and glared back up the hill. Behind and below him, the land kept its eerie silence.

'Good idea!' Mandy followed his lead. 'Come on, John! If they won't listen to reason, we'll have to find another way of stopping them!' She joined James, leaping on to a low boulder, and looking determined to see off the three men with their guns.

Saville stared down at them and shook his head. He put his hands in his pockets and strode back up to the ridge. 'Down! Stay down!' he ordered the dog. For a few moments he stood and talked with the two lads.

'I only hope this works!' Mandy whispered to John and James.

'Well, *I'm* not moving,' John replied between clenched teeth. He stood alongside James and Mandy. 'James is right; we're staying right where we are!'

'Forever?' Mandy bit her bottom lip. What had

they got themselves into now? The men were still discussing their next tactic.

'For as long as *they* stay!' John promised. 'And I'll be here for as long as there's any chance of them coming back!'

'Could be a long wait.' Mandy glanced at him. The wind had brought colour back to his cheeks. His head was up, his face looked brave and clear. 'Anyway, good for you. After tonight we can get Lydia to use her new phone to send down warnings to Animal Ark or to the Fox and Goose, whenever she sees them crossing the back of her place with their guns. It'll mostly be in the evenings. And we'll drop what we're doing and be up here like a shot – oops!' She laughed at her choice of words.

'Great!' The wind blew John's hair straight back. 'As long as we're around they won't be able to shoot any more rabbits!'

'Maybe!' James added, in his sensible, clear way.

They waited, confidence rising, and they watched as Dennis Saville shrugged and muttered one last instruction to the lads. Then he led them and the dog off over the ridge out of sight.

Mandy, James and John cheered. 'Brilliant!' John cried. 'That's the first battle won, at any rate!'

With huge sighs of relief, they ran back to the ash trees and John's usual lookout spot. They crouched down. Soon peace and quiet returned to the high fields. No more gunshots. No more man-smell to scare the rabbits. Now the pasture and the hills beyond were alive with mother and baby rabbits, lolloping, crouching, scuffling, nibbling, nipping, and combing their ears in the calm evening air.

'One more thing!' Mandy said, when she could catch her breath at last. James studied the rabbits with a small, secret grin on his face as he listened to her. 'Ask us why we came up here when we did! Go on, ask us!' She couldn't hide her own excitement at the news she was about to give.

John dragged his own glance away from the rabbits. 'Go on, then. Why?'

'Your dad sent us.'

'Oh!' he grunted.

'To tell you—'

'To get back home for supper?' he growled.

'No! To tell you you can keep Button and Barney after all!'

'Where? At home?' John's mouth hung open. He grabbed hold of Mandy's arm.

'Yes, at home! He changed his mind!'

John whooped and fell flat on his back. 'Tell me I'm not dreaming!' he gasped.

'You're not dreaming. You can keep the rabbits,' James repeated. 'Come on, let's go!'

They gathered John's things, dragged him up off the ground, and headed for home.

But Lydia cut them off as they made their way down past High Cross. 'You three haven't been getting yourselves shot at, have you?' she called. 'I heard all the noise up there!' She came up to them with a worried frown.

'No!' Mandy laughed. 'Not quite.' She told Lydia what had happened.

'Hmm.' Lydia was still frowning. 'I'm on your side,' she told them. 'Call me soft-hearted, but I hate the idea of taking a gun to the poor creatures as much as you three do. On the other hand, I don't want you to risk getting yourselves shot!'

'We won't!' James promised. 'But if you do see Dennis Saville up there again, can you ring and tell us? We've got a plan to stop them shooting in the nursery warren.'

Lydia nodded. She took John inside to bathe his grazed face in warm water and disinfectant.

'We just need to be there. That would be enough,' Mandy explained. 'They'd never carry on shooting while we're there.'

'Let me think about it,' Lydia said. 'Perhaps I can come up with a better plan.'

'What?' John winced as she dabbed his graze with cotton-wool.

'Maybe I can get them to give into the temptation of freshly-baked scones whenever they're passing this way. That would soon put paid to their rabbiting; hot tea and fresh scones!' Lydia's eyes twinkled.

'I'm not sure.' John stood up and looked at Mandy and James.

'Well, leave it with me. Perhaps I can think of something else as well.' Lydia drained off the bowl of water at the sink.

Mandy nodded. She could trust her old friend to help them out. 'Come on,' she said, anxious to get John back home.

They said goodbye to Lydia and ran on, down past Upper Welford Hall, then past Beacon House. Mandy waved to Imogen Parker Smythe. The little girl swung moodily to and fro on the swing her father had slung from a branch of one of their huge beech trees. The plump, pig-tailed seven-year-old was slow to wave back. She had her heated swimming-pool and her enormous garden, but she didn't seem to have any friends who would come and play. Mandy usually saw her all alone, scowling, or running inside to her mum, whenever she passed.

Mandy, James and John gathered speed down the steep hill, and ran down past the golf-club, past the tennis-courts, and over the old bridge to the crossroads and the Fox and Goose.

Julian Hardy looked relaxed and comfortable in a blue open-necked shirt as he lounged in front of the television. In the bar, his staff were getting ready for the evening trade. Sara sat at a table by the window. She was writing out wedding invitations on squares of cream-coloured card edged with silver. She looked up and smiled at the three of them, then laid down her pen.

'Hello, son!' Mr Hardy made room for John on the sofa. He put an arm along the back of it, close to his shoulder. 'Hey, have you been in the wars?' he asked. He'd noticed the raw graze on John's cheek.

'I slipped on a rock, that's all,' John said. 'Something had scared the rabbits, and I was just trying to sort it out when I slipped and lost my footing.' He stared meaningfully at Mandy and James, as if to warn them not to go into detail.

'Well, never mind, no real harm done.' Mr Hardy grinned across at Sara. 'When shall we go and collect Barney and Button, then?'

'First thing tomorrow?' she suggested. Mandy could see that Sara was going to enjoy this almost as much as anyone else in the room.

John's grin stretched from ear to ear. 'Fantastic! Thanks, Dad!'

'Thank Mandy and James, and Sara here. She threatened to divorce me if I said no to the rabbits!'

'And we're not even married yet!' she joked.

John turned towards her. 'Thanks, Sara.' He looked round the room at them all. 'Oh, great! Oh, fantastic! Oh, brilliant! . . . Wow!' he said.

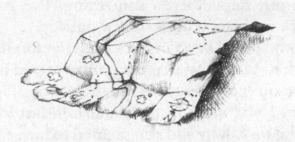

Seven

'Nice to see that you two have made friends again,' Jean commented. She peered over her glasses from behind the reception desk at Animal Ark.

James Hunter had arrived early for the trip into Walton. Sara had promised to wait at the Fox and Goose while Mandy and James travelled over to the pet shop with John and his father. She knew they could help choose the right food and so on, so they'd arranged to meet up at the pub at nine o'clock.

Now James coloured up under Jean's gaze.

'We never fell out in the first place!' Mandy objected. 'James has always been my best friend!'

'I've just remembered something! I've got to padlock my bike!' James darted outside.

Mandy flicked her hair back from her forehead. 'See what you've done? You've embarrassed him!'

Jean smiled. 'He's such a nice boy, James Hunter. I was quite lost without him last week, when he went away and you seemed to have taken up with the Hardy boy. I missed his smiling face!' She smiled. Her own grandchildren lived too far away for her to see them often.

'John Hardy is nice too,' Mandy protested. 'Once you get to know him.' She remembered to write a name and phone number into the appointment book from a phone call she'd taken just before James arrived. 'You know, he was great yesterday. He stopped Mr Western's men from shooting all the rabbits up at High Cross!' She delivered the tale of John's heroic dash up the hill. ' . . . And then he came face to face with the barrel of a gun and he never even flinched! Imagine! Only inches away from his nose. It was just like on TV!'

Jean tutted. 'You're exaggerating again, dear.'

'No, I'm not. Oh, well, maybe just a teeny bit! But most of it's true! And now he's going to get the reward he deserves. His dad says he can have the two baby rabbits from the pet shop in town. Isn't that great?'

Jean's eyebrows shot up. 'I thought Julian Hardy had enough on his plate, poor man, coping with everything single-handed.' Jean went to straighten the chairs back against the wall, ready for surgery to begin.

'Well, he won't be single-handed after he marries Sara, will he? And *she* likes pets. And anyway, he did say yes. We were there at the time!' Mandy checked her watch and ran a brush through her hair, getting ready to go.

'Hmm, well, he must be going soft in his old age, then.' Jean chatted on regardless. 'Funny that; rabbits seem to be popular at the moment. I had a phone call only yesterday from someone who wanted to know about inoculations for them, and so on. The little girl was so excited she could hardly get the word out. I told her to bring her rabbits along to the surgery this Saturday.'

'Well, I'm not surprised they're so popular. They're gorgeous creatures.' Mandy thought of the fluffy brown babies in Pets' Parlour, and of her own three rabbits happily munching oats out in the back garden. She glanced out of the window on to the drive. 'Here's Simon now!' She went out to join James, and they crossed paths with Animal Ark's young nurse who, as ever, looked bright and cheerful as he turned up for work.

'Don't do anything I wouldn't do!' he called after them.

'As if!' Mandy replied. They were in high spirits themselves as they headed for the Fox and Goose.

They rode over to Walton in Mr Hardy's smart green car. John sat in the front, silent with excitement, almost gripping the sides of his seat in his eagerness to be there. No one said much during the fifteen minute journey; they just looked out across the moor, spotting curlews overhead, plus the odd seagull, and high above, a sparrow-hawk gliding on the air currents.

Mr Hardy parked in the town's central carpark. Together they crossed the main street. Mandy waved at Mr Cecil, hard at work inside his chocolate shop. He was filling the windows with home-made chocolate assortment boxes. Down the road they could spot the red lettering over the window of Pets' Parlour, and the much dimmer, more cluttered interior.

'Come on!' John insisted, breaking into a run for the last few metres.

They looked into the window at the muddle of dog leads, baskets, mice cages and budgerigar mirrors. There was a gap where Button and Barney should have been. John shot an anxious look at his father.

'They must still be inside,' Mr Hardy remarked. 'Having breakfast. Come on, let's go in and see.' He opened the door to the stuffy smell of birdseed and fish food. Across the dark room, the blue, red and silver fishes darted across their bubbling tank. James was the last one in. He closed the door to the loud tinkle of the shop bell.

'Yes, please? Can I help you?' Geoff, the friendly young shopkeeper, came out from the back room, his red shirt covered in stray wisps of straw, his sleeves rolled back. 'I hope I didn't keep you waiting.'

Julian Hardy nudged John forward to the counter. Mandy and James stayed quietly in the background. Their eyes swept the shelves for any sign of the rabbit hutch. A nervous feeling had begun to clutch hold of Mandy's stomach.

'I've come about the rabbits,' John began. He put both hands on the counter to steady his nerves.

Geoff studied him more closely. 'I'm sorry,

which rabbits?' He looked puzzled.

John carried on. 'I know it must have seemed a bit strange, me not coming straight back for them yesterday, but can I collect them now, please? I'd like to take them home.'

Mr Hardy stepped forward to help out. 'Actually, to be fair, it was me who caused the delay, not John. I thought we wouldn't be able to cope with Button and Barney. But then I thought better of it. He can have them after all, and we promise five-star accommodation at the Fox and Goose!' He jollied the mood, which seemed to have gone awkward and flat.

Behind the counter, Geoff began to frown. 'Button and Barney? The little brown rabbits?' He coughed and cleared the back of his throat, then shook his head.

Mandy's chest thudded; one dreadful, heart stopping moment.

Geoff went on. 'Look, I'm sorry, but you're too late. I'm afraid I've already sold those two, just yesterday afternoon. Don't worry, it was to a very good owner.' He shrugged and looked uncomfortable. 'You're out of luck there, I'm afraid.'

The life drained from John's face. His eyes

stared slowly round the shelves, as if this was some terrible joke and Button and Barney could be found lurking in a dark corner. 'But I already paid for them!' he stammered. 'They were *my* rabbits! You can't have sold them to someone else!'

Mandy saw from the stricken look on her friend's face that his world had collapsed. He stared as Geoff explained what must have happened. 'It wasn't me you bought them from, was it?'

Slowly John shook his head. 'No, it was someone else. A lady.'

Geoff nodded. 'That was Mrs Kearney. She was looking after things in the shop that day. She obviously forgot to tell me that she'd sold the rabbits to you!' He sighed and then shrugged at Julian Hardy. 'I'm very sorry. He's obviously upset, and I don't blame him. It's a bad mistake on our part. But I'll tell you what!' He turned to John. 'I'll put your name to the top of the list, and I'll tell you when the next two rabbits come up for sale. I'm expecting to take in another litter in a couple of weeks,' he said. 'You could come back then. In the meantime, I'll refund your money.'

'I'll be away at school,' John said in a hollow voice.

'But I can bring Mandy and James back here,' his father offered. 'They can help me choose some more rabbits.' He stood, hands in pockets. 'Look, John, it's not a disaster. We can still get you some pets.'

He shook his head. 'No thanks.'

'Why not?'

'Because it's Button and Barney I want. I bought them myself, and I don't feel the same about having any others. Thanks.' He turned stiffly away.

Julian Hardy shrugged at the shopkeeper. 'It looks as though we'll have to leave it for now,' he said.

Geoff nodded. 'Sorry about the mix-up.' He spread his palms and returned the shrug. 'I do feel really bad about it.'

'Never mind, it can't be helped. It doesn't matter.' He smiled and herded James, Mandy and John out of the shop.

Mandy heard the doorbell ring behind them. *Yes, it does matter!* she thought. *It means the whole world to John!*

She glanced at James, uncertain what to do next. Button and Barney had been whisked away from under their noses. She felt empty and sad, and yet she could only guess how disappointed John himself must feel. They trailed back to the carpark in complete silence.

'Sorry,' Mr Hardy sighed, as they sank into their car seats. 'I can see that this is all my fault. I shouldn't have held things up. I really am sorry, John!'

John pulled his seat-belt across his chest. 'Oh no, not at all,' he said. 'It's nobody's fault. It's just one of those things.'

How can he say that? Mandy wondered. She knew John must be feeling dreadful!

When they got back to the Fox and Goose, John got out of the car and went straight to his room. Mandy looked at Mr Hardy, who nodded that she should follow him up. She took the stairs two at a time.

Mandy opened John's bedroom door. He sat cross-legged on the floor. The walls were covered in diagrams and sketches. Rabbits stared down at him from the bathroom door, from his wonderful photographs still scattered all over the carpet. He was surrounded by them. But he hadn't got what he really wanted. All he wanted was Button and Barney to clean and feed and care for. Two live creatures to help him get over the changes that had come charging into his life.

'I thought you might like some company,' said Mandy.

'Thanks, Mandy, but I'd rather be on my own,' John replied in a quiet voice.

'I understand,' Mandy said. 'Call me tomorrow, and we can go up to High Cross together.' John nodded a reply, but Mandy wondered if he really would call. She quietly closed his bedroom door.

Feeling rather helpless, Mandy went downstairs.

After the disaster at the pet shop, Mandy and James didn't hear a word from John. Sara popped into Animal Ark for coffee one morning and told Mandy's mum that he was drifting round the house like a ghost. 'Like he's not really there,' she said. 'And he's out all the time; every chance he gets, he's up roaming round on that farm. His dad's nearly out of his mind with worry. We really don't know what to do.'

Emily Hope gave Sara a sympathetic smile. 'Give him time,' she advised. 'There are so many new things for him to get used to all at once.'

Mrs Hope saw her old school-friend to the door, and shook her head sadly. As she went to begin surgery, Mandy realised that even her mum had no decent solutions.

She heard too from Lydia that John Hardy now spent all his time among the High Cross warrens. Lydia rang up one teatime, worried that she hadn't seen Mandy up there with him during the last few days. 'I thought you might be ill,' she said. 'I got so used to you coming along too that I began to wonder what had happened. Have you two fallen out?'

'No. But John said he wanted to be by himself. He said he can concentrate on his work better that way.' Mandy fiddled with the half eaten cheese-on-toast on her plate. She'd lost her appetite and spent her own time worrying what was happening to John. Lydia's phone call did nothing to put her mind at rest.

'Hmm. It's not good for a boy of his age to be alone so much.' Lydia let a big pause develop before she went on. 'Mandy, I don't suppose you could—'

She jumped in without allowing Lydia to finish. 'Come up to High Cross? Yes, of course I can. James is here too. We'll both be right up!' She jumped to her feet and looked in James's direction.

'Oh, good. I'm sure it'll help to cheer him up. He looks so . . . lonely, you know. It's very cut off up here. I'm sure he'd prefer to have some company.'

'OK?' Mandy signalled to James. He nodded. 'OK, Lydia, we're on our way.' She put down the phone. Whether or not John would prefer to have company, Mandy leapt at Lydia's suggestion.

She and James hopped on to their bikes and pedalled up the hill. It was evening; John was certain to be hanging round the warrens at this time of day. The rabbits would be feeding and basking in the low sun. That, anyway, would be a sight worth seeing.

Sure enough, John's rucksack sat abandoned at the foot of the ash tree. Down past the farm, they could see Lydia leading the goats in for milking. Then, higher up, beyond the far pasture, they spotted John. He sat still as a statue on a low rock, huddled over a sketchbook. All round him rabbits grazed, nipping and nibbling at the grass. The hillside would spring to life whenever they moved; hopping, kicking and darting to the next juicy leaf. John was there right in their midst, but they ignored him.

'He looks like part of the scenery,' James

whispered. 'I bet he wishes he could stay here forever.'

'Poor John,' Mandy sighed. 'Let's wait here until he moves. We don't want to scare them all away.' They stood by a wall, watching and waiting.

When the rabbits sat bolt upright, twitching their ears to listen out for danger, Mandy and James saw John glance behind. There must have been a tiny sound, up over the horizon. The rabbits stared and twitched. Another sound. They fled. Dozens of white tails bobbed and were gone. John stood up and turned to face the high ridge.

Two figures appeared. They carried shotguns and swaggered down the hill.

'Dean and his friend!' Mandy gasped. She ran forward across the empty pasture. 'Not again!' But this time there was no farm manager to keep the lads in check.

'I think that's Steve Burnley with him,' James told her.

The two youths were bearing down on John, who just stood waiting, camera round his neck, sketchbook at his side.

'He got expelled for bullying in his last year. I know his younger brother, Frankie.' James sounded worried. 'Have you seen their guns?'

'Yes, and I've got this feeling that John's likely to do something rash again, the strange mood he's been in lately!' Mandy began to shout and wave her arms, trying to distract Dean and Steve's attention.

But John turned on them as they clambered over the last low wall on to the common ground. 'Go away!' he yelled. 'I can deal with this!'

On a level with John, Dean came to a halt. 'Not you again!' he said scornfully. 'I've had just about enough of you!'

'Tough!' John retorted. 'Because I'm not moving!'

Dean laughed. 'Big man!'

John stood his ground.

Dean's friend, Steve, curled his lip and took up position on the far side of John.

'Wait!' James warned Mandy. 'Better see what happens next!' He pulled her to a halt.

'I said I'm not moving!' John insisted. His chin was up, he stared back at them.

'Do you think we can't make you!' Dean taunted. He tapped the barrel of his gun, then grinned.

James and Mandy gasped.

'Look, sonny, just stand out of the way, why don't you?' Steve advised. 'We've got a job to do here; Mr Western's orders. And we always do what we're told, don't we, Dean?' Swiftly he swung his gun round in the direction of some distant hawthorns. He took a shot at them. The sound cracked and echoed across the valley.

Mandy jumped, but John didn't move a muscle. She half turned away, afraid to look.

'Go on, shoot! But I'm still not moving!' he yelled. 'I'm staying right where I am!'

'Now, no one's shooting anything round here!' A calm voice started up close by, just behind James. Lydia had marched up from the bottom pasture, leading Houdini on a short rope. The goat's head was down, horns at the ready. He'd picked up Lydia's serious tone. 'I suggest you two just put away those guns, and listen to me for a minute.'

John waved them back. 'I'm not moving from this spot!'

'Who said anything about moving?' Lydia said mildly. But she stood firm, Houdini at her side. Dean glanced at the goat and frowned at Steve. Together they backed off a step or two. 'I expect you'd like a word of explanation,' Lydia continued. 'I can see that this must all be rather puzzling. Now, I want you two to go back to Mr Western and tell him this piece of news.'

Steve's lip curled again. 'What's she on about?'

Dean shrugged, but he didn't dare speak. Houdini stared him in the eye.

Lydia drew a brownish paper from her work jacket pocket and began to open it out.

'What I have here is a map of High Cross land,' she explained. 'Dating from the time when my grandfather farmed here. Now, it's an old map but it's a good one.' She beckoned Dean and Steve across. Reluctantly they went and bowed their stubbly heads over Lydia's paper.

'I had some idea that Mr Western and Dennis

Saville might be mistaken,' Lydia went on. 'So I went to my desk the other day and unearthed this map, just in case. See – I was right!' She pointed a finger at a faint dotted line. 'The High Cross boundary cuts across the ridge and down by those hawthorns over there. That means the area where we're standing isn't common land after all!'

Mandy took a deep breath of surprise and relief.

Lydia looked from Steve to Dean. 'You can see for yourselves, it's High Cross land.'

Dean ducked his head and grunted. 'But Mr Western says we have to keep back the rabbits,' he complained.

'That may well be,' Lydia agreed. She folded the map and put it back in her pocket. 'And you have to follow orders whenever you can; I can see that. But not on *my* land, you don't!' She looked calmly at them. 'So you'd best go back and tell Mr Western that from me. Tell him it may not be worth anything as farming land, but I fancy it does rather well as an old-fashioned nature reserve. There's every variety of clover, wild cowslip, and that pretty pale lilac flower which we called milkmaids when I was young. Besides, there's the rabbit nursery.' She smiled at John, then gazed gently round. 'And

this is the way I like it, just as it was in Grandfather's time!'

Dean and Steve knew when they were beaten.
If nothing else, they didn't like the look of
Houdini's sharp horns. 'OK, OK,' Dean said, as
the goat stamped and strained at his rope, 'we're
on our way. We'll tell him, then he can't blame
us.' He muttered to Steve as they backed off; 'It's
not my fault if he lives next door to a rabbit lover,
is it? It's nothing to do with me.'

Lydia kept on smiling and nodding at John,
Mandy and James as the two lads made their way
back up the hill, guns drooping, shoulders
hunched. 'Well done, Houdini!' she said proudly.

He tossed his head and stamped.

'Is all that true?' Mandy demanded. She pointed
to the map bulging in Lydia's pocket. 'How come
you made this discovery all of a sudden?'

Lydia's eyes crinkled shrewdly. 'According to
this map, it's true; we're standing on High Cross
land.'

'But?' Mandy knew Lydia well enough to know
there was more to it.

'But Grandfather was an argumentative sort.
He had the map drawn up in a dispute against
Mr Western's own grandfather. This was over sixty

years ago. And as far as I know, the two old gentlemen never settled their quarrel, and the dispute is still in the hands of some dusty lawyer's clerk.' She laughed mischievously.

'In other words?' James said.

'In other words, I don't know whose land it is!' Lydia smiled broadly. 'But those two weren't to know that, were they? And it'll take Sam Western many months to go back to the lawyers and work it all out to his satisfaction. If he can be bothered to go to all that expense over a piece of rough old land like this!'

'Lydia!' James and Mandy chorused together. They hopped around at the success of her little scheme.

Quietly, John bent to pick up his pencil. 'Thank you very much, Miss Fawcett,' he said. he stood awkwardly. 'Thanks, James. Thanks, Mandy.'

His words set a seal on the incident, and now it was plain that he wanted to be by himself again. He sat back on the rock and bent his head over his work.

Lydia nodded for James and Mandy to come away. 'Give him time,' she advised. 'I think that's what he needs.'

That's what everyone says, Mandy thought. *But it doesn't seem to work!*

She and James followed Lydia and Houdini through the long grass. 'He doesn't have any more time,' Mandy told her. 'He goes back to school on Sunday, and I'm really worried about him.' She turned to James. 'You see what I mean about him? It's like he's locked himself up and thrown away the key. I don't think he can ever bear to speak about losing Button and Barney!'

James nodded. They came to a halt in the farmyard.

'What would it take to put things right?' Lydia asked Mandy. 'You know John better than most, I suspect.'

Mandy sighed. 'Button and Barney,' she replied. 'That's what it would take. But they were sold to someone else by mistake earlier in the week.'

They stood together in the dusk.

'I've got it!' James said suddenly. 'If Button and Barney are the only things that'll help, what we have to do is set out and find them, isn't it?' He looked eagerly at Mandy. 'See? If we found the lucky owners and tracked the rabbits down, at least John would know where they were. We might even be able to get them back for him!'

Mandy saw it in a flash; James was right. 'Sometimes I could hug you, James Hunter!' she cried, with a mad urge to fling her arms round him. 'You have the best ideas!'

Lydia laughed as James ducked and darted away. 'Keep her off me!' he yelped.

'Don't worry, you're safe!' Mandy spread her arms wide and spun round on the spot like Superwoman. 'Da-da! Let the quest to find Button and Barney begin!' she announced. 'Pets' Parlour, here we come!'

Eight

James and Mandy were waiting on the doorstep of Pets' Parlour when Geoff turned up looking rumpled and sleepy. It was half-past eight in the morning.

'Hi, it's us again!' Mandy said. 'I bet you wish you could get rid of us!'

He grinned, opened the door and invited them into the shop. 'So what can I do for you this time?' Geoff hung his keys on a hook behind the counter and flicked the switch on a kettle which sat on a nearby shelf. 'Go ahead, talk to me. But don't expect me to take much in at this time in the morning. Not until I've had a cup of coffee!'

'Don't worry, we'll be quick,' James promised. 'We just need a little bit of information.'

Mandy took a pen and piece of paper out of her jacket pocket. She looked up eagerly, ready to scribble down the name and address of Button and Barney's new owners.

Geoff rubbed the top of his tousled head and yawned. 'OK, try me!' He nodded to a middle-aged woman with curly brown hair who'd just followed them into the shop. 'Morning, Mrs Kearney!' he said.

'Can you tell us who took the baby rabbits that John Hardy had bought?' James blurted out. 'You see, he bought them first, so it's him who should really have them, isn't it? And we thought we might be able to track them down for him.'

Mandy's pen hovered over the paper.

Geoff looked doubtful. 'I don't know about that . . .'

'It's OK, we're not planning to go off and kidnap them. Or bunnynap them!' James promised. 'But we did think we could talk to the other buyers and see if they would let John have the rabbits back.'

'They might agree, once they hear the full story,' Mandy put in.

'Maybe you're right.' Geoff frowned and shook his head. 'And I can see that you two wouldn't go and do anything daft.' He glanced again at Mrs Kearney who was just buttoning up her overall, ready to start her day's work.

'Then what's the problem?' James glanced anxiously at Mandy. Their plan seemed to be coming to a full stop before it had begun.

'The problem is, I can't tell you exactly who went off with Button and Barney. These people came into the shop, chose them and paid cash for them. They didn't even give me their name.'

Mandy's hopes came crashing down. She stuffed the pen and paper back into her pocket, at a loss for words.

James was deep in thought. 'But what did they look like, these people? Do they ever come in here for other things? Won't they be coming back to buy food and bedding for the rabbits? Haven't you seen them round town since? Don't you have a clue who they might be?'

'Whoa, steady on!' Geoff held up his hands in protest. 'One thing at a time!' He poured milk into his coffee and stirred it. 'I can tell you what they looked like, but I don't know if it will help much. They were a fairly ordinary couple, a man and wife. I can't say I noticed that much about them. He was tall and well-dressed. She was neat and slim, and well-groomed. I think she was wearing gold earrings. She had blonde hair. His hair was darker, I think.'

'Didn't they have a child with them?' Mandy forced her brain into action, once she was over the first disappointment.

Geoff shook his head. 'No. They wanted to buy the rabbits as a surprise Easter present for their little girl. It was very hush-hush. Apparently she'd been wanting a pet for ages. They were passing by and thought Button and Barney would be just the thing. Easter bunnies.'

James sighed. 'You were right, it doesn't help much. And you're sure you've never seen them before?'

'I swear. But like you say, they might come back for rabbit food and so on. I could always find out more for you then.'

Mandy shook her head. 'No, today's Saturday. John goes off to school tomorrow. We have to track these people down today, to try and get Button and Barney back before he leaves home. That's the plan at any rate.'

All three looked at one another. Mrs Kearney stood in the background, looking uncomfortable. 'Don't worry, nobody's blaming you!' Geoff called out. 'It's just been a bit of bad luck, that's all.'

A gloomy feeling had settled on Mandy.

'Thanks.' Mandy nodded and smiled briefly. 'Thanks for all your help.'

'No worries. Sorry it didn't work out.'

The bell rang as they left the shop. Mandy turned, one foot on the step. 'Oh, we haven't given up,' she promised. 'Not by a long way! This is just a small setback. We've got all day to sort it out!' She closed the door and stepped down on to the street. She breathed in deeply as she zipped her jacket.

'OK, next idea?' James asked. They passed a newspaper shop, Cecil's Confectionery and a chemist's. People queued outside a bread shop, waiting for it to open.

'We could advertise in all the shops,' Mandy suggested. The cards in the newsagents' window had brought this to mind. 'You know; a message in the Wanted section. "Wanted: two brown rabbits from Pets' Parlour. Would the new owners please contact Animal Ark, Welford

703267." If they ring up, we can tell them the whole story.'

'It's worth a try,' James agreed. So they spent half an hour going up and down the High Street, writing out cards and paying to stick them on clear display in all the newsagents' windows and on the notice-board in the town library. 'It's a weekend, so town should be busy,' James said hopefully. 'Plenty of people will read the notices!'

'The trouble is, we don't have much time.' Mandy stood back from the library notice-board. 'What now?' she said with a sigh.

'I suppose we could go over to York. There are loads more pet shops there. We could try them all to see if they've got any brown baby rabbits that look the same as Button and Barney. Then we could go back and tell John we'd found them after all!'

'You mean, *lie*?' Mandy took a deep breath.

'It's only a white lie. And it's for a good cause.'

'I know. But it's a bit risky, isn't it?'

'Shh!' The assistant behind the polished wooden counter pointed to a notice above their heads. It read, 'Silent Reading Area'.

Mandy and James blushed and slunk out of

the library. They stood on the street, opposite the railway station, wondering whether to risk a trip to York. 'Do you think we'd get away with it?' Mandy asked. 'I mean, John is a real rabbit expert now. He's bound to notice the difference. You know what he's like. He probably knows every whisker and hair on Button and Barney's head.'

James sighed. 'You're right. Anyway, I just realised; I spent all my money on those Wanted cards. I couldn't afford to go to York on the train, even if we decided it was worth a try.'

'Me neither. I've only got enough for the bus back to Welford.' Mandy felt another emergency plan flare and fade. 'If only we weren't so short of time!' Tomorrow John would pack his huge suitcase and drag it across the carpark at the Fox and Goose. He'd be off to school, then home again at half-term for the wedding. But there'd be no pet rabbits sitting cosily in his back garden under the apple tree.

'I suppose we'd better go back home,' James decided. 'We've done all we can here. I can't think of another single thing!'

She was forced to agree. 'John will be up at High Cross already, you realise? He'll stay until dark, all by himself, with his rabbits and his sketch-book and camera.'

'I know.' They both sighed.

'I'd like to go and join him, but I don't think I can face him just yet,' Mandy decided.

'It's his last day.'

'I know. But let's go back to Animal Ark first and have one final think about it. I need to tell Jean about our Wanted notices, just in case someone rings up. After that, what do you say we take sandwiches and biscuits up to High Cross? I bet John hasn't even thought of that. He's bound to be hungry.'

James nodded, and they climbed, heavy-hearted, on to the Welford bus. It wasn't often they had to give in where animals were concerned. They could find good homes for kittens, and put up strong fences for goats. They could rescue orphan hedgehogs. But they couldn't magic the twin rabbits out of thin air, and they couldn't make one sad boy happy.

'Cheer up; the holiday isn't over yet, you know!' Mandy's dad called as he climbed into his Land-rover to set off on his morning round. He gave James and Mandy a cheerful wave.

Mandy could hardly raise a smile.

Mr Hope wound down the window and studied her serious face. 'Tell me about it later. Or talk to Mum after surgery. I'm sure we can sort something out.'

Not this time, Mandy thought. She tried to smile back at him. 'Thanks, Dad.' They went inside, to the busy waiting area of Animal Ark.

Toby, Mrs Ponsonby's mongrel dog, came tottering out of a treatment room. He wore a big white plastic cone around his head and looked very sorry for himself. The cone knocked clumsily against the doorpost and he yelped.

'Oh, poor Toby! Poor doggy!' His fussy, middle-aged owner bent to scoop him off the floor. 'Did he hurt his poor little self? Oh, diddums!' She hugged him, and staggered out across reception.

'What's he done to himself?' Mandy stroked Toby gently on the nose. She could see a small, open sore on the dog's back. Mandy knew he had to wear the plastic cone to stop him from nipping at it and making it even worse.

Mrs Ponsonby raised her arched eyebrows from behind her fancy pink glasses and mouthed a secret word: 'Fleabite!'

'Oh, dear!' Mandy sympathised. She knew how they itched. 'Did he go and scratch it too hard?'

'Shh, dear! Yes, I'm afraid Toby was a naughty little doggy!' He wasn't so little. Mrs Ponsonby's legs had begun to buckle under his weight.

'Here, let me help,' Mandy offered. She took the miserable mongrel and set him down on his own four feet. Then she led him carefully out to Mrs Ponsonby's car. 'Don't worry, that wound will soon clear up. It's nice and clean now. It should be better in a few days, then Toby will be good as new!'

'Thank you, Mandy dear!' Mrs Ponsonby stowed her precious dog into the special compartment at the back of her car. She tugged at the jacket of her powder-blue suit to straighten it, then fixed her straw hat more firmly on her head. 'I must say, you're not looking quite yourself today, dear. You're a bit peaky. Is there something the matter?'

'No, I'm fine, Mrs Ponsonby. Thanks!' Mandy helped her to close the back door on Toby. 'I've got a problem on my mind, that's all.' She waved and went inside once more.

On the doorstep, she paused to see who was

turning into their drive as Mrs Ponsonby drove out. 'Oh no!' she groaned out loud. 'Just what I need!'

'Trouble?' Jean asked. She was wearing a flowery dress in white, blue and green, with big white buttons down the front. She looked summery and breezy, but surrounded as usual by a muddle of opened letters, papers, catalogues and bills.

James came across to the door. 'Uh-oh!' His mouth turned down at the corners. 'What are *they* doing here?'

'Exactly!' Mandy's eyes narrowed. She watched as Mr Parker Smythe stepped out of his posh black car and came towards the surgery.

'Since when did they need a vet?' James wondered. Both Mandy and he were only too well aware that the family owned a tennis-court, a helicopter and a swimming-pool. But as far as they knew, they had no pets.

'Hello,' the tall man said. His thinning hair was smartly combed, and he wore a posh grey suit. He looked strict, but he spoke to them pleasantly as he strolled into reception.

Mandy stared hard at his car. Inside, sitting behind tinted glass windows, she spied the blonde head of Mrs Parker Smythe and the chubbier shape of Imogen's pale face. To Mandy's surprise, the girl was actually looking cheerful. She pressed a button to slide down the window, then leaned out eagerly, watching for her father's return.

In the reception area, Jean was talking to Imogen's dad. 'That's quite right, Mr Parker Smythe. Your appointment with Mrs Hope is for ten o'clock. Just bring them inside and take a seat over there. I'm sure you'll be seen shortly.'

Mandy and James slid inside the reception room as Mr Parker Smythe came out. 'Jean, what are they doing here? What's going on?' Mandy whispered. 'I never knew Imogen had a pet!'

'Ah, you wait and see,' Jean replied, smiling sweetly. 'I think you're really going to like these two!'

Soon the surgery door opened again and Mr Parker Smythe backed awkwardly in. He carried a bulky, square shape. Imogen had to hold the door for him to get through.

'Careful!' Mrs Parker Smythe warned from behind in her high, silvery voice. 'That's a good girl, Immi! Let Daddy come right through. Now try not to get too excited, or you'll upset the poor baby rabbits!'

Mandy gasped and held on to the counter for

support. James stared at her wide-eyed. 'Did she say baby rabbits?' Mandy repeated.

'What did I tell you?' Jean beamed at them. 'I knew you'd both gone mad on rabbits lately. You and John Hardy!'

Mr Parker Smythe put the hutch down gently on the shiny floor. Slowly, a brown shiny nose appeared through the hole in the wooden partition of the hutch. Then two brown ears, two bright, shining eyes. One rabbit hopped into view. A second identical one came after.

'Button!' Mandy cried.

'Barney!' James followed her across and they both crouched down by the wire mesh at the front of the hutch.

The two baby rabbits sniffed at their new surroundings and stared out wide-eyed. An ear twitched, a paw scuffed in the straw. They sniffed the disinfected air.

'Like them?' Mr Parker Smythe inquired. He stood back, hands in pockets.

Slowly Mandy stood up and stared at Imogen.

'It was love at first sight as far as Immi was concerned,' he explained. 'Now we can hardly drag her out of the garden to go to bed at night, with these two to look after!'

Mandy took a deep breath. They'd found what they were looking for. But now it was going to take all her tact and skill to get Button and Barney safely back to John Hardy!

Nine

'Hello, Imogen.' Mrs Hope put her head round the treatment room door. 'We're all ready for Button and Barney now. Let's take a look at them, shall we?' She smiled at Mandy. 'Why not get your white coat and come and give me a hand?' she suggested. 'Simon's caught up next door with a spaniel with an injured paw.'

Mandy's head was spinning, but she did as she was told. With clumsy fingers she fastened the buttons on her white lab coat and followed Mr Parker Smythe and the rabbits into the treatment room.

'Can Immi come too?' Mrs Parker Smythe

pleaded from outside. 'She promises not to be a nuisance!'

'Of course she can. Come in, Imogen,' Mrs Hope said. 'Just close the door nice and tight, so the rabbits can't hop about and escape. That's right. Now, let's see what we have here!' Gently she lifted Button out of the hutch.

Emily Hope's calm voice had a soothing effect. Mandy told herself to think straight. Perhaps there was a way of sorting this out. OK, so Imogen Parker wasn't the kindest and most generous person she'd ever met. She probably didn't even know what the word sharing meant. But there had to be a first time for everything! She watched as her mother handed Button over to his new owner and bent forward to take Barney from the hutch.

'I'm glad you've brought them along, Mr Parker Smythe.' Mrs Hope inspected Barney's ears, then gently massaged his bottom jaw to open his mouth. She peered inside. 'Rabbits can easily fall ill with small infections, especially of the eye and ear. They need vaccinations, to be repeated every twelve months or so. The sooner we protect them against disease, the better.'

Barney nestled comfortably in the crook of her arm while she ran her fingertips over his abdomen and chest. She smiled. 'But he's certainly a healthy little chap at the moment!' She gave her verdict and handed him to Mandy. Then she began her examination of Button.

Mandy cradled the lightweight ball of warm fur, holding Barney close against her chest. His round, pretty face stared up at her, ears flat, nose twitching. Her mother began to prepare a syringe, while Imogen took Button and stroked him, laying her cheek against the soft brown fur of his back.

'Shh, Button. No one's going to hurt you! Shh!' Imogen half sang in the rabbit's ear. Her lips were parted in a soft, round shape. She crooned and

stroked her precious pet. Mr Parker Smythe stood back, watching his daughter with quiet satisfaction.

Even Mandy had to admit that this was a new girl who stood before her. The spiteful, selfish child who stamped her feet and swung moodily on her garden swing was gone. In her place was a sweet, loving seven-year-old.

Oh dear! Mandy frowned. How could she spoil Imogen's day by suggesting that she give Button and Barney back to John Hardy? She couldn't just say that they really belonged to John because he was the one who'd bought them in the first place! This was much more difficult than she'd expected.

'Hush, Button, there, there! That didn't hurt too much, did it?' Imogen scooped the rabbit back off the table as soon as Mrs Hope had finished the injection. The tiny creature quivered at the sharp needle, but he soon calmed down under Imogen's gentle touch.

Next it was Barney's turn. Imogen insisted on being the one to hold him too, while Mrs Hope went to work once more. So Mandy took Button from her and put him back in his hutch. He settled quietly into the clean straw.

'It looks like you made a good choice,' Emily

Hope said to Mr Parker Smythe. 'I know that you've been looking around for a pet for Imogen for quite some time. You must be very pleased to have found just the right ones!' She stood back, peeling off her surgical gloves.

'Oh, it's marvellous,' he agreed. 'You should have seen Imogen's face when we gave them to her. It was a picture!'

Oh dear! Mandy took a deep breath. *Why can't life be more simple?* She helped Imogen to fasten the front catch on the hutch. Button and Barney were both snuggled into the straw. This was a situation she hadn't expected to face; either Imogen or John was bound to end up broken-hearted.

'There *is* one thing, though.' Mr Parker Smythe drew Mrs Hope to one side. 'As you know, we've thought and thought about pets for Immi, and often we've decided that we're just too busy to fit them in. You know, I work away quite a lot, and we have a house in Tuscany which we like to visit whenever we can. We'd be there right now, except that I have some business I need to clear up.'

Mrs Hope nodded. She put her head thoughtfully to one side, pushed back a wisp of red hair and listened hard.

'Anyway, we took the plunge with these two rabbits, and we're all thrilled to bits with them both. But I promised my wife that I'd ask you what you thought we might do with them during the holidays. You see, it's quite a problem for us, having pets and travelling about so much.'

If Mandy had been a rabbit, her ears would have shot up. As it was, she sprang upright and stared across the room at the grown-ups. *Maybe . . . just maybe!*

'You want a reliable bunny-sitter?' Mrs Hope considered the problem. 'For school holidays? I take it that Imogen doesn't want to part with them during term-time, when she's at home?'

'Oh, no!' Imogen gasped. 'And I won't ever go on holiday ever again, if it means leaving them all alone, with no one to look after them properly!' She was stung to tears at the prospect.

'Immi!' Her father smiled uncomfortably. 'You know we've already discussed this! You promised not to make a fuss, remember?' He shrugged at Mrs Hope.

'No, no, she's quite right. You do need a good, firm arrangement. So many people just go off and leave their pets without proper food and water, let alone exercise. You simply wouldn't believe it!' She paused, arms crossed, wondering what was the answer. 'But I'm afraid we don't do a boarding service here at Animal Ark. We don't have the space, you see. But we could put up a notice for you. There's a notice-board out in the waiting-room. Perhaps that would lead to something?'

'No need!' Mandy stepped forward. She clasped her hands in front of her to stop them trembling. 'I think I've got the answer!'

There was no such thing as magic in the real world, she knew. But this had just come close. And in an instant, she was about to make one sad boy happy!

Everyone at Animal Ark agreed that it was a brilliant idea. Mandy burst out into reception to tell James. 'Fantastic!' he gasped, rocking back on to his heels. Jean smiled broadly from behind her desk. Even Mrs Parker Smythe looked relieved. 'Are you sure that's all right, Immi? John Hardy does sound like just the right person to look after your rabbits while we're away! And since you haven't decided on names, yet, I think Button and Barney sound perfect.'

Imogen nodded. 'I suppose so.' She cocked her head sideways, looking serious and grown-up. 'And I do like the names.'

Now Mandy was all action. 'Now, let me ring John's dad to see what he thinks,' she said. 'If he says yes, why don't you and Button and Barney come and check to see whether you think the Fox and Goose is OK?'

Imogen thought about it. She peered wistfully into the hutch. 'OK,' she said slowly, her frown easing. 'If you're sure it'll be all right, Mandy.'

'More than all right! John loves rabbits, and he knows everything about them. He'll take really good care of them, don't you worry!'

'When would he have them?'

'Just whenever you have to go away, during the holidays.'

'Half-term,' Mrs Parker Smythe said. 'That would be the first time we'd have to leave them.'

'And maybe tonight?' Mandy asked. 'Just so Button and Barney can get used to John before he goes back to school. Then they won't be so nervous when they go there at half-term.'

'Good idea.' Mr Parker Smythe had relaxed. The crisis was over. He wanted another quick word about the rabbits with Mrs Hope before they left.

Meanwhile, Mandy reached for the phone to explain everything to the Hardys.

'I'm sorry, Julian's not in,' Sara said. 'And John's up at High Cross, of course!' She had listened carefully to the news. 'But I think it's an absolutely great answer to the problem. I tell you what, let's keep it a secret from John. You bring the rabbits over here for this trial run, and I'll find somewhere to hide them for when he comes in. I just want to see his face when he discovers them. It'll make his day! Well, it'll change his life, as a matter of fact. Thank you so much, Mandy!'

The phone clicked and Mandy went ahead, making sure that Imogen was happy with all their plans. 'Thanks for letting John have Button and Barney for tonight,' she told her when they had reached the Fox and Goose. 'I know it's hard for you to let them go.'

'Yes, but they will be all right, won't they?' Imogen was trailing after her father across the pub carpark. She watched anxiously as he took the hutch in through the back garden.

'Come in, I'll show you,' Mandy promised. 'Sara said she'd find just the right hiding-place for them; somewhere secret where John won't spot them when he first comes in. Come on, let's go and see!'

They went upstairs, along the crooked corridor, into John's room.

James and Mandy went in ahead of Imogen, who hung back. Then she crept in behind them and stared round at the walls covered in photos and sketches; dozens of rabbits, hundreds of rabbits; close-ups, long distance, at play or feeding. 'Where are they?' she whispered. 'Where's Button and Barney?'

'In here!' Mr Parker Smythe called out. 'Through this door. What do you say to this, Immi? Bunnies in the bathroom!'

He held the door open wide and pointed to the two little brown rabbits peering curiously round the white tiled space. 'Satisfied? Now let's say goodbye for now and leave Mandy and James to settle them down. We can come back and collect them early tomorrow. That's a good girl; I'm very proud of you.' He took her by the hand.

Imogen sniffed. Her mouth puckered. She bent down close to the hutch. 'Goodbye, Button! Goodbye, Barney! See you tomorrow!' She whispered.

By teatime, Mandy and James could hardly bear

to wait any longer. They were certain that John would stay up at High Cross until dusk; another two or three hours of unbroken suspense.

'Let's go on up there!' James suggested. 'We could persuade him to come down early.'

'No way!' Mandy bit her lip. 'He won't come until the very last rabbit's disappeared down its burrow. It's his final day. Wild horses wouldn't drag him away!'

'OK. Anyway, he'd probably suspect something.' James sat down again on the grass in the pub garden. It was a clear evening, with a tint of pink in the sky. Dusk tonight would be long and late.

'No, we just have to wait.' Mandy sat cross-legged under the apple tree. White blossom drifted on to the grass. Glasses clinked and customers chatted in the bar. 'Anyway, Button and Barney are both asleep.'

'Well, they've had a busy day.' James leaned back on his elbows.

Soon Sara brought out a tray of lemonade and crisps. 'Julian's just got back from town,' she told them.

'And?' Mandy got to her feet. 'What's he say?' Surely Mr Hardy wouldn't object to the new plan; not after all this!

'Come here!' Sara waggled her finger at them.

They crept indoors and up the stairs. Inside John's room, Mr Hardy was busy fixing big white display boards on to steel frames. He wanted to arrange his son's sketches and photos into an artistic display before John came home. He turned quickly and saw them peering in.

They lent a hand, pinning up the pictures, making sure they were straight. But it still wasn't even dusk by the time they finished. Mandy glanced at her watch, then at James.

Mr Hardy stood back to judge the effect of their work. 'Do you think he'll like it?' he whispered. 'It's a big surprise!'

Mandy and James nodded. 'It's not the only one!' James added.

'Thanks for your help,' Mr Hardy whispered. 'Now why don't you two scoot up to High Cross and meet up with that son of mine. Tell him I said it was time he got himself back home. But don't let on. I want everything to stay a complete surprise!'

Ten

John sat on his low rock by the nursery warren. His sketchbook lay across his knees. His camera still had its lens cap fixed firmly in place. He sat in the fading light. All around, the rough grassland dipped and rose; hazy green, alive with rabbits.

'Shh!' Lydia warned. She came out of the house to walk with Mandy and James across to the far pasture. They were ankle-deep in grass and buttercups. 'I've had my eye on him all day, poor little mite. It breaks my heart to see a boy so alone.'

'Let's wait until the rabbits have gone in before we interrupt him,' James whispered. They came to a stop by the low wall and stood watching.

Mandy longed to run across and send the rabbits scattering across the hillside. She wanted to run up to John and give him the good news. But she kept her promise to his dad. They studied the mist rising slowly from the valley. It crept amongst the trees, over the patchwork fields. 'Has there been any more trouble with Dean and Steve?' she asked Lydia.

Lydia gave a wicked little smile. 'Not a squeak. Sam Western, their boss, came to see me though. According to him, the old land dispute was settled in favour of Upper Welford Hall. In other words, John over there *is* sitting on common land!'

'But?' James prompted.

'But I didn't let him get away with that, let me tell you!' She laughed. 'I told him to go and check his facts with the Land Registry. Meanwhile, he'd better keep Dennis Saville and his lads off *my* land!'

Mandy grinned. 'Phew!' Mr Western was known as a loud-mouth and a bully. He wasn't popular, but he did have friends in high places.

'Don't worry.' Lydia stood, hands in pockets, collar turned up. 'That man's a stickler for laws and lawyers himself. He won't dare send men out here with their guns while there's a question mark over who owns the land. When our friend John comes back home in a month or two, I guarantee he'll still be able to come up to this warren and find it just as it is now. Peace and quiet; that's what we like.' She breathed in deeply and threw her shoulders back. 'Peace and quiet!'

At last the light faded from the hill. The mist rose and the rabbits went to ground. John sat on in the damp twilight.

Mandy glanced uncertainly at Lydia.

'Go on, you two. It's time for you all to go home. You go and fetch him now.' She smiled at them both and said goodbye. 'Take care of that young man for me, and tell him there's a cup of tea for him at High Cross any time he cares to drop in!' She wandered off across her field, back to the house.

John looked up at Mandy and James as they trudged through the wet grass towards the rock. He uncrossed his legs and tucked his sketchbook under one arm. 'Hi,' he said in a flat voice. 'It's OK, I've finished here. I was just about to come down.'

'Your dad says you have to come home,' James told him. 'They say you've been up here all day.'

'Well, they don't have to worry about that now,

do they? After tomorrow I'll be gone, and they'll be alone together, just those two!'

'Oh, I don't think they want to get rid of you,' Mandy put in. 'In fact, I'm sure they don't. They've been really worried about you since—'

'Never mind!' John jerked to his feet. 'Anyway, it was a waste of time you two dragging yourselves all the way up here. I was on my way without needing to be told!'

Mandy nodded and kept her head down. John was in no mood to be friendly. They walked silently across the fields, making their way through the mist, guided by fence-posts and trees, until they reached the lane leading down into the village.

'It'll be dark before we get back,' James warned. 'Or just about, at any rate.'

Mandy and he chatted on about Lydia's goats, about school on Monday; homework they hadn't done and friends they would see. John walked in silence, locked away, lost in his own thoughts.

He didn't even notice when they walked on past the crossroads with him, instead of turning off to their own houses. He walked on through the village, head down, his dark figure striding two or three steps ahead. James and Mandy jogged the final stretch to catch him up. They entered the pub garden together.

They were greeted by the buzz of customers drinking in the bar. It sounded cosy and warm. But John went straight upstairs, not knowing or not caring that the other two still followed. His door stood open. He went in, unzipped his jacket and flung it on the bed with his sketchbook and camera.

'Surprise!' Mr Hardy stood with one arm round Sara's shoulder. He revealed the new gallery of John's work, waiting for a reaction.

John hesitated and blinked.

'What do you think?' His father came forward. 'Do you like it?'

'Yes, thanks, Dad, it's great.' John attempted a smile, but his voice gave him away. 'But you shouldn't have gone to all this trouble.'

'No trouble,' Mr Hardy said uneasily. 'Don't you think they look really professional? We'll have to talk about you taking it up as a job when you leave school.'

John shrugged. 'I don't know.' His own rabbits stared silently back at him from every angle.

Then Sara came forward and took him by the hand. 'Surprise number two,' she said gently. She

led him through to the bathroom.

Button and Barney had done what all rabbits do; they'd woken up to feed and play as night fell. They bobbed and hopped about inside their hutch, which rested on two planks of wood, carefully placed across the width of the white bath. As John approached, they hopped forward to the wire mesh, and poked out their noses in greeting.

'Carrot?' Sara offered. She handed two pieces to him.

He took them, too stunned to say anything. Button and Barney curled back their lips to show their long front teeth. They waited for their treat.

Mandy watched as John's blank face broke into a smile. The rabbits set to and nibbled. He crouched there with all the patience in the world, waiting until every scrap of carrot was gone.

Then he stood back. Without saying a word, he went up, put his arms round his father's neck and buried his face in the soft blue wool of Mr Hardy's best golfing sweater.

That evening they celebrated. John dashed downstairs to consult Ernie Bell about building a wire run for Button and Barney. 'Can it run the length of the whole garden, so they have lots of space to come out and feed?' he wanted to know.

Ernie sipped his beer. He winked at Mandy. 'Oh, aye, I reckon it can.'

'And will it be strong enough to keep them in, so they can't escape?'

'Aye. I'll make it just like the run I made for my Sammy, only not so high. Sammy, being as he's a squirrel, likes to climb a bit, see.'

John nodded. 'Rabbits like to dig. They won't be able to dig their way out, will they?'

'No problem. I'll put a good barrier along each edge, well dug in. Matter of fact, I've already promised one to the Parker Smythes up at Beacon House. It looks like I'm going to have my work cut out.'

John backed off, satisfied. Button and Barney were going to live in the lap of luxury in both their houses.

Walter Pickard, sitting across the table, tutted. 'I don't know, young man. You'll be wanting one of them Jacuzzi things for them before long!'

'Rabbits don't like water!' John laughed.

'Aye well, then, it'll be an 'utch with a patio and a sun umbrella!'

Mandy got up to go. 'James's dad has just arrived to give us a lift,' she told John.

'Yes, and I've got to go and pack,' he said. 'And check up on Button and Barney, of course.'

'Don't worry, they'll be OK,' she grinned. 'They're probably fast asleep again.'

'Thanks to you,' he nodded. He breathed a deep, happy sigh. 'I'll be back in six weeks. Ernie says the run will be ready by then.' He looked away, scratched his ear and gave a dry cough. He was blushing as he turned back to her. 'Er, Mandy . . .'

'What?' She saw Mr Hunter and James hovering by the door. 'Look, John, I've got to go!'

'Will you write to me?' he asked in a rush. 'Tell me how Button and Barney are getting along up at Beacon House. I mean, it's OK if you don't want to; you don't have to!'

'Of course I will!' she promised. A smile swept across her face. 'Any excuse to go and visit those bunnies!'

'Rabbits!' he said sternly. 'Er, Mandy, do you think you could manage to write to me, say, once a week?' he stammered.

'Twice!' she promised again. 'Three times! Whenever there's any news!'

'Oh, thanks!' John had turned crimson to the roots of his hair. 'Now I know it's not going to be half as bad!'

As it happened, John wrote first. A letter fell on the mat at Animal Ark on the Tuesday of the following week. Mandy was still in her pyjamas, with slippers wet from going out across the dewy grass to feed her own rabbits. She yawned as she opened the scribbled note:

Dear Mandy,

How are Button and Barney? Have they settled in at Beacon House? Tell Imogen not to feed them too much lettuce; it's too rich for them to have every day. I got an A++ for my project. Sorry if that sounds like boasting. I hope James is OK.

Love, John
P.S. Don't forget to write back soon about Button and Barney.

She wrote:
Dear John,

Button and Barney are fine. Ernie's started to build the run at Beacon House. But guess what? We all made a mistake. We thought Button and

Barney were both boy rabbits. All right then, male rabbits. But Mum says we were wrong. Barney's a male, but Button's a female! Mum says she's absolutely sure. There's no doubt about it.

Mr Parker Smythe wanted to book Button into Animal Ark for her operation. But Imogen wants them to have one litter of babies first. (Sorry, kittens!) Her mum and dad said yes. So guess what again? Button and Barney could have babies soon! Isn't that great? Just think – baby Buttons and Barneys! What could be better?

Love, Mandy

He wrote back a one-line letter:
Dear Mandy,

Great news. OK, so I guess I don't know everything about rabbits!

Love, John.

LUCY DANIELS

Donkey
— on the —
Doorstep

Illustrations by Shelagh McNicholas

Hodder
Children's
Books

a division of Hodder Headline plc

Donkey on the Doorstep

Special thanks to Jenny Oldfield

Text copyright © Ben M. Baglio 1995
Created by Ben M. Baglio, London W6 0HE
Illustrations copyright © Shelagh McNicholas 1995

First published as a single volume in Great Britain in 1996
by Hodder Children's Books

One

The old donkey stuck his hairy brown face over the stable door. He tilted his head to one side as he watched Mr Hope fighting to save the life of the Greenaways' show horse, Ivanhoe.

Mandy had come along to watch her father at work, but the horse had reacted badly to the vet's treatment for nettle-rash. His limbs began to shake, his eyes rolled, and he started to sway. To make it worse, the donkey's worried face continued to stare at them.

Mandy's mouth went dry and her heart thumped. She knew her dad was a good vet; one of the best; but now his skill was being tested to the limit. Ivanhoe crashed to the ground and his legs pedalled the air.

Are you sure you know what you're doing? the donkey's stubborn face seemed to demand. He stood on the doorstep shaking his head.

'Get out of the light, Dorian!' Stephen Greenaway backed the donkey out of the doorway to give Mr Hope more breathing space. Mandy crouched down beside the horse to cradle his head. Ivanhoe's skin quivered all over in reaction to the vet's antihistamine drug.

'He will get better, won't he?' Mandy whispered.

Her father licked his dry lips. 'I don't know. I've only seen this twice before. We'll have to wait and see.'

Outside in the stable yard, Dorian stamped his feet and brayed.

The beautiful horse lay helpless. Mandy knew it was serious and the end could come any moment. An iron grip seemed to clutch at her throat as she blinked back the tears.

'Steady on, boy. Steady on!' Mr Hope ran his hand up and down the animal's fine neck. 'Don't give up on him yet,' he whispered to Mandy. Then he went over to the anxious owner who stood with his arms crossed.

'Ivanhoe,' she pleaded softly, kneeling over him. He was a lovely thoroughbred, a black and white pinto Arabian. Mandy pictured him out on the moor top, cantering in the wind with Andi Greenaway on his back, and in the lanes down into the village. He was one of the finest horses in this part of Yorkshire, a prize-winner at the Welford Show. And now he lay stretched out in the straw, taking great shuddering breaths. 'Get up, boy. Come on, you can make it!'

She glanced up at the two men framed in the doorway, saw the donkey still trying to poke his nose in from behind. For a moment Mandy wished with all her heart that she wasn't a vet's daughter, that she didn't live at Animal Ark, and that she didn't have to sit by and watch beautiful creatures die like this.

But that moment passed. The horse raised his head, then he eased himself on to his chest. Mandy gasped and sat back on her haunches. 'That's it. Come on, boy. Come on!' She stared as he got shakily to his feet.

'Good lord!' Mr Greenaway looked stunned.

Mandy's dad's face broke into a grin. Mandy jumped up. Stephen Greenaway heaved a sigh of relief and shook Mr Hope by the hand. As Ivanhoe stood and pawed the cobbled floor, his iron horse-shoe struck a spark. He'd recovered as suddenly as he'd collapsed.

Dorian butted and barged his way back into the stable. He came up to Ivanhoe to check him over. A bit shaky, a bit dazed; and no wonder! The donkey nuzzled up to the Arabian's head. *Trust them and their newfangled medicines*, he seemed to say. *All that was wrong in the first place was a touch of nettle-rash!*

Mandy gave a delighted laugh. She heard her father explain to Mr Greenaway. 'Ivanhoe must have suffered an unusually severe reaction to the medicine,' he said. 'One chance in ten thousand. But he's a fine, strong horse with plenty of will power, and that's seen him through. I wouldn't be surprised if having the old donkey fussing about in the background didn't help him as well. They seem pretty good friends, those two.'

'They always have been,' Stephen Greenaway agreed.

Mr Hope scratched his bearded chin and asked if the horse was taking any other medication before they'd called him in. 'I think we may have mixed two drugs without realising. That could have brought about the drastic collapse.'

Mandy heard their voices grow more distant as they walked across the yard towards the house. She wanted to stay with the patient, just in case. She put one arm round Ivanhoe's neck, and one arm round Dorian. The donkey blinked back at her with his huge, almond-shaped eyes. It was easy to imagine what he must be thinking now. *When you've lived as long as I have*, he seemed to say with his wise old expression, *you learn to let nature take its course. Some of these young vets, they don't realise that.*

Mandy laughed at him and scratched his nose. 'Yes, yes, we know,' she murmured. 'You've been around an awful long time, and no one knows better than you do, Dorian. We all admit that!'

Eventually she tore herself away from the two friends. She took her jacket from a hook by the haynet and gave Ivanhoe one last gentle stroke on the muzzle. Dorian, not wanting to be left out, barged in for his share. She scratched his bony head between his ears. When she closed the stable door and looked back, Dorian was pulling himself up to his full twelve hands, standing there and peering out. He flicked his long, pointed ears and bared his teeth in what looked like a smile. His stiff, upright mane was neatly trimmed, his dark muzzle and rubbery lips curled upwards at the corners. He was obviously snickering goodbye.

Mandy crossed the Greenaways' yard in the evening sunlight. It struck her full in the face with its warm orange glow. She had to shield her eyes to make her way to the old stone porchway of Manor Farm.

'In here, Mandy,' her father called from the kitchen.

She joined them in the low-beamed, quaint old room.

'How's Ivanhoe?' Mr Hope asked.

'He's fine. As good as new, and the nettle-rash has gone too.' She'd checked the horse's flanks for the round, flat spots. They had seemed to vanish before her eyes. He was a perfect specimen once again.

'Thank heavens for that,' Stephen Greenaway chipped in. He reached for his car keys in the middle of the solid kitchen table. 'Will there be any after-effects, do you think?'

Mr Hope shook his head. 'Unlikely. You were saying you've got buyers coming in to look at him?'

Mandy held back a gasp of surprise.

Stephen Greenaway was a tall, brisk, fit-looking man with short, dark hair and a tanned face. He nodded. 'Yes. That's why we were so keen to be rid of the rash. We're trying to sell him. Andi's really upset about it, of course. It's a hard decision for us to make, but it has to be done. She knows that if you want something in this life, you have to go for it one hundred per cent. That might involve giving something up too. In this case, the horse.'

Mandy bristled at his tone as he pronounced the word 'horse'. *Ivanhoe has a name,* she wanted to point out. Mr Greenaway talked about selling him as if he was a car.

'Why does Andi have to give him up?' she asked.

Mr Greenaway glanced at his watch. 'She's fourteen now. She has to concentrate on other things.' He looked out of the window up the drive.

'Exams?' Mandy knew school work could sometimes crowd out a pastime like riding.

'No, tennis.'

She stared back at him. How could anyone consider giving up a horse like Ivanhoe just for the sake of a game? Even though Mandy and her best friend, James Hunter, liked to play tennis, she would still always put animals first.

'Here's Andi and her mother now,' he said, giving her a brief smile. 'Why not ask her?'

Mandy heard a car crunch down the long drive.

Manor Farm stood well out of the village, further down the same lane as Animal Ark and Lilac Cottage, her gran and grandad's place. It was tucked away in the valley with two or three acres of land, but it was no longer a farm. The Greenaways had turned it into a lovely, luxurious home, with plenty of room in the grounds for Ivanhoe and Dorian. Mr Greenaway was the manager of a successful premier league football team. He travelled seventy-five kilometres to work and back each day. He was a busy man.

'I'm glad the horse made it all right,' he told Adam Hope. 'Would you tell Silvia she doesn't need to put the buyers off from coming over after all. But ask her not to agree to a price until we've talked it over, OK? She'll take care of your bill, Adam. Thanks very much. Sorry, I must dash.' And he strode out to his gleaming black sports car, with only a brief wave for his wife and daughter.

'Don't frown, Mandy,' Mr Hope warned. 'You'll get wrinkles!'

'Well!' she said. 'Tennis!' She felt too angry to put her feelings into words.

'Andi's a good player; county standard. They think she could even become a professional eventually. To get that good you have to practise for hours every day!' He rummaged in the pocket of his leather jacket for his own car keys. 'Come on, let's go and have a word with Silvia. We've done all we can here.' And he led her out of the kitchen, back into the warm rays of the setting sun.

As soon as Andi caught sight of the Animal Ark Land-rover parked in their yard, she ran to meet them. She clutched a tennis bag in one hand and was wearing her sports gear; a trim blue and white track suit and white tennis shoes. Her long hair, blonder even than Mandy's, was tied back in a high pony-tail. Her face looked worried. 'What's wrong? It's Ivanhoe, isn't it? Is he OK?' She began to dash towards the stable, followed by Mandy, Mr Hope and Mrs Greenaway.

Whoa there, steady on! Dorian, the donkey, stood at the stable door, mouthing and shifting gently from hoof to hoof. He seemed to have everything under control, as usual. He nodded towards Ivanhoe in his quiet, dark stall, then he stepped back to let them enter; but only Andi and Mr Hope. *Not too many visitors, or you'll tire him out,* he seemed to suggest. Mandy and Silvia Greenaway took the hint and waited outside.

Andi checked Ivanhoe and saw her horse standing untroubled and healthy, nibbling at his hay. She took a deep breath and came back out into the yard, squinting in the sun. She flung a relieved arm round Dorian and rested her head against his soft brown neck. 'Thank heavens he's OK. Come on, boy, let's get you out into the paddock.'

The donkey, suddenly docile and meek as a lamb with Andi, nodded and walked on.

'Do you want to come?' Andi invited Mandy.

Mandy checked with her dad. She didn't need a second invitation. Soon she strode alongside Dorian and his mistress. She began firing donkey questions at Andi. 'How often do you groom him? How do you trim his mane? Aren't they supposed to be very stubborn animals?' she said in a rush.

Andi laughed. She opened the paddock gate and followed Dorian into the sloping field full of buttercups and clover. 'Don't let Dorian hear you call him stubborn. He won't like it. "Clever" is OK, though. Donkeys are very intelligent, aren't they, boy?' She let him poke his round face close to her own. 'See, he understands every word I say. And he's brilliant with Ivanhoe. To tell the truth, thoroughbreds can be a bit highly-strung, but

Dorian has a knack of calming him down. Don't you, boy?' She fondled the donkey's chin and sighed. 'He's going to miss him when he goes.'

'What about you?' Mandy asked. 'Aren't you going to miss him too?'

Andi sighed. 'I try not to think about it too much. As for Dorian, it's as if he understands every single thing that goes on around here. Sometimes I think he's even talking to me!' She blushed and smiled at Mandy.

Mandy grinned. 'I know what you mean.' She gazed down the sloping meadow to the stream at the bottom, where hawthorn trees provided shade beside the fresh water. *This must be a brilliant place for a horse and donkey to live*, she thought. 'Do you really have to sell Ivanhoe?' she pleaded. Andi was obviously fond of her animals, in spite of her tennis.

Andi hugged Dorian round his neck and buried her face in his coat. The donkey leaned his cheek against her shoulder. *There, there,* he seemed to say.

'Dad and I agreed. He has to go. He's worth a lot of money, you see. It'll help pay for my tennis coaching.' She sighed and her eyes filled with tears.

Yes, she does love them both, Mandy thought.

Andi looked up. She spoke sadly. 'I don't think we'll get much for you though, Dorian! You're not worth anything!'

Dorian sniffed and tossed his head. It was true; he was an old, ambling, shambling donkey with a hairy face and a girth like a barrel.

'Lord knows what we're going to do with you, though!' Andi sounded as though she would break down completely, then she pulled herself together. They heard Silvia Greenaway and Adam Hope leading Ivanhoe across the yard down towards the paddock.

'Dad's right, as usual. I love Ivanhoe and Dorian to bits, and I'll miss them dreadfully. But I have to concentrate on my tennis if I want to get really good.'

'But why not keep your animals? Why do you have to get rid of them?' Mandy tried hard to see the Greenaways' point of view.

Again Andi sighed. 'Now is the right time. Dad's got a new job and we all have to move down south. The new house doesn't have any grounds to keep animals in.'

Mandy nodded. 'I see.' She still studied the pinto as Mrs Greenaway turned him into the paddock.

He was fifteen hands, head and shoulders above stumpy Dorian. His neck arched gracefully, his face was long and slim, his white mane flowed against his black and white shoulders. He picked up his dainty feet like a dancer poised to pirouette. He was magnificent. *How can Andi bear to lose him?* she wondered.

Once Adam Hope was satisfied with Ivanhoe's full recovery, he passed on Stephen Greenaway's message about the buyers.

Silvia leaned both elbows on the five-barred gate and nodded. She gave her daughter a small, sympathetic pat on the back. 'Such big changes,' she sighed. She spoke softly, with a foreign accent. Mandy knew she came from Finland, and Andi had inherited her blonde hair and pale grey eyes from her. Mandy thought Silvia looked sad and uncertain as she looked out across the field and the valley beyond. 'And Welford is so beautiful, so peaceful.'

As she left with her father, she carried his heavy bag full of medical supplies and instruments and swung it up into the back of the car.

'Hop in, Mandy. We'd better get a move on.' They were running late. They had two more calls to make; one to Bleakfell Hall to reassure Mrs

Ponsonby about Pandora, her poorly Pekinese, and then on to Susan Price's place with an anti-worm injection for Prince, her pony. It was a typical round of evening calls for the busy practice at Animal Ark.

Not so fast! Dorian had decided he liked them after all. The donkey came trotting up the paddock and along the fence, craning his stubby neck and braying loudly. His short black mane stuck up like a Mohican haircut, and he showed them his old, yellow teeth. Mandy laughed. She couldn't resist going over to him one last time. 'What do you think of Ivanhoe now, old fellow? We did a pretty good job in the end, huh?'

He turned down the corners of his mouth and jerked his head.

'Come on, we're the best there is!' She scratched his chin and gave a cheeky grin. He sniggered. She ran and hopped into the Land-rover, leaning out to give Dorian a final wave.

'He's going to be one lonely donkey when Ivanhoe goes,' she said to her dad. 'And then what? When the Greenaways move on, I don't suppose anyone will want him!'

Mr Hope gave her a sideways glance. 'Don't look at me, Mandy! No waifs and strays at Animal Ark.

That's the rule, remember!'

Mandy nodded. It was a rule they had because they were already short of space at home. Mandy had to be content with her pet rabbits and all the animals brought to Animal Ark for treatment. There was no chance of Dorian coming to live with them. They pulled into the driveway and headed up to the road.

A car was signalling to come down the Manor Farm drive. 'This could be the people who want to buy Ivanhoe,' Mr Hope said. He gave way and pulled on to the grass verge to let it pass, then swung back on to the narrow road. 'Pandora will be wondering where on earth we've got to.' He put his foot down and the Land-rover sped off. 'I expect Mrs Ponsonby's nerves will be all on edge by the time we arrive!' He winked at Mandy.

Mandy smiled. She loved being out on the round with her dad, even if it meant coming face to face with fussy Mrs Ponsonby. She turned to see Dorian tilt back his head and bray at the top of his voice as the buyers' car approached. He kicked his heels and galloped out of sight. Though he was past his prime, he could still get a move on.

Soon he was a dark speck vanishing noisily into the shadow of the hawthorn trees.

No, thank you very much! he seemed to say. *I don't like the look of this new lot at all!*

Two

'Well, *I* don't like the look of them!' Mrs Platt and Mrs Ponsonby were deep in conversation on the doorstep of Animal Ark. Mrs Platt's poodle, Antonia, growled at Mrs Ponsonby's Pekinese. It was several days after Pandora's latest false alarm, and the dog looked perfectly well to Mandy. She got off her bike and eased her schoolbag from her shoulders. Mrs Ponsonby waved Pandora's paw in greeting.

'We don't know where they've come from, do we?' Mrs Platt insisted. She lived with Antonia in a tidy bungalow and kept busy by helping Mandy's gran to arrange flowers for the church. But she was no match for bossy Mrs Ponsonby.

'Who, dear, who? Whom don't we like the look of?' Mrs Ponsonby tried to disentangle her stout legs from the lead of Toby, her other dog, a tough and friendly mongrel. Mandy obligingly offered to help. She stooped to straighten out the lead.

'Those traveller people. They've parked or camped or whatever you call it just down the lane from here, past Dorothy's place. In full view of their cottage! Dozens of them in their scruffy van. Poor Dorothy!' Mrs Platt sighed. 'I'm sure *she* doesn't like the look of them any more than I do!'

Mandy freed Toby and frowned as she stood up. 'I don't think Gran minds, Mrs Platt. Anyway, she says they've parked on common ground. Everyone has a right to use it.'

Mrs Ponsonby raised her eyebrows. 'But dozens of them, you say?' She turned to Mrs Platt.

'Four.' Mandy was quite definite. 'Two grown-ups and two children. They're a family.' Gran had told her all about them since their arrival last weekend. 'And two dogs.'

'See! *And* they have long hair!' Mrs Platt said darkly.

'Who, the dogs?' Mrs Ponsonby looked confused.

'No, silly, the parents. *He* wears an earring!'

'Well, that's not a criminal offence, so far as I know,' Mrs Ponsonby pointed out. 'But bringing flea-ridden dogs into Welford is a different matter.'

'I'm sure their dogs are perfectly healthy,' said Mandy, her blood beginning to boil. 'And Gran says the family is very friendly – and harmless.'

'You wouldn't say that if they camped on *your* front doorstep!' Mrs Platt looked put out. She snatched Antonia away as Mandy leaned forward to give her a gentle pat. Then she flounced off.

'Never mind, Mandy dear,' Mrs Ponsonby whispered.

They went into reception together, where Jean Knox, the receptionist, tried to keep order amongst the assorted dogs, cats, rabbits and guinea-pigs. 'There are some people round here with very old-fashioned ideas. You just have to put up with them!' Mrs Ponsonby announced.

Mandy smiled. She'd never looked on Mrs Ponsonby, with her pink and blue flowered hats, as a pioneer of forward thinking in the village. But just then, Simon, their nurse, stuck his head out of the treatment room and spotted her. 'Oh great, you're back,' he said. 'Mandy, I need an extra pair of hands in here. I don't suppose you're free?'

She leapt into action. Reverend Hadcroft's cat, Jemima, was kicking up a bit of a fuss about having her temperature taken. Mandy held her gently on the table. She calmed her down, while Simon continued the examination.

And then it was one busy chore after another until well into the evening. Mandy put on her white coat to assist her mother with the insulin injection for a diabetic fox-terrier. Then she helped to prepare two cats for spaying. She loved the work, and felt it would help her own training as a vet when she finally left school.

So it was late when she and her exhausted parents finally finished supper. Then Mandy remembered the rabbits. 'Can I take them the leftover lettuce?' she asked.

Emily Hope was sitting on the patio with her feet up. It was a beautiful warm evening. The sun on her hair made it look even redder and softer than usual. It had brought out her skin in deep brown freckles. 'Mm-mm,' she murmured, without lifting her head.

Mandy drifted out into the garden at the back of the house, down to the far corner where Flopsy, Mopsy and Cottontail sat and twitched their noses at the smell of the lettuce. They hopped and thumped as Mandy approached.

She changed their water and cleared out the dirty bedding, replacing it with sweet, clean straw. The shadows began to stretch long and deep over the lawn as Mandy went back to the house. She headed for the surgery, to get rid of the rubbish.

'Oh, hello!' she said, startled. She turned the corner to find a visitor. His front hooves were on the doorstep. He seemed to be trying to press the surgery bell with his blunt nose. It was Dorian.

He shook his head impatiently. *I've been hanging*

around here for ages, waiting for someone to show up!

'Dorian, nice of you to drop in!' Mandy said with a grin. 'But do they realise back home that you just popped out for a visit?'

The donkey stood firm on the doorstep.

'Don't you think you ought to let them know? They're bound to wonder where you are.' Mandy rubbed his nose a little sadly.

Dorian lifted his top lip and tilted his head to one side.

'It's late, Dorian,' Mandy said. 'I think I'd better get you back home.'

Dorian blew down his nose. He was in a huff as she took hold of his halter. He backed down from the doorstep, but then he dug in his heels.

Mandy soon gave up trying to lead him off. She didn't want to force him, yet she knew his escape from Manor Farm must be causing concern. 'Dad!' she called out. 'Can you come and give me a hand?'

Adam Hope came running round the side of the house. 'Well, blow me down!' he said. His old-fashioned phrase set them both chuckling. 'If it isn't old Dorian!' He stood in his shirt-sleeves, quite taken aback.

'I told you he liked us in the end!' Mandy laughed. 'After I told him we were the best vets around!'

'That may well be,' Mr Hope mused, 'but how are these best vets going to get the old chap home?'

Dorian stood stock still, legs rigid and caked in dry mud.

Adam Hope looked him up and down. 'Tell you what. You could give him a brush down while I ring Manor Farm and let them know where he is.'

Mr Hope went off for the grooming brushes and soon came back. Mandy set to work, first with the stiff brush to clean the mud from round Dorian's fetlocks. Then she used a softer brush on his mane, neck and chest. 'Might as well get you spruced up while you're here,' she told him.

Dorian agreed. She heard him give a deep sigh as he felt the brush whisk away the hayseeds and dust caught in his long hair.

'Here, try this.' Emily Hope came out into the yard with a hoof-pick. 'If he's been in mud, his hooves will need cleaning out.' She watched as Mandy lifted each foot in turn and picked out the mud and stones from the hoof. 'You know something,' she said with an amused grin. 'I think that old donkey knew just what he was about when he decided to come visiting you, Mandy Hope!'

'Hairdresser and pedicurist at your service!' Mandy chipped in.

'You've got a friend for life there,' Mrs Hope decided. They both turned as Mr Hope came back out of the house.

'No reply from Manor Farm,' he said.

Dorian tossed his head and clicked his tongue. What did they expect?

'I'll walk him back anyway,' Mandy volunteered. 'It's only down the lane. There won't be any traffic. And I can turn him into the paddock if there's no one around.'

They agreed that this was the best idea. Mandy handed Dorian's rope to her dad, then she rushed inside to ring her friend, James Hunter. She had to postpone a game of tennis, arranged for that evening. 'I've got to see a man about a donkey,' she explained quickly. 'Sorry, James. How about tomorrow?'

James sounded resigned. 'A donkey? What are you on about, Mandy?'

'I'll tell you tomorrow. Must dash!' She hung up.

Outside, she found Susan Price sitting in the lane, all shiny and smart in her hard hat, astride an equally well-groomed Prince. 'Hello, Mandy. I didn't know you had a donkey!' she said with a smile. Many pony people were snooty about donkeys, and it annoyed Mandy. She felt Dorian's neck muscles stiffen and heard him sniff.

'He's not ours, worse luck,' Mandy replied. Susan sat upright, with her dark hair pulled neatly back under her black hat, her boots spotless. 'I'm just about to walk him home.'

'I couldn't exactly see you riding the old boy over the jumps at the Welford Show!' Susan grinned down at them both.

Mandy frowned as Susan and Prince cantered away.

'Come on, Dorian, I'm your number one fan,' Mandy coaxed. 'Be a good boy now and take no notice of pony snobs like Susan. They go for looks, not personality. And they don't know the first thing about donkeys!'

Dorian looked down his nose at the disappearing duo. Prince high-stepped his way between the hedgerows with Susan perched elegantly on top. The donkey gave a loud, wicked bray. Then he led off down the drive from Animal Ark, heading down the lane in the opposite direction to Susan and Prince; quite happy to go home now, in his own good time, at his own pace.

'Take care!' Emily and Adam Hope both laughed. 'And don't be late back!'

* * *

Mandy and Dorian headed as one into the setting sun. OK, so he was stout and knock-kneed, with a sway-back. He wouldn't win any prizes. He was hairy and nosy and stubborn, with a will of his own. He'd been everywhere, seen everything. As they strolled past Lilac Cottage, Mandy thought he must be a donkey with a long and fascinating history. She was lost deep in thought when her grandad stood up straight from piling luggage into their camper van. He and Gran were getting ready to set off in a couple of days on one of their touring holidays. He spotted Mandy over the gate.

'A penny for your thoughts!' he called.

Mandy jumped, then waved. 'They're not worth it, Grandad!' She stopped to explain where she was going with Dorian.

'Oh, I just saw the Greenaways' car heading home a few minutes ago,' he told her. 'They should be in by the time you get there. There are big changes afoot at Manor Farm, I hear.'

Mandy nodded. 'Have they managed to sell Ivanhoe, do you know?'

Grandad nodded and pocketed his car keys. He came to the gate for a proper chat. He was looking brown and relaxed in his checked shirt and waistcoat. 'Yep. I saw the horse box drive down there yesterday. Do you reckon that's why this old fellow got itchy feet?'

'Well, wouldn't you?' Mandy pointed out. 'If you suddenly got left all alone?'

'Not likely!' he laughed. 'No, I love a bit of peace and quiet. But your gran is always going on about the Women's Institute and rhubarb jam and what not!' He winked at her.

'Grandad!'

Mandy's gran had come down the path, followed by a complete stranger; a man dressed in jeans with long, dark hair and an earring. 'What's that you say?' She raised her fist in mock anger. 'I can hear you calling me names behind my back, you old rascal!'

Gran came right out into the lane and greeted Mandy with a hug. She patted Dorian's neck. 'Mandy, this is Jude Somers. Jude, this is my favourite granddaughter, Mandy Hope.'

Mandy grinned. 'I'm your *only* granddaughter, Gran!'

'Exactly. My son and his wife had the good sense to adopt Mandy when she was a baby, I'm happy to say. Mandy, Jude lives in the van down the lane. He came to fetch fresh water from our tap.'

'Oh!' Mandy realised this must be the unwelcome traveller that Mrs Platt had complained about. He was skinny and long-limbed, with skin that had begun to burn and wrinkle in the sun. He said hello to Dorian and made a fuss of him. Mandy immediately warmed to him. She said she was walking the same way and they set off up the lane together.

'Welford's a nice little place,' Jude said. He strode alongside Dorian and Mandy. 'We like it round here. There are some friendly people.'

'Like Gran and Grandad?'

'Yes. They're going to let us use their outside tap for our water, even though they're going away themselves. I call that friendly!' He smiled at Mandy.

She grinned back.

'Not everyone's like that, I can tell you,' Jude continued.

'No.' She remembered how Mrs Platt had complained about the travellers.

'Anyway, we'll stick around for a while and look for work; gardening, odd-jobbing, anything. We'll have to see how it goes.'

Mandy nodded, while Dorian nuzzled Jude's pockets.

But they had to split off after a few minutes of easy conversation. Jude's battered old van came into view, parked on a flat piece of grassy land. The site was surrounded by young silver-birch trees and backed by an old drystone wall. The wall marked the limit of Manor Farm land, so Mandy knew they were nearly at their own journey's end.

Two children came running from the step at the back of the red van. They were dressed in T-shirts and shorts of bright, clashing colours and patterns. Their mouse-coloured hair hung over their eyes, and their faces were red as berries from the sun. They ran to Jude and clambered round him, then turned their noisy attention to Dorian. One jumped up at his neck, the other demanded to be lifted straight on to his back.

'Hang on!' Jude put down his water container and tried to look stern. He introduced Mandy to his kids; Skye, who was five, and Jason, three. Still they shouted for a ride on the donkey, and soon got their way. He lifted the pair of them up on to Dorian's broad back, and walked steadily down the lane.

'Good boy, steady!' Mandy encouraged him, as she led from the side. She was amazed by how good-tempered he was with the children, who

squirmed and giggled and slipped about like two peas on a drum. Then they whooped and slithered off his back without warning, running to tell their mum of their adventure.

Their mother was a small, slim woman with short hair dyed a dark maroon. She stood on the grass with two thin, whippet-like dogs sitting to heel. She wore earrings in the shape of dangling silver moons and stars. They caught the light as she picked Jason up. She squatted him on her hip, took Skye by the hand, and gave Mandy and Dorian a friendly wave. Jude nodded goodbye.

Dorian looked at Mandy. He pushed out his

bottom lip to pass judgment. *Nothing wrong with them at all.*

Mandy laughed. 'Come on, boy, let's get you home!' she said.

She was glad to see both Greenaway cars in the yard as she and Dorian finally arrived. The stable door hung open and empty, a reminder that Ivanhoe had moved on to a new home. She decided to go up and knock at the kitchen door to tell them Dorian was back. Then she would offer to lead him into the paddock. But as she crossed the yard, she heard raised voices, so loud and angry that she stopped in her tracks, half-embarrassed, half-afraid.

'Don't bother me about it! And don't make such a fuss!' Stephen Greenaway shouted. 'If you must know, I'm *glad* the stupid donkey has gone missing! At least it saves me the trouble of having to get rid of him!'

Mandy felt Dorian go rigid. Donkeys did this when they were afraid; they didn't bolt like horses, they just stood still. And no wonder Dorian was frightened of Mr Greenaway's angry words.

'What do you mean? We're not going to get rid of him just like that, are we?' Andi's voice rose above her father's. 'You promised we'd find a good home for him!'

Silvia Greenaway's voice, much lower and softer, tried to cut in. 'Stephen, please! This isn't making things any easier! Please try to calm down.'

Mandy hesitated beside Dorian, not knowing what else to do.

'Calm, nothing! She has to come to terms with leaving those animals behind! We've been planning it for long enough, and now it's all gone through. We're leaving Manor Farm, Andi! We've sold up. We've got to be out in a week. Just get it into your head once and for all, and accept what's happening, for heaven's sake!'

There was dead silence. 'I'm trying, Dad. I really am!' Andi began to sob.

Her father's voice softened. 'Listen, this is a good move for all of us, Andi. A better job for me. A chance for you to get the best tennis coaching in the country. This school in London produces world circuit players!'

'But I'm not sure I want to go there any more! Mum, I really don't want to leave Manor Farm. What will happen to Dorian?' Andi sounded as if she was in agony.

'We'll try to find him a good home, like we

said,' Silvia Greenaway promised.

'Who'll want to buy him? No one! He's thirty years old!' Andi wept and wept.

'Maybe, maybe not.' Stephen Greenaway held firm. 'But it's too late to change our minds. The house is sold. Now, come on, Andi, this is a real step up the ladder to success!'

Andi stopped sobbing and sounded suddenly calm. 'Well, I've decided not to go. I'll never pick up another tennis racket for as long as I live!'

'Andi!' Her mother's protest fell on silence. 'Please be sensible. This move is for the best.'

'That's not the point. I won't leave Dorian. I'd rather give up playing tennis!'

Mr Greenaway turned away in exasperation.

'Wait, Stephen. Let her calm down. She'll soon see why we want her to do this. Just wait,' Silvia pleaded.

Mandy edged Dorian across the yard to the kitchen door. She raised her hand to ring the bell. Dorian stood, edgy and restless, at her side.

'I can't wait for her to see sense! We've got a week to get out of this place, that's all! The new people want to move in almost immediately. The whole world can't come to a stop over one ridiculous donkey; you know that!'

Mandy saw Silvia nod and admit he was right. Andi glanced at the doorway and spotted Mandy and Dorian. She gave a gasp.

Stephen Greenaway, standing with his back to the door, delivered his final word. 'Like I said, if the old fool never comes back, so much the better! If he does, I'll get straight on the phone to the market. I'll send him down there right away!'

Mandy's heart sank. The market for a thirty-year-old donkey meant only one thing – the slaughterhouse. She saw Andi rush towards Dorian as though to save him from this dreadful fate. In her own confusion, Mandy gave him one quick hug and fled across the yard. She left him trembling on the Greenaways' doorstep.

'You hear me! That donkey has to go!' Stephen Greenaway insisted.

Mandy ran off up the drive, the dreadful words drumming in her ears.

Three

There was no life in Mandy's game as she played tennis against James next day. Her forehands flopped into the net, her lobs fell short. Today she couldn't care less whether she won or lost.

'Forty-fifteen!' James yelled. He gathered balls from the back of the court and began to imitate a commentator's voice as he stood to serve. 'And it's James Hunter serving for the match! Will his one hundred and twenty miles per hour cannonball delivery outclass his off-form opponent?' His voice was low and urgent. He threw the ball up and served. Across the net, Mandy swung at it and missed.

'Game, set and match!' James leapt into the air. His brown hair fell over his eyes as he landed. He took off his glasses and wiped his forehead, then set them back firmly on his nose. He trotted over to join Mandy on the bench at the side of the court. 'Bad luck,' he told her. He was grinning away at his victory.

'Well done. Sorry it wasn't much of a contest.' Mandy hadn't lost the match on purpose. Her mind was still on the scene at Manor Farm. Andi obviously hadn't stuck to her threat to give up tennis and stay with Dorian. There she was, dashing about on a distant court, in the middle of a serious training session with her coach. She hit the ball with perfect style and timing. It shot low over the net. She was a really excellent player, Mandy had to admit. 'I was finding it hard to concentrate,' she confessed to James.

'Excuses!' James laughed. Then he grew more serious. He backtracked over what might be upsetting Mandy. 'This couldn't have anything to do with the donkey you had to see a man about yesterday, could it, by any chance?'

She sighed. 'Right first time.' James knew her very well. She explained everything; how Stephen Greenaway had forced Andi into selling her beautiful thoroughbred horse, and was now set on getting rid of poor Dorian. She spread her hands, palms upwards. 'It's not that I'm against tennis. I just don't see how anyone can think it's more important than looking after an animal, that's all. Especially if that animal's been part of the family for years and years!'

She turned sideways to involve her grandad. He'd come down to the tennis-courts to trim the grass around the pavilion before he went away on holiday. He was in his summer hat, a straw trilby with a smart black band, and a blue, open-necked shirt. 'I'm telling James about Dorian,' she explained. 'Have you seen him today?'

'No, but I heard him.' Grandad strolled across, garden shears in hand. The air smelt of cut grass. 'He was kicking up a fuss as usual. Why?'

'I'm worried about him, that's all.'

Mandy and James picked up their rackets and headed for the gate with Grandad. They came out into the lawned area by the green and white pavilion.

'I know what you're thinking!' James declared. He flung down his racket and leaned against the veranda which ran the length of the pavilion. 'You think you should have stayed to save that donkey. Just like that!'

She had to admit it was true. 'I don't think I should have just left him there.' She remembered Dorian's sad, forlorn face as Stephen Greenaway had pronounced the death sentence.

'Mandy, dear, he's not *your* donkey,' Grandad reminded her. 'You couldn't just whisk him away without asking.' He settled down into a canvas chair on the veranda, legs outstretched, arms folded.

'I know. But Andi said she wouldn't play tennis ever again if they went ahead and got rid of Dorian. But look at her now!'

For a couple of minutes they watched Andi's athletic smashes. Her face was grim and determined as she struck the ball.

'People say lots of things in the heat of the moment,' Grandad sighed. 'Mind you, it would be a shame if the old chap ended up as dog-meat.'

'*Grandad!*' Mandy was shocked.

'Sorry, love. Not very tactful, eh? I didn't mean to upset you.'

James jumped in to swing the conversation round. 'How long have they had Dorian down at Manor Farm, Mr Hope?'

It set the old man off down memory lane. 'Ten years or more. I can remember seeing that young lady over there perched on his back, a little blonde scrap of a thing, and she couldn't have been more than three or four at the time. Before that, he served on the Golden Mile in Blackpool, I believe.'

'The Golden Mile?' Mandy loved to hear her grandad talk.

'The beach. Dorian was a beach donkey before he retired, so I hear. Up and down those sands, come rain or shine. They wore little brass name tags round their necks, I remember, and their bridles jingled all day long. When the donkeys packed up to go home for a well-earned rest, all the kids trailed after them with their buckets and spades. Next day there they'd be again, queuing up with their sixpences for a ride on the donkeys.'

Grandad was lost in the past. 'Well, eventually Dorian got pensioned off. If I've got it right, Silvia Greenaway found him at a donkey stud somewhere on the coast, miles away from here. She brought him back for Andi, and he's been at Manor Farm ever since.'

'Until now,' James concluded sadly.

'Yes, now everything's changing.' Mandy imagined crowds of children in bright swimsuits riding up and down the beach on Dorian's broad back. No wonder it dipped now, and his old knees turned in with the strain. She was glad he'd had almost a dozen peaceful years here in Welford. But it made it all the more cruel to turn him out now, in his last days.

'The trouble is, donkeys live too long,' her grandad said. He got up from his chair and pulled down the brim of his hat to shade his eyes. 'Children grow up and grow out of their faithful old friends.' He sauntered off to attack a weed that had dared to force its way up through the tennis-court netting.

'I would *never* grow out of Dorian!' Mandy said, half-cross, half-sad.

'No, but you're different,' James replied.

They watched Andi whack the ball over the net. 'Good shot!' her coach called.

When Mandy finally cycled home to Animal Ark, she had only one picture in her mind. It was a picture of Dorian's face; drooping, sad-eyed, abandoned.

'Hello, Mandy love, it's Gran!' The cheery voice spoke down the phone early next day. It was a Saturday, just one hour before they were due to set off on their holiday. 'We've got an emergency here at Lilac Cottage,' she said. 'Well, your grandad calls it an emergency. He's out in the garden trying to get a donkey off his vegetable patch. He says you'll know what to do!'

'I'll be right there, Gran!' Mandy's heart lurched as she rang off. Dorian again! She hoped it was just a friendly visit, nothing worse. By this time she'd begun to imagine gangs of men hustling Dorian up a ramp into a smelly horse box. She pictured their struggle to cart him off to market. Perhaps Dorian had seen them and bolted? She rushed down the lane on her bike to her grandparents' house. Grandad was face to face with a muddy, messy donkey standing four-square in his spinach bed. Both looked as though they'd been pulled through a hedge backwards. Grandad's white hair stood on end, as he hung on to Dorian's halter. Dorian had dug all four hooves into the rich soil.

'Can you do something, dear?' Gran wiped her hands on her flowered apron. Donkey and man stared each other out in a battle of wills.

'Yes, but Grandad will never get Dorian to go like that, not by pulling him from the front in a tug of war.' Quickly and carefully Mandy stepped

between the rows of peas and beans into the middle of the spinach bed. She came up alongside Dorian's left shoulder. 'Let go, Grandad!' she said softly. She took the donkey's halter close to his mouth. Then she pushed him with a stiff wrist and said, 'Walk – walk – walk!' in a rapid, firm voice.

Years of routine on Blackpool beach made Dorian obey. He stepped confidently over Grandad's beautifully tended spinach without damaging a single leaf.

Gran clapped and cheered. Grandad stood scratching his head and shaking it. 'Well, I'll be!' he stammered.

'You'll be what, Grandad?' Mandy couldn't hide a giggle. Dorian was easy to manage if you knew how.

'Never you mind!' Gran stepped in smartly. 'Say thank you to your granddaughter, Tom, before she takes this cantankerous old chap home for us.'

Grandad came round at last from his ordeal. 'Who are you calling cantankerous?' he teased.

'Not you; Dorian!' Gran winked at Mandy. She saw that her face had dropped into a frown. 'What's wrong, love?'

'Gran, do I have to take Dorian back?' she pleaded. She'd come to the donkey's rescue once more. Surely she wasn't just meant to take him back home so they could sell him to the highest bidder? Dorian seemed to agree. He nodded his head wisely and nuzzled close to Mandy's side.

'Yes, you do.' Grandad stepped in to overrule Gran, who'd begun to soften. 'He's obviously escaped again, through the stream and up the muddy bank opposite, by the look of him. Now it's time to go home. The game's up, old chap.' He patted Dorian's neck to show there were no hard feelings.

Gran sighed. 'Uh-oh, don't tell me. It looks like you got too fond of someone again!' She hugged

Mandy round the shoulders. 'Your grandad will tell me the full story, but now you'd better take Dorian back. And give me a hug and say goodbye. You won't see us for over a week, you know.'

Mandy hugged her grandparents goodbye. 'Have a good holiday. Come on, Dorian,' she said reluctantly. 'Walk on. Good boy.' They set off down the lane under a grey, overcast sky. Dorian walked sulkily beside her. She swung a hazel switch behind her back and tapped him on the rump when she felt him begin to drag his feet.

Dorian's face was sullen and blank. He stared straight ahead. For once in his life, he didn't want to go home.

He insisted on stopping by the common for a word with the Somers family. Mandy gave each of the children a quick ride on Dorian's back. This time it was the mother who was in charge. There was no sign of Jude.

'Hi, my name's Rowan,' she introduced herself. 'Jude's gone for a scout around,' she told Mandy. 'We've heard they might try to move us on soon.' She didn't sound upset or worried. Instead, she held out her arms for Skye, who wanted to fling herself from Dorian's back, free-fall. They laughed as she landed safely.

'Oh, they can't do that! You're not doing any harm.'

Rowan smiled. 'That doesn't seem to be the point.' Her earrings hung prettily against her dark skin. Her teeth were white and even.

'But you'll be homeless!' *Like Dorian*, Mandy thought.

'Oh no, we're never homeless.' Rowan bent to pick up her little boy and pointed to the van. 'We're like tortoises, aren't we, Jason? We always carry our home with us!' She reached into a plastic washing-up bowl sitting on the metal step and fished out a bruised apple for Dorian. 'Thanks for the rides,' she told him.

He bowed his head gallantly and walked on.

Perhaps he'd spied Silvia Greenaway walking up the lane to fetch him, because he put on a burst of speed and trotted willingly to her.

'Oh, Dorian, you bad boy!' she scolded him in her gentle voice. She turned to Mandy. 'Thanks for bringing him back. Dorian probably went looking for Andi down at the tennis-courts, didn't you, boy? Poor lad, I think he realises that all good things come to an end,' she added. 'It's amazing what this animal can understand! He's forever watching in at the kitchen door for Andi, and when he sees her go off, there's not a fence or a wall in the whole of Yorkshire that would keep him in.'

Mandy nodded. She handed over Dorian's halter. 'When do you have to move?'

'On Thursday. Dorian has to go on Wednesday, don't you, lad?' Silvia sighed helplessly. 'We'll all miss Welford. But there you are.' Slowly she led Dorian off. 'Even Andi seems to have accepted it.' She turned and waved to Mandy. 'Come on, Dorian, walk on, boy!'

That afternoon Mandy worked alongside Simon in the surgery. First they revived a dazed frog that had been in a collision with Walter Pickard's push-bike. They made sure that the victim was fit to be released back into his pond. Then there were the usual croaky canaries, moulting mice and gasping goldfish. Simon and Mandy helped each one as best they could. Then they heard Mrs Ponsonby's loud voice out in reception and realised that Pandora was to be their next patient; both heaved a weary sigh.

'This I could do without,' Simon admitted.

'Me too,' Mandy agreed.

But Mrs Ponsonby soared in with her snub-nosed

pet. 'She's got the snuffles, my dears! She thinks it's hay fever, don't you, darling? She must be allergic to pollen, poor thing!' Splendid in her pink glasses and turquoise hat, Mrs Ponsonby stood Pandora on the table and awaited their verdict.

Simon looked Pandora straight in the face. The dog rolled her big, dark eyes. 'Now, I'm sure it's nothing serious, Mrs Ponsonby. I'll just give her a quick once-over. It may well be something that will clear up by itself without treatment; probably nothing at all to worry about.'

Soon he was able to confirm this diagnosis. 'Right as rain,' he said.

Mrs Ponsonby scolded Pandora for making such a fuss. 'Tut-tut! You and your imagination, my pet lamb! You're always letting it run away with you!' She scooped the brown furry creature into her arms. 'And I was so afraid she'd picked up a nasty bug from those horrible dogs belonging to those travellers. I didn't want to tell Pandora that, of course. It would worry her far too much! But they were horrible scruffy creatures, with all sorts of dreadful creepy-crawlies teeming all over them, I shouldn't wonder. Poor little Pandora didn't realise the harm she might come to! She's such a friendly girl!'

'Oh, I don't think Pandora could pick up anything from those two fellows,' Simon said. He sounded quite sharp. 'I saw them with Jude Somers outside the Fox and Goose earlier today. They looked in perfectly good nick to me.'

'Jude Somers? You don't mean to tell me that you're on *speaking* terms with those people?' Mrs Ponsonby had changed her tune since she'd spoken to Mrs Platt. Now she seemed dead-set against the travellers.

'I certainly am, Mrs Ponsonby,' Simon said even more curtly.

Mrs Ponsonby drew herself up as she stood by the door. 'I must say, I'm surprised at you, Simon. It's people like that who drag down the tone of this village. Why, one of those dogs actually came up to Pandora and tried to . . . well, you know!'

Mandy felt the corners of her mouth twitch.

'Of course, Pandora made her feelings quite plain.' Mrs Ponsonby continued to hold her nose in the air.

'But I don't see the problem.' Simon seemed determined to have his say, and Mandy admired him for it. Though he was a mild-mannered, studious type with his round glasses and spiky fair hair, he could stand firm if he had to. 'They're parked on common ground, aren't they?'

Mandy decided to back him up. 'They're really very nice, Mrs Ponsonby. And I'm sure their dog was only being friendly!'

Mrs Ponsonby sniffed, and the flowers on her hat trembled. '*Common* ground is the proper place for them!' she retorted. 'For common is what they are, and the sooner they're gone the better!' She and Pandora swept out of the door in a terrible temper.

Mandy looked at Simon. 'Count to ten!' he said.

She took a deep breath instead. But when Mandy cycled down past Gran and Grandad's empty house, after breakfast next morning, she was sad to look down from Lilac Cottage into the dip of the common, and see only a patch of flattened grass; no battered van, no smiling children.

Her spirits sank. The Somers had been forced to move on. And now there seemed little hope for Dorian too. Sunday was creeping towards Monday, and the final deadline for the poor old donkey was approaching.

Four

Dorian had no intention of taking the decision to sell him off to Walton Horse Market lying down; or standing up for that matter. In fact, he'd no intention of getting sent there at all. Before Sunday was over, he'd gone missing again.

'Hello, Welford 703267?' a frail voice asked as Mandy picked up the phone.

'Hello, this is Welford 703267, Animal Ark,' Mandy said breathlessly. She'd rushed in from the garden to answer it. 'Can I help?'

'Oh dear! Oh yes, I certainly hope so. Joan, it's eating the asparagus fern! Oh my!' The female voice fluttered helplessly.

'Miss Marjorie?' Mandy put one hand over the phone and signalled for James to come in from the garden. It looked as though their plan for a quiet stroll down to the tennis-courts would have to be put off. 'Hang on a moment, I think we're going to be needed.' She turned back to the phone. 'Miss Marjorie? Is there anything wrong?'

Marjorie Spry was one of identical twins who lived by themselves in a huge old house on the Walton Road. The Riddings was a dusty, old-fashioned place covered in ivy, and the twins were eccentric old ladies. But they'd given a good, kind home to Patch, a homeless kitten, and Mandy was anxious to help them when she could.

'Oh dear! Now it's eating the yucca! Oh, shoo! Oh dear, Joan, put away that umbrella. You'll frighten the poor thing!'

Mandy could hear the panic in the old lady's voice. She had a sudden flash of realisation and her blood ran cold. 'Miss Marjorie, you don't have a donkey down there by any chance, do you?'

'Oh yes, dear! How clever of you! As a matter of fact we do. That's why I'm telephoning. You see, I have absolutely no idea what to do. I can spy him now through the window. He's got himself into our conservatory, and I must say he has rather a healthy appetite. He's eating all our plants!'

In the background, Mandy heard a crash and a little squeal from the other sister, Joan. Her mouth fell open and her blue eyes widened as she imagined the chaos at The Riddings. 'Hold on, Miss Marjorie; we'll be right over!'

'Oh, yes please, dear! Oh my! Joan, don't do that! Oh, good gracious! Now look here, just a minute!' There was another crash. The phone went dead.

'Come on!' Mandy urged a bewildered James. 'Let's go!'

They ran out, grabbed their bikes and helmets, and cycled up the lane into the village. 'It's Dorian. I don't know exactly what's going on,' Mandy panted. 'But the sooner we get there the better!' They pedalled fast and furious, out along the Walton Road. Soon the pointed towers and ivy-covered walls of the ancient house came into view.

A figure flew down the grand front steps to greet them as they flung down their bikes and ran up the gravel drive. Marjorie Spry was dressed in a bright flowered dress, her wispy grey hair coming loose from its bun, her thin arms waving like windmills. 'Oh, here you are, dears! This way, this way!' She ran with little tottering steps round the side of the big house to the conservatory at the back.

Mandy and James chased after her into the glass extension. Its iron arches soared overhead on beautiful branching pillars. Its glass panes, green with moss and decades of hothouse growth, let in a misty sunlight. The inside was a jungle, thick with shiny tropical leaves and bright orange and pink flowers. For a moment they stood still, hit by the fierce, muggy heat.

'There!' Miss Spry put one hand to her mouth and gasped. She pointed. 'Oh, Joan, do come down and behave yourself,' she said crossly.

Joan Spry was perched like a parrot on a high ledge at the back of the conservatory. She gave little, bird-like jerks of her head, and jabbed at the enemy with fierce pecks of her pointed nose. 'You don't frighten me!' she squawked, though she cowered on the ledge. Brawny Dorian stood nose to nose, a sullen look in his eyes. There was a trail of vine leaves hanging from his mouth.

'Can you do something?' Miss Marjorie pleaded. 'I'm afraid Joan will do the poor creature some damage!'

James hid a smile. He frowned at Mandy. 'Shall we creep up on him from either side?' he

suggested. Dorian hadn't spotted them, so intent was he on bullying the twitchy old lady.

'No, we'd better not surprise him from behind,' Mandy whispered. 'He wouldn't like that.'

Joan Spry flapped a thin hand at him. Dorian didn't even blink. He began to chew contentedly.

Mandy decided on blunt tactics. 'Dorian, come here!' she called out in a severe voice.

The donkey's head froze. *Uh-oh!* His eyes rolled sideways. Down went his head and he shuffled round awkwardly to face the music.

'I should think so too!' Mandy saw him hang his head in shame. She glanced round at the smashed clay flowerpots and tumbled, half-eaten plants. 'I should think you *are* sorry, Dorian. And so you should be!'

Miss Marjorie tripped forward to help her sister down from the ledge. 'Now don't be too hard on him, my dear. He's only doing what comes naturally.'

Miss Joan glowered from her sister to Dorian and back again. She stood safe on firm ground again and began to pick stray cactus spines from her hair. 'I'll give him what comes naturally!' she threatened.

'Now, Joan, don't make a fuss. We like animals

here. We like kittens! We like donkeys, remember!'
She came up to Dorian who'd sidled obediently
up to Mandy. 'Take no notice. My sister likes you
really,' she explained.

'No, I don't!' Joan snapped.

'Yes, you do!'

Mandy heard them launch into one of their
famous rows. 'Let's help clear up,' she suggested
hastily to James. She began to scoop earth back
into flowerpots and stand them upright, glad to
see Patch, the twins' cat, sitting quietly in an old
cane chair in a far corner of the conservatory. He
let the argument roll over him, lying in the sun
on a faded cushion. He was obviously used to it.

'Will Geoffrey be able to rescue the plants?'
Mandy asked. Their old gardener worked long
hours to keep the place in good order. She
propped some broken stems against their canes,
and waited for the twins to run out of steam.

' . . . I don't!'

'You do! Anyway, he's a lovely old thing! I could
have a better conversation with that donkey than
I could with you any time!' Miss Marjorie said,
crushing her sister Joan with a final burst of spite.
She turned to Mandy. 'Geoffrey's no longer with
us,' she told her.

'Oh, I'm sorry . . .' For a moment Mandy was lost for words. The crabby old gardener was part of the furniture at The Riddings, in his baggy old corduroys and flat cap.

'No, no, he's not dead. He's retired and gone to live with his sister in York.' Miss Marjorie's glance alighted on James. 'You don't happen to know of an odd-jobbing gardener, do you?' It seemed from the glint in her eye that she thought James was the very thing; sturdy, young and agile. She'd have him clipping the lawns before he could say Jack Robinson.

'Don't be silly, he has to go to school!' Miss Joan crowed.

'Oh!' Miss Marjorie looked crestfallen.

'Even in *your* day, boys still went to school until they were fourteen, you know!' Joan was triumphant.

Mandy began to lead Dorian out on to the terrace. She was glad to be in the fresh air again – the Spry twins weren't always as shy and helpless as they seemed!

'Oh well.' Miss Marjorie glanced at James as though she hadn't quite given up hope. The twins stood side by side, watching Dorian go, gentle as a kitten. Their flowered dresses were a riot of colour out on the stone terrace. They watched wistfully, hands clasped, feet spread like wading birds, as their uninvited four-footed guest departed. 'If you do hear of anyone who would like a gardening job . . .' Marjorie Spry called, but Dorian had had enough and was already plodding down the drive with Mandy and James in tow. He rolled his big tongue round his teeth and looked back doubtfully at the scatty old ladies.

Mandy paused, while James picked up their bikes at the gate. 'You know, I'm sure Dorian realises what's in store for him!' She thought gloomily of him penned in amongst the broken-winded horses and all the other miserable, old creatures that nobody wanted. They walked in silence towards the village, minds working overtime on solutions to Dorian's problem.

But finding a home for an aged donkey was not as easy as finding homes for adorable young kittens. You couldn't hang a 'For Sale' sign round his neck and leave Dorian in the carpark outside the Fox and Goose, as if he was a used car. Everyone in the village had a friendly word for Dorian as he ambled through with Mandy and James, but no one could give him a home.

Mandy stopped outside the pub. 'Hi,' she said to Ernie Bell and Walter Pickard, two old men who sat outside the door. Across the yard, Walter's cat, Tom, lay sprawled along the wall top, while young Tiddles, Ernie's cat, chased butterflies in the garden. Ernie and Walter both loved animals. Even now, Ernie sat with his pet squirrel, Sammy, perched on his shoulder.

Walter grinned and let Dorian investigate his pint of beer. Sammy peered at the donkey's huge face and darted on to Ernie's other shoulder, out of danger. 'You two look a bit down-in-the-mouth,' Walter observed. 'What's up? Not sunny enough for you?' It was his joke about the lovely weather.

Mandy sighed. She was too upset to explain Dorian's problem to Walter. He lived in a tiny house across the pub yard, in the same row as Ernie. Neither had any space for a donkey.

'Did you know donkeys lived in the desert? It's their natural habitat.' Walter came out with this scrap of information. 'I expect they like this heat.'

'Well, I never!' Ernie shook his head and took a long swallow from his glass. 'So where are you off to with this old chap?'

'Home,' Mandy said in a hollow voice.

Walter and Ernie turned curiously to James for an explanation.

'Not for much longer. He belongs to the Greenaways at Manor Farm. They're moving, so they have to get rid of him.'

'That's a shame,' Walter said, scratching Dorian's nose, but the two old men were more interested in Stephen Greenaway. They launched into a discussion about the merits of his new football team. Dorian poked his nose through the pub door and made a friendly nuisance of himself.

'Greenaway's a good manager. He's tough all right,' Walter said. 'They say he's one of the hardest men in soccer.'

Mandy overheard. 'You can say that again. He's not even trying to find a decent place for Dorian. The man's got no heart!'

'Uh-oh!' Ernie winked at Walter. 'Why do I feel another favour coming on?'

Mandy smiled. Ernie was a retired carpenter who'd often helped them in the past. He would be grumpy at first, but really he was kindness itself. 'I would ask you if I thought it possible, Ernie, but even you couldn't build a stable and put it in your tiny back yard!'

'Ah, no,' he admitted. 'Sammy here might object

to that.' The squirrel scuttled down his arm into his lap and clung to Ernie's waistcoat.

'Looks like you're stuck,' Walter said. 'Unless, of course . . .' He leaned sideways to squint down the main street. Mandy heard the smart click of horseshoes on the tarmac road. Mandy followed his gaze and recognised Susan and Prince, heading towards them. 'I bet those Collinses would have room for one small donkey on that ranch they call a home!' Walter decided.

'If only!' Mandy said wistfully. She expected Susan to ride straight by.

But Susan was in the mood for a chat. She pulled Prince up and smoothly dismounted. Then she led him across. 'Still taking in waifs and strays, I see,' she said to Mandy. She gave Dorian's chin a friendly scratch. 'I was talking to Andi Greenaway about him this morning. She seemed really upset about having to let him go.'

Dorian thrust his nose at the pretty, horsey newcomer.

'Steady on!' Susan laughed, almost over-balancing backwards. 'Prince here will be getting jealous!'

'Er, Susan!' Mandy suddenly grabbed Dorian's halter and beckoned her towards a private corner of the carpark. 'I don't suppose . . . ?'

'No, I'm sorry, Mandy, I honestly couldn't!' Susan said, shaking her head. 'I'd love to take him in, I really would. But my mum would have ten thousand fits. She says Jim has much too much on his plate as it is, looking after Prince as well as the garden. It just wouldn't be fair to ask him to take on anything else!'

Mandy could see Susan's mind was made up. She knew there was no point in pleading.

James had joined them and stood stroking Dorian's neck. Dorian lifted his head and tutted. 'Well, it was worth a try,' James suggested.

'I'm sorry, Mandy.' Susan had the last word.

'OK, then!' Mandy's mouth set in a determined line. A sudden, desperate idea had just formed in her mind. 'I've got one last plan!' Mandy, James and Susan put their heads together. 'Overnight,' Mandy muttered. 'If Dorian could stay at your place for just one night . . . I'd tell him to stay quiet . . . no one need know! Please, Susan!'

Susan narrowed her eyes and bit her bottom lip.'OK, Mandy. But if my mum and dad find out, I'm in deep trouble!'

'They won't!' Mandy promised.

Then James spoke out. 'Mandy, are you sure it's

worth the risk?' He looked worried.

Mandy glanced at Dorian's wide, trusting eyes. 'Yes, it's worth it!' she said. 'Come on, let's go!'

The Beeches was Susan's splendid, ranch-style home. Susan split off from the others at the gate and rode alone up the front drive. Mandy and James turned and led Dorian down a path that ran along one side of the garden. It was overgrown with hawthorn bushes, and daisies grew underfoot. They'd arranged to meet up with Susan in the stable block at the back.

'Shh!' Mandy warned Dorian. He'd spotted the luxury stables and was bursting to look them over. 'We have to wait here!'

James gritted his teeth. 'What if he starts kicking up a fuss in the middle of the night?'

'He won't. Will you, Dorian?'

The donkey blew out his cheeks and shook his head.

At last, Susan, still in her riding gear, crept out to the back gate to let them in. 'It's OK, there's no one around,' she told them. 'We should be able to make it without being seen.'

They tiptoed across the stable yard. When he reached his new, five-star quarters, Dorian didn't even hesitate. Straight in through the door; best quality hay, a bucket of oats, a handful of carrots. Bliss!

'Be a good boy!' Mandy whispered. 'If you're spotted, don't worry. Susan will say she's arranging for the horse box to take you home tomorrow morning. But it's better if no one sees you!' She rubbed Dorian's nose and spoke gently. 'So don't go arguing with Prince here and making a noise. I'll come and fetch you early tomorrow, OK?'

Dorian sniffed the air as Prince shifted in the stall next door. He snickered quietly, then munched his hay.

Mandy glanced behind at James and Susan. They still looked worried.

'Do you think we're doing the right thing?' James whispered.

Mandy turned to them. 'I don't like this either,' she confessed. 'But which is the worst thing? Keeping Dorian hidden here while I work out a safe place for him to go? Or sending him straight off to the horse market?'

James and Susan both nodded. There was no arguing with that.

'So we'll keep him here for one night. I'll come early tomorrow morning, and I'll set off with him before anyone's up. I just have to make one phone call tonight.'

'Who are you going to call?' Susan leant forward. The secret plan made her feel tense and excited.

Mandy was thinking ahead. She still had one arm round Dorian's neck. 'First, I have to find the name of that donkey stud, the home for donkeys where Dorian came from in the first place. Then I'll have to ring them up. I'm sure they'll take him back once I explain what's happening.'

James and Susan nodded. 'And you'll trek over there with him?' James asked. 'How far do you think it will be?'

'It's near the west coast somewhere, according to Grandad. Dorian and I can do that in two days if I plan the route properly, and take food and everything. I'm sure I can do it!' she insisted.

James nodded slowly. 'If anyone can, you can,' he agreed.

'I'm not so sure.' Susan looked doubtful. 'Why don't we just tell someone? Your mum and dad would know what to do.'

But Mandy shook her head. 'Dad is adamant that we shouldn't take in homeless animals,' she recalled. 'No, this is something I have to work out by myself!' She pictured stealing away before dawn on an early morning trek out of Welford, up on to the moor as the sun lit the sky. 'Don't tell anyone! Promise!'

They promised. 'Oh, Mandy, I only hope this works!' Susan whispered. Her eyes gleamed in the dull light.

'Me too!' Mandy cried. 'But what else can we do? It has to work!'

Five

Mrs Hope looked oddly at Mandy. 'You haven't finished your tea!' She pushed a bowl of strawberries and cream across the table towards her.

'Pass them this way if you're not hungry!' Her dad looked longingly at the bowl. His own was already empty.

Mandy gave him a little smile. She was wondering how soon she could put her plan into action. First of all, she needed to find the address of the donkey stud from a book on the surgery shelf. Then she would plan her journey there with Dorian.

'What's on your mind, Mandy?' Mum asked, her suspicions aroused.

For a moment, Mandy considered again whether she should let her mum and dad in on the plan to save the donkey. But she knew what they would say; that it was a good idea, well meant, but that she'd no right to take Dorian from his rightful owners. *No*, she decided once and for all. 'Nothing.' She sat in their homely kitchen, at a table piled high with homemade bread and cakes. Her spoon was poised in mid-air.

'Fresh strawberries from the garden,' Dad tempted her.

Mandy dipped her spoon into the bowl. 'Sorry, Dad.' Perhaps she'd better eat up after all. This could be her last proper meal for some time. She only hoped that Dorian would have the sense to stock up on the best quality hay on offer at The Beeches.

She ate her strawberries slowly. She must try to act normally. She mustn't go to bed too early, though she had to be up before dawn; she mustn't let them overhear the phone call, she must pretend that nothing was different.

There was a loud knock at the door.

'I'll go!' Mandy jumped off her chair and rushed to answer it.

'What's got into her today?' she heard Mum ask. 'She's a bag of nerves.'

'She's up to something . . .'

Mandy could hear them discussing her as she shot to the front door.

She opened it. Susan Price grabbed her by the wrist and pulled her over the step. Her dark hair hung loose out of its pony-tail. She was dressed in a white T-shirt and denim shorts. 'Mandy!' she gasped. 'You've got to come quickly!'

'Why? What's wrong?' Mandy's heart sank like lead. 'It's Dorian, isn't it?'

'Good guess!' Susan snapped. 'That stupid donkey! You told him to wait at my place until morning, didn't you? As plain as anything. Well, he didn't. He's gone!'

'Oh, Dorian!'

'Yes, "Oh, Dorian" is absolutely right!' Susan stood with her hands on her hips. 'And I thought you said he was supposed to be clever! Do you know where he's headed for now?' She almost spluttered with annoyance.

'No. Where?'

'Let me explain! I heard this dreadful noise through our back door. My mum dropped her best teacup, she was so surprised. There was Dorian with his head stuck through the door, bellowing at the top of his voice. My mum screamed. Dorian bolted. He charged straight across our front lawn down to the road. I set off after him. He was going at a gallop.' Susan stopped to draw breath.

'Where? Where is he?' Mandy demanded.

'Listen! He was heading down the road. And you know it's a dead end from where we are. There's only one place he can go.'

'Oh no!' Mandy pictured the scene.

'Oh yes! The tennis-courts!' Susan was practically in tears. 'They'll blame me, they'll say it's all my fault. I tried to head him off, but he wouldn't listen to me! So I came straight to tell you, Mandy. Your plan for tomorrow is off. It hasn't worked!'

Mandy's mind worked quick as a flash. No point hiding things from her parents now. She would have to own up later. Right now she needed their help.

'Dad!' she yelled. 'Can you drive us down to the tennis-courts, please? It's important. Dorian's escaped again.' She didn't plan to tell him where from; that would have to wait.

Mr Hope came out, car keys at the ready. 'Come on, hop in, you two.' They all jumped in the

Animal Ark Land-rover. He started up the engine. Emily Hope came to the step to watch them drive off.

'We'll be back as soon as we can!' Mr Hope shouted. He turned to Mandy, sitting in the middle seat. 'Just stay calm. Save the explanations until later.'

Mandy gulped and nodded. Her father was brilliant in an emergency. 'It's not Dorian I'm worried about,' she gasped. 'It's the tennis-courts.'

'And what the players will do to him if they catch him, I expect.' Dad nodded and swung the car expertly round the bends. 'I know that tennis club crowd. Those grass courts are their pride and joy!'

'Dorian's hooves will make an awful mess of them!' Susan giggled in spite of herself.

'Exactly!' Mr Hope's eyebrows shot up into his forehead. 'Hoof-marks all over the place. It doesn't bear thinking about!'

They arrived at the tennis club and leapt out of the car, then stopped dead. To their surprise, everything was calm and peaceful.

'No Dorian?' said Mr Hope. He stood and scratched his head.

The hard smack of tennis balls hitting taut

strings greeted them. Couples dressed all in white chased them across the green courts. Over to the left, to one side of the pavilion, Mandy spied Andi Greenaway involved in a friendly game with her parents and James Hunter.

'He was headed this way, honestly!' Susan protested.

'Well, let's just hope he got diverted,' Mr Hope said.

They watched balls whizz over the nets. Scores were called. Other players sat on the grass and sipped cold drinks. It was a perfect Sunday evening.

Suddenly an ear-splitting noise from the river shattered the calm. Mandy panicked. She ran down the side of the pavilion towards the river. 'Dorian!' she yelled at the top of her voice. 'Stay where you are. Don't move!'

'Ee-aw!' Dorian scrambled up the river-bank. His head appeared. He opened his mouth, showed his yellow teeth and bellowed. 'Ee-aw! Ee-aw!'

Andi stood on court, glued to the spot. Stephen Greenaway flung down his racket. He clutched at the wire-netting fence which separated him from the donkey. James quickly ran out to join Mandy round the back.

Dorian had mounted the bank, covered in mud.

Happy to see Andi, he began to trot towards the courts.

'Someone stop that thing! He's going to charge the fence!' an elderly club member shouted. 'Don't let it near the courts!'

A swarm of players made for the scene. They stood shoulder to shoulder, a human barrier.

'That's it. Go forward. Drive it back! Don't let it set foot on the court!' The old man marshalled his troops. His white hair blew in the breeze as he strode to the front line.

Dorian stopped short. He was cut off from Andi by a thin white line of angry tennis players. They

all waved their rackets at him. He decided on a swift change of plan. With a glance at Mandy and James, he veered to one side and trotted off along the river bank.

'Thank heavens!' James heaved a sigh of relief. Adam Hope and Susan had just caught up with them, in time to see Dorian's broad brown rump heading upstream.

'Panic over?' Mandy's dad inquired.

'Not quite.' Mandy pointed back to where Stephen Greenaway had pushed his way to the front of the gang of tennis players. Now he set off in hot pursuit of Dorian. 'We'd still better get to him first, I think.' She ran as fast as she could after the disappearing donkey.

He trotted calmly along the river-bank, past Mrs Ponsonby walking her two dogs in the evening sun. Mandy ran after him, leading James, Susan and her dad. They were followed by the three Greenaways and some of the keener tennis players, all going hell-for-leather. Mrs Ponsonby pressed herself back against the trunk of an oak tree to avoid being trampled. Pandora growled fiercely. Toby leaped to join the chase. But the commotion only encouraged Dorian to break into a gallop and surge ahead.

'Whoa!' Mandy saw a tall, skinny figure step bravely in front of Dorian and begin to wave his arms. She recognised Jude Somers, the traveller, trying to head him off. She was only half-glad as she saw the donkey halt and try to change tack. Jude flung himself round the runaway's neck. Mandy put on a final spurt, desperate to be the first to reach them.

'Jude!' She gasped out her astonishment. 'I thought you'd packed up and gone!' Behind her, the others were catching up.

Jude Somers hung on to Dorian's tufted mane, then lunged for his halter. 'We did. But we didn't go far. There's a small lay-by just upstream from here, well out of the village. We decided to stop there for a bit.' He grinned as he handed the rope to Mandy. 'You don't seem too pleased to see me.' His brown eyes looked bemused by the whole frantic scuffle. Toby bounded by to greet Jude's two dogs. 'Here, boys! Here, Joey! Here, Spider!' Jude whistled them to heel.

Mandy had time to notice their sleek, brindled coats, their graceful pointed faces as they settled quietly beside their master. Joey and Spider. She even grinned back at Jude. But she was too worried to relax for long. 'Why didn't you just stay

put, like you were told, Dorian?' she demanded.
'You were perfectly safe where you were!'

Dorian rolled his eyes. He ducked his head as
his mistress caught up with them. He nuzzled up
close to her, shutting his eyes, sighing deeply.

Andi fell on his neck, nearly sobbing. Soon
everyone crowded round. Stephen Greenaway
seized Dorian's halter from Mandy.

'Oh, please!' Mandy cried out. She felt her dad's
hand on her shoulder.

'Stand to one side,' Mr Greenaway ordered. He
looked over Mandy's head, trying to ignore his
own daughter's sobs. He looked straight at Mr Hope.
'Do you think you can get this idiot thing back up
to Manor Farm in your Land-rover?' he asked.

Dorian stamped his feet and tossed his head.
Mr Greenaway took no notice.

Mandy's dad frowned. 'We have a ramp up into
the back. Yes, I should say we could just about fit
him in.' He sounded calm but cool.

'Fine. Let's go.' He didn't waste words. His face,
red with the effort of the chase, showed that his
mind was made up. As he pulled Dorian round to
face the way they'd come, Mandy leaned forward
to take Andi's hand.

Mr Hope shrugged. 'Thanks for your help,' he

said to Jude. Then he turned to Mandy. 'You can make your own way back home whenever you're ready, OK?'

She nodded. James and Susan were still here to lend a hand with Andi. 'We'll walk back with Andi to Manor Farm, then follow you to Animal Ark.' She felt like crying herself. She never thought the day would end in such disaster.

Sadly they stood and watched a dejected Dorian being led off along the path. His tail swished, his head went down. He was beaten.

Jude Somers looked genuinely upset. 'I seem to have stuck my foot in it; I didn't realise.' He stood, hands in pockets, watching the retreating procession. Joey and Spider lay low, chins at ground level, while Toby bounded all around.

Mandy shook her head. 'You weren't to know. Heaven knows what we were going to do if Dorian had got all the way to the road, in any case.'

Andi sniffed and gradually pulled herself together. 'It's not your fault. It's not anyone's fault. Thanks for trying to help.' She put on a brave face, ready to walk back to the club.

But the day wasn't over. Mrs Ponsonby still had to roll up and have her say. She toiled up the pathway, carrying Pandora. 'Oh, Toby darling!

There you are. Thank heavens!' Her face was pinker than her glasses, pinker even than her hat. She panted up to them. 'What did those nasty doggies do to you, then?' She bent down to catch hold of lively Toby, then stood up and looked down her nose at Jude and his two perfectly well-behaved dogs.

'They didn't do anything to Toby, Mrs Ponsonby,' Mandy began. She heard James and Susan warning her to be quiet. 'They're beautiful dogs!'

'Oh, you're mistaken there, my dear!' Mrs Ponsonby backed off. She eyed Jude with distrust, then she smiled a superior smile. Without another word, she turned and strode away, one dog under each arm.

'Ouch!' Mandy whispered. 'Sorry!'

Jude smiled. 'Don't worry, we're used to it. Some people take against us just because we're travellers. We have to learn not to mind.'

'I think it's a shame!' Mandy protested. She bent down and patted Joey on the head.

'It's because we're different, that's all. People can't cope with us. But we like the life, so we have to put up with some abuse. If it gets too bad, we just move on.' He looked up at the fluffy white clouds. 'It looks as if we'd better get ready to do that again before too long, now they know we're here.'

'Oh no!' Mandy felt it was all her fault. 'Do you have to?'

Jude nodded. 'We're used to that too. We're planning to look for work. Don't worry about us.'

James stepped forward, looking as if he was about to say something. But Jude turned quickly, whistling to the two dogs. They streaked ahead, and he didn't look back to say goodbye. He walked with his long, loping stride, head up. 'Never mind,' James murmured. 'It was just an idea.'

'What?' Mandy only half heard.

'Nothing. It doesn't matter.'

Sadly they all set off downstream. Dorian had already been whisked out of sight, on his last journey home to Manor Farm. They trailed along the green footpath after him, without a glimmer of hope in their hearts.

Six

Things looked serious by the time Mandy finally got back to Animal Ark. She'd confessed her plan to save Dorian to Andi, and now she was weary from the long walk home. Their parting at Mandy's gate had made her feel wretched. Andi's springy stride had slowed to a heavy trudge. She kept her eyes fixed on the ground and had hardly said a word, all the way up from the tennis club.

Mandy stood with one hand on the gate, trying to find something useful to say. But the words stuck in her throat. She could only think of Dorian and how they'd let him down. 'Sorry, Andi,' she whispered at last.

Andi glanced up at her. 'It's not your fault, Mandy. At least you tried. It's more than I did.'

She sounded so flat and hopeless that another lump rose in Mandy's throat. She nodded quickly and half ran up the path into the house.

Inside, everything was unusually quiet. Her dad wasn't humming hymns for choir practice, or pedalling on his exercise bike, or doing any of the usual things he did on an evening off. He sat with Mrs Hope at the kitchen table, obviously waiting for Mandy to arrive. They looked up as she walked in, her lip already trembling, her eyes not quite free of the awkward tears that kept welling up.

'I'm sorry, Mum. Sorry, Dad.' She hovered by the door. 'It was all my fault. I wanted to save Dorian by taking him back to the old stud. But I realise I should never have tried to keep him hidden in the first place.'

Emily Hope gave a faint smile. 'It's a classic case of wanting to help and ending up making things much worse, I'm afraid.'

'Was Mr Greenaway very mad?'

Mr Hope nodded. 'That's putting it mildly. I think I saw steam coming out of his ears.'

'Oh dear.' Mandy slumped into a chair next to the open fireplace.

Her mother came over and crouched beside her. 'You have to understand, Mandy, a man like Stephen Greenaway can't bear to be made to look a fool. Trying to ghost his donkey away from under his very eyes feels that way. I can see his point.' She spoke gently. 'Whatever you think about his treatment of Dorian, your mistake was to try and trick him.'

Mandy took a big gulp. 'I know, Mum. I did it on the spur of the moment. I'm sorry.'

Mrs Hope smiled and gave her a hug. 'Well, next time . . .'

'There won't be a next time!' Mandy pointed out. 'There'll be no more Dorian to worry about after today. Mr Greenaway will see to that!'

Adam Hope got up from his chair and came and leant against the fireplace. He gave Mandy one of his lopsided grins. 'Tell me, how did you plan to get Dorian all the way over to the donkey stud?'

Mandy blushed. 'I was going to head across country, along the bridle-paths.'

'Then he could live out his retirement in peace and quiet?' Mandy nodded.

'Good idea,' her mum agreed. 'Full marks for content, love. Nought for style.'

At last they could all relax and laugh about it. 'You think a donkey stud could be the solution for old Dorian, then?' Her dad pursued the idea as if it was worth considering.

Mandy took a deep breath. She got up and began to walk around the kitchen, almost back to her old self. 'Yes, I do. If he has to leave Manor Farm, it's the best sort of place he could go to. It'd be like an old people's home for donkeys. They'd take good care of him, especially if we got him back to the place he first came from.'

'Did you mention this to Andi?' Mrs Hope asked.

'Yes, but she was too upset to talk about it. I just said goodbye to her in the lane. She's on her way home now.'

'Funnily enough,' Mr Hope cut in, 'the same idea occurred to me as I drove old Dorian back home. I was sure we could do something better for him than sending him off to market. As a matter of fact, I mentioned the Welford Sanctuary to Stephen, just as an idea. I thought Betty Hilder might offer Dorian a welcome there.'

Mandy gasped and ran up to him. 'What did he say?'

'He told me to mind my own business, I'm afraid.'

'Oh!' Mandy stepped back, her hopes crushed.

'But . . .' Her mother clasped her hands together and raised them under her chin. 'Your dad came home and discussed it with me. We thought we might offer to buy Dorian from the Greenaways ourselves. Then we could take him off to this stud, if it seems OK.' She talked slowly, to let it sink in.

Mandy felt she had to sit down. 'I don't believe it!' she said. 'Oh, Mum, that's brilliant!'

'He won't cost much. Practically nothing. We'll give Stephen a fair market price and take Dorian off his hands for him. We feel the same as you, Mandy. The old boy deserves a better end than the one that lies in store for him at the horse market. We both decided that it's something we'd like to do.'

Mandy leapt up into her mother's arms. She was speechless. Then she ran to her father and hugged him too.

'I'll ring the Greenaways first thing in the morning,' he promised. 'And I'll make the offer.'

'Why not tonight?' Mandy wanted to rush to the phone that second.

Mrs Hope laughed. 'No, just let things calm down a bit at Manor Farm. We all need to sleep on it, and Stephen will be feeling better by morning.

Give him a chance to get over the tennis club fiasco!'

'First thing in the morning?' Mandy asked. It seemed a long way off.

'Very first thing,' her mum said. 'Now settle down with a book, or watch some television. Get a good night's sleep. Tomorrow we'll sort everything out, OK?'

Mandy was torn; she felt half-relieved, half-afraid. One more night; then Dorian would be safe.

At nine next morning, Mr Hope picked up the phone to make his offer for Dorian. Mandy hopped from one foot to another as she stood by him in the reception area at Animal Ark.

'Hello, Silvia? It's Adam Hope here,' he began in a breezy voice. 'How are you?'

Mandy noticed his face fall and a frown set in.

'Is something wrong?' he asked.

Mandy stood still. She felt the excitement slipping from her.

'Oh dear, that's very bad news. Yes. Is Stephen there with you? Good. Well listen, just hang on. We'll be right with you. Try not to worry. Yes, OK. I'm sure we can sort this out. Yes, bye.' He put down the phone with a dazed look.

'Dorian's gone missing again,' he said.

Mandy's shoulders sagged. Just when they were on the point of solving everything!

Adam Hope sighed. 'Even worse. Andi's gone with him.'

'They've run away?' She felt herself go pale.

He nodded. 'Apparently. She left a note saying she couldn't bear to let Dorian go. Getting rid of Ivanhoe was bad enough. She said she was sorry but she hoped they understood.'

Mandy was stunned. 'You mean she's given up everything for Dorian's sake after all? Her tennis, everything?' She could hardly believe her ears.

'Yes. She says she's not coming back. She's gone for good.'

Mandy followed her father out of the surgery, leaving her mother and Simon to cope with the appointments. They ran to the Land-rover and made for Manor Farm as fast as they could.

They drew up and ran across the stable yard, into the kitchen, where they met the two haggard faces of Andi Greenaway's parents. A letter lay open on the table in front of them. Silvia Greenaway's trembling hand rested on top of it.

Stephen Greenaway scarcely looked up. His eyes were glazed, his hair out of place. 'We only just found the note, Adam, a few minutes before you rang. I can't believe she would do this.' He shook his head. 'Two days before she was due to move off to a new life, with everything to look forward to. Why would she throw it all away?'

Mr Hope put a hand on Stephen Greenaway's shoulder. 'Look, don't worry. They can't have got that much of a start. Andi's old enough to look after herself without coming to any real harm. We'll soon track them down.'

'Do you think we should ring the police?' Silvia Greenaway asked.

'No, not yet!' her husband suddenly stood up. He ran his fingers through his dishevelled hair. 'Let's go and scout around for ourselves first. Do you have time to lend a hand, Adam?' He seemed desperate to avoid too much fuss.

Mr Hope nodded. 'Of course. But look, once we've cruised round the local roads and if we still haven't managed to track them down, I suggest you involve the police.' He nodded again at Silvia.

'Yes, but not yet. We'd look pretty stupid if she turned up in an hour or two, looking sorry for herself. Kids often do, you know.' Stephen Greenaway was firm.

Mrs Greenaway agreed. 'OK. I'll take my car.

We'll set off in three different directions. That way, surely we should find her soon!'

They all ran for their cars. Mandy followed her father. 'Dad, I'll set off on foot,' she decided. 'I think we need someone to do that; looking for hoof-prints, for a sign to show which direction they took. Is that OK?'

He nodded. 'Good idea. Check in back here as soon as you can.' He jumped back into the Land-rover and sped off up the drive in the dusty wake of the worried parents.

Mandy watched the three cars speed off. Her idea was to go down to Dorian's paddock to check for clues. But first she went to the empty stable and glanced in. No doubt Dorian had been out in the field all night in such mild weather, but she wanted to check something out.

Yes, just as I thought, she said to herself. Andi had taken Ivanhoe's tack from its hook, and a saddle too. She obviously planned to ride Dorian to freedom. Now Mandy knew she must look for heavier, firmer shoe marks; ones that showed he was carrying extra weight on his back. Quickly she ran to the paddock gate, vaulted it, and began her search.

She criss-crossed the sloping field, heading for

the stream at the bottom. For a second, she wished
James was there to help, but she was determined
to do the best she could.

She expected to find the evidence she needed
in the softer ground at the edge of the water. Sure
enough, she saw Dorian's oval-shaped prints sunk
deep into the mud, heading straight into the
shallow water and out the other side. Then they
led off up the far bank, turned left, away from the
narrow farm road, and across more fields. 'Yes!'
Mandy let out a little yelp of triumph. Her hunch
had paid off; the trail had begun.

She plunged into the stream and waded through

the cold water, without even stopping to take off her shoes.

Mandy looked carefully for the route which Andi and Dorian must have taken. All the fields were enclosed, with only one gate. So she headed across from gate to gate, careful to stop and check the telltale hoof-prints at each one. She sprinted across the middle sections of the fields, until she finally came to a halt on a road which ran along the valley side, heading up on to the moor top. Which way now? Far off, on a distant peak, Welford's Celtic cross stood out as a landmark. Mandy looked up and down the road, scanning the grass verges for more of Dorian's prints.

In the distance, from the direction of the village, she saw a dark speck on a bike hurtling down the road towards her.

'Mandy, wait!' a voice called. The bike came nearer. It was James yelling at her to stop.

'Thank heavens!' she gasped. 'Am I glad to see you!'

He joined her, breathless and windswept, swooping down the hill into the final dip, heather to one side of the road, green pastures to the other. The breeze blew the grass in silvery waves.

James told her that he'd heard from Simon what

had happened. He'd rushed along to help, and spotted Mandy heading across country.

She explained how she'd found Andi and Dorian's trail. 'But now I'm stuck. The prints fade just here. They must have gone on the road for a bit. But which way?'

James looked all round. 'I reckon they'd go where it's quietest, where there's less chance of being spotted. Up towards the moor?'

She agreed. 'Let's follow the road that way then. We'll have to watch out for more prints cutting off across the moors. OK?'

They set off again. Sooner or later, Andi and Dorian would stop for a rest. James and Mandy could hope to gain some ground, so they watched out for a sighting somewhere on these long sweeps of moorland. They could see for miles; it was a crystal-clear, bright day.

James left his bike at the point where Dorian's tracks began to cut across country again. They tramped for what seemed like several kilometres, with the rough heather pulling at their feet and ankles. They raised bees from yellow gorse flowers, and trampled bilberries underfoot in their rush to cover the ground. Still there was no sign of the runaways.

But up ahead, almost on the crest of the moor, they had to cross another tarmac road, where they came to a large, flat area covered in gravel. This was where car drivers pulled off the road to sit and look at the view. Mandy was all set to wave at the Somers family, whose van was parked there, then to head straight on. There was no time to lose. But James stopped short and ran across to their van.

Rowan Somers jumped down to meet him. The back doors stood open, and when Mandy followed James, she saw little Skye and Jason playing happily inside. They had washing-up liquid and small wire loops which they were blowing through. Their shiny bubbles floated out of the van doors, up into the blue sky. The children laughed and pointed.

'Hi!' Rowan greeted them, friendly as usual. 'You two look hot. Fancy a cold drink?'

James nodded. 'We can't stop long. We're looking for Andi and Dorian.'

Rowan's clear-eyed gaze stared steadily back. It gave nothing away. She handed them mugs full of orange juice.

'I just remembered something I meant to tell Jude earlier.' James gulped the drink. Mandy stood to one side, wondering what he was up to.

'Here's Jude now.' Rowan pointed. He was walking with the dogs up a sunny slope of grass and heather.

Jude waved a greeting. 'Jude, you know you mentioned that you were looking for work?' James reminded him.

'Still am. We're planning to go from farm to farm to see if they need extra hands. We'll find something sooner or later.'

'Well, listen,' James gabbled on. 'I just thought I'd tell you that there's some work back in Welford. It might not be what you're looking for, though.'

'We're not fussy,' Rowan told him. 'We can't afford to be.'

'It's a gardening job,' James explained. 'At a place called The Riddings. With two old ladies.'

Mandy's eyes widened. 'James, hang on a minute. Are you sure?' She couldn't imagine the eccentric Spry twins getting on with Jude and his family.

He shook his head. 'Like I said, it was just an idea.'

'Well, thanks.' Jude seemed surprised and pleased. 'It'd mean cutting back the way we've just come, but it might be worth it. I've done a bit of gardening in my time.'

'Great!' James grinned. He was ready to set off again.

'I hope it works out,' Mandy said. But privately she wasn't too optimistic about Miss Marjorie and Miss Joan hitting it off with the travellers. 'Anyway, you haven't seen Andi and Dorian this morning, have you?'

Rowan folded her arms and looked down at her bright red laced boots. 'Well,' she said doubtfully.

Mandy saw she'd put her on the spot. She would have to explain. 'You probably know that they've run away to try to save Dorian's life. But what Andi doesn't know is that my mum and dad have already worked out a plan to buy him and find a place in a donkey stud for him; a kind of rest home. We're trying to track her down so we can tell her the good news.' It all rushed out in one long sentence. Mandy ended up breathless. She was sure that Rowan and Jude knew more than they were saying.

Rowan blushed. 'Well, I suppose that's different.' She glanced at Jude.

Jude hooked his hair behind one ear and nodded. 'Andi did ask us not to say anything, but we've seen her all right. She says they'll grab Dorian if they find her, and they'll send him off for good. It'd be curtains for the poor old guy.'

He pursed his lips as he considered the problem. 'She seemed pretty uptight about it, so we agreed not to say anything.' He took a deep breath. Mandy crossed her fingers. 'But Rowan's right; this is different. We really trust you two, you know that?'

James and Mandy nodded.

'Well, like I say, we saw her. And you're about to go way off track if you keep going this way.'

'We just lost Dorian's prints.' Mandy pointed back down the road.

'Yes, you've got to go back, turn right, and take that hidden bridle-path there. That's where they were headed about an hour ago.' Jude shaded his eyes with one hand and pointed with the other. 'Andi was planning to reach Moorcliff before dark tonight. That's another thirty kilometres.'

Mandy nodded excitedly. 'Thanks, Jude! Thanks very much!' She was about to rush off when she had second thoughts. 'What time is it, James?'

He checked his watch. 'Five to twelve.'

'Hey, I think we'd better get back to Manor Farm and check in. Dad told me I should.'

James shrugged, uncertain, but Rowan stepped forward. 'Sounds like a good idea. Give them the news about Moorcliff. They can get a full search party out there before evening.' She looked at Jude and he nodded. 'Look, hop in the van with us. We'll drive you back down. It'll be quicker.'

Mandy jumped at the chance. 'Thanks. We can be there in twenty minutes.'

'Come on, then.' Jude piled them into the van. Skye and Jason giggled and cuddled up close. Jude turned in the wide gravel space and revved the engine. The battered old van chugged off along the moor road, back to Welford.

'I hope we're doing the right thing here,' Mandy whispered to James. Part of her wished they'd followed Andi and Dorian on foot. But this was more sensible; they'd let the Greenaways know what was happening and put their minds at rest. She just wished the Somers' van was faster. Its top speed was about thirty kilometres per hour, as it spluttered and coughed its way down the hillside. Meanwhile, Andi and Dorian headed in the other direction, across the wild moor top.

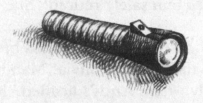

Seven

Mandy and James jumped down from the Somers'
van at the Welford crossroads. They stood and
watched it chug slowly out on to the Walton Road.
Then they quickly ran up the lane to Animal Ark.
Mandy spilled out the news to her mother.

'Let's phone Manor Farm right away,' Emily
Hope said.

But Mandy put one hand on her mum's arm as
she reached for the phone. 'Tell Mr Greenaway
where they're heading, and tell him we'd like to
buy Dorian from him at the same time!' she
pleaded. 'Then we'll know they're both going to
be safe, both Andi and Dorian. Please, Mum!'

Mrs Hope nodded. 'OK, Mandy. That's good thinking. I'll get him to agree to sell Dorian to us, so we can see him safely retired!' She dialled the number.

Mandy stood close by with bated breath.

' . . . Yes, that's right, Silvia. Mandy seems to know exactly where Andi's headed.' Mrs Hope's voice stayed calm in all emergencies. 'Look, we've finished surgery here. Why not come over and discuss what to do next? We've a little plan of our own to put to you. Yes, I'll put the coffee on!'

She put the phone down and nodded. 'Well done, you two. This looks a lot more hopeful!' She told them that Mr Hope and the Greenaways had driven round in circles all morning, without seeing a single sign of the runaways.

Mandy went to the bookcase in the lounge to fetch a local map. By the time her father, and Mr and Mrs Greenaway strode up the path, she and James had pinpointed Moorcliff and found the quickest route there. Soon everyone circled round.

'I know that village,' Dad said. 'It's out of our area, but Tony Marsden, the vet there, is a friend of mine. It's tucked away in the middle of nowhere, way off the beaten track.'

Stephen Greenaway nodded. 'I know it. There's

a pub there called The Red Lion.'

Mr Hope nodded. 'A church and a few houses, that's all.' The village sat at the foot of a sheer limestone cliff. Above that, there was a stretch of strange rocks and standing-stones, famous for their wild location. 'The locals call it The Valley of the Giants.'

Silvia looked worried. 'It sounds like a dangerous place.' She turned to Mandy. 'Are you sure Andi is making for Moorcliff?'

Mandy said she believed everything that Jude had told them. 'I thought maybe the best idea would be for everyone to drive up there and form a search party. We can set off from the village. There's plenty of time to get there by car and start looking. Andi won't expect us to arrive there before her.'

'You mean she'll be busy looking over her shoulder, expecting us to follow? So she won't realise what lies ahead,' Mr Hope thought aloud.

Mandy nodded again, then she took her mother to one side while the others studied the map. 'Mum, did you ask Mr Greenaway about buying Dorian?'

'Yes. He agreed!' Emily Hope smiled broadly.

'He promised?'

'Yes. He admits it was tough on Andi to send the old chap off to market. So that's all sorted out.'

Mandy breathed a sigh of relief. In that case, she'd do her level best to help with the search.

'Listen.' Stephen Greenaway went to stand at the Hopes' kitchen window and spoke as he looked steadily out on to the lane. 'I'm grateful for all your help. Especially to Mandy and James here; that was good thinking. But I feel that from now on we ought to crack this problem by ourselves. There's really no need to put yourselves out any more. I'm sure we can manage.' He turned, hands in pockets, smiling confidently.

'Oh, it's no trouble!' Mandy's dad assured him.

Mandy felt worried. The bigger the search party, the better, surely?

'No, look, we really want to help!' her mother put in. 'What are neighbours for? We wouldn't dream of letting you cope with this by yourselves. I know how worried you must both be!'

Silvia Greenaway spoke up. 'Oh thank you, Emily. You're sure you don't mind?' She looked and sounded relieved.

Mandy sighed. What a lot of time they were wasting, being polite. She was impatient to be off.

'Let's go and check again with Jude and Rowan,' James suggested, as the grown-ups finished their coffee. 'We've got time, haven't we?'

'I'll run you down there,' Adam Hope agreed. 'I wouldn't mind checking over what they have to say. After all, as far as we know, they were the last people to see Andi and Dorian.' He'd already arranged his route along the dale to Moorcliff, and now promised to meet up with the others there. 'Come on, you two, let's go!'

Soon they were on the move again, windows open, breeze blowing through the Land-rover, and heading for Welford. 'Where are we going exactly?' Mr Hope asked.

'The Riddings,' James said. 'Jude's gone there to look for work.'

Adam gave a low whistle. 'If you say so!' He pulled off the road and turned into the driveway of the big old house.

Sure enough, there was Jude's red van. Skye and Jason sat cross-legged on Geoffrey's perfect lawn, playing with Patch. Down the side of the house they could hear more voices.

'We don't!'

'We do!'

'Don't!'

'We do, Joan,' Miss Marjorie sighed. The old ladies were standing outside their conservatory, face to face, arms outstretched, like two colourful scarecrows. 'You know perfectly well that we do need a new gardener. We agreed. When Geoffrey left us, we said we'd find somebody else to do his work!'

Jude and Rowan stood nearby, hands behind their backs, looking puzzled and patient. Rowan raised a hand to say hello to Mandy, James and Mr Hope. But still the sisters scrapped on.

'There's a whole family of them!' Miss Joan snapped. 'Even children! And you know I can't stand strangers!'

'But Mrs Somers has offered to do our cleaning, Joan. Though Lord knows why.' Miss Marjorie sighed and glanced through the window at piles of old newspapers and years of dust. 'She seems quite keen to tidy the place up. They will park their van in our big garage and work for us here for as long as they can stand it!' She poked her sharp face even closer to her sister's. 'It'll liven the old place up, so there!' And Miss Marjorie, the boss, turned and shook hands with Jude and Rowan. Miss Joan stormed off.

'Well, I'm glad that's settled!' Marjorie Spry

said. 'Ah, Mandy!' She came over with a delighted smile. 'Let me introduce you to our new gardener, Jude Somers.'

Mandy smiled back. 'We've already met, Miss Marjorie, thanks. It's him we've come to talk to actually. You don't mind, do you?'

Miss Marjorie shook her head and smiled, then went in to sort out her sister.

James grinned broadly at the success of his plan. He gave a thumbs-up sign to Rowan. Meanwhile, Mandy asked Jude if he would mind repeating the story about Andi to her dad. 'We're going to drive up to Moorcliff now,' she told him. 'So we'd be glad if you could remember any other little detail.'

'Anything at all,' Mandy's dad said.

Jude thought carefully, biting his forefinger between a set of even, white teeth. 'Well, like I said, she was riding the old donkey down the bridle-path, heading into the next valley, towards the reservoir at Tindle. She planned to get to Moorcliff before dark.'

'Did she say what she was going to do when she got there?' Mandy asked.

'She said she knew of a place to sleep at a farm over there; a kind of youth hostel. She was hoping to find that, then head on east tomorrow.'

'What time was it when she left you?' asked Mr Hope.

'Around eleven, I think. Look,' he said, as if he had something important to say. 'I feel pretty bad about all this. I could see she was uptight about something. I think maybe I should have tried to talk her out of carrying on.'

'No chance. From what I know of Andi, she's a very determined girl!'

'That's right,' Mandy agreed. 'I don't think anyone could change her mind.'

'OK.' Jude nodded. 'Thanks.'

'No. Thank *you*!' Adam Hope shook his hand.

'We'll let you know how we get on.'

Jude watched them climb back into the Land-rover. 'I hope you find her. I wouldn't like to be out on that moor alone at night!'

His words echoed in Mandy's thoughts. The journey up to Moorcliff was bound to be tense. The road was narrow and twisting, across some of the wildest, emptiest stretches of moorland in all of England.

They arrived at the village green in Moorcliff just after three o'clock. One side of the deep valley already lay in shadow, the other in bright sunshine. Mandy spotted Stephen Greenaway's car waiting for them in the small carpark at The Red Lion. Opposite the pub was a church with a squat grey tower, and beside that a row of low stone cottages, with moss growing on their long, sloping rooves. There was no one on the village green; only a solitary black cat stalking through the grass. Behind them loomed the steep white cliff after which the village was named.

Stephen Greenaway beckoned them across, map in hand. 'Any news?' he yelled.

'First off, we have to look for a farm bunkhouse,' Mr Hope answered. 'Maybe someone should wait there to see if Andi shows up. The problem is, we don't have the name of the farm.'

Mandy scoured the village for signs of life. 'Let me go and ask in that little shop!' she suggested. She ran over the green to the end house in the row of cottages. She'd spotted a sign over the door saying 'Newsagent'. She dived inside and soon emerged. 'It's Bridge Farm Bunkhouse!' she announced. 'Along the riverside, turn right at the stone bridge, then first house on the left, up a long lane.'

The whole group followed her directions, but only the Greenaways went ahead on foot, up the track to the square farm building. Mandy and the others agreed to wait by the bridge, keeping an eye open and deciding how to split up. They wanted to go off looking for Andi and Dorian before evening began to draw in, to make sure they didn't get lost on the way through the bleak Valley of the Giants.

'I reckon we've got two or three hours to search,' Emily Hope said. 'Then we should meet up back here again to reconsider.'

'We'll find her!' James promised. 'She can't just vanish into thin air, can she?'

Soon Stephen and Silvia Greenaway returned.

'Mrs Russell, the farmer, says she'll keep an eye open for Andi. We've told her what to expect.'

'You mean a tired girl and a stubborn old donkey?' Mrs Hope tried to lighten things. 'Not easy to miss, when you think about it.'

'Don't you believe it.' Stephen Greenaway scanned the horizon in every direction. 'When Andi decides to do something, she does it properly. Including disappearing!' He pointed to a hillside strewn with dark rocks. 'That's the bridle-path coming down the moorside from the direction of Welford,' he said. It was already in deep shadow. 'It's the Valley of the Giants. That's where I think we should head for, then fan out and start the search.'

Everyone agreed, and the tramp through the heather began again. They criss-crossed the slope between high rocks. Mandy smelt the peat underfoot and felt the ferns brush against her legs. She screwed up her eyes and gazed around. For miles ahead there was nothing but rocks and moorland, the dark horizon and the eggshell blue sky.

Two hours later, when they finally scrambled to the top and looked down on acre after acre of open countryside, their hopes sank. If a girl on a donkey had been anywhere nearby, anywhere within say fifteen or twenty kilometres, they'd have spotted her by now. 'Not a single hoof-print!' Mandy sighed. She felt exhausted. James sat next to her on a flat rock and shoved a hand through his hair. 'I never thought it would be this hard!' she moaned.

He agreed. 'I guess she changed her mind and went off in another direction.'

'Oh no!' Mandy thought of all the time they'd wasted on the wrong trail. Andi and Dorian could be many kilometres away by now, heading south or north. Who could tell?

Reluctantly everyone agreed they should head back down into the village. 'I'll stay there,' Mr Greenaway volunteered. His face was drawn, his voice quiet. 'I'll stop over at Bridge Farm, just in case Andi finally turns up. You never know, she might have come by a different route.'

'I'll stay with you,' Mr Hope offered.

But Mr Greenaway asked him to take Silvia home. 'There's got to be someone at the house, in case Andi shows up there. One person ought to be enough here.' He squeezed his wife's shoulder. 'Try not to worry too much.'

She took a deep breath. 'If there's no sign of

Andi when I get back home, I'm going to telephone the police.'

He nodded. 'OK, do what you think is best.
Here's the farm telephone number. Ring me if
there's any news. Now, off you go. I'll scout around
here until it finally gets dark. We'll just have to
keep our fingers crossed.'

'I've had mine crossed all day!' Mandy whispered
to James. There was a pink glow in the sky as the
sun settled into the branches of the trees in the
churchyard. She thought of Andi trekking with
Dorian across the empty spaces, miserable and
alone.

No one spoke much as they split off from Stephen
Greenaway and drove in the Land-rover out of the
sleepy village. By the time they reached Welford,
dusk had fallen. Everyone's thoughts were fixed
on the lost pair.

Emily Hope asked her husband to stop at
Animal Ark. She wanted to drop Mandy and James
there. 'Wait inside,' she told them gently. 'We'll
drive Silvia down to Manor Farm. Dad will drop
me off there and then he'll drive straight back
here. OK?'

Mandy nodded. Her mum squeezed her hand.

Then the car was gone, down the lane out of sight. Mandy and James, leg-weary and footsore, trudged up the path and opened the door.

'All for nothing!' James sighed. 'What shall we do now?'

Mandy flopped in a chair by the kitchen table. 'Don't ask me. It looks like it's up to the police from now on!' She gathered her last scrap of energy and took some lettuce leaves from the vegetable rack. 'I'm just going out to feed the rabbits,' she told him. 'It won't take me long.' She walked through the surgery, a short cut into the back garden. The cool air soothed her as she trod across the grass.

'Mandy!' James's voice cut through the still air.

She dropped the bundle of leaves. 'What is it?' She ran back towards the house. James's shout had come from the direction of the front door. She could hear a thumping, rattling, stamping noise. She turned the corner. Dorian!

The donkey kicked at the door. A deep, chesty sound warned them he was getting impatient. He tossed his head as Mandy ran up to him. James flung the door wide open and ran out.

'Andi?' he shouted. 'Where are you?'

There was no reply.

'Here, boy! Steady!' Mandy reached out for his bridle, but he reared up and brayed. His loose saddle slipped sideways, stirrups swinging. 'Oh, Dorian, where's Andi?' Mandy pleaded. 'What are you doing back here all by yourself? I wish you could tell us!'

James tried to reach out and catch the donkey by a length of rope coiled round his saddle, but he too had to back off. Dorian's hooves were up, pawing the air. He charged off down the drive, then turned to look at them.

'Dorian!' Mandy said again.

He trotted up. Again she tried to catch him. He tossed his head, his eyes rolled, he trotted away down the drive.

'James, he's trying to tell us where Andi is!' Mandy gasped. 'Oh, clever boy! Steady! We understand!' She turned to James. 'I think she must be in trouble.'

They stared at the riderless donkey. There could be no other explanation.

'Wait, I'll grab a torch!' Mandy said. 'It'll be dark soon.' She dashed into the house then rushed out again, torch in hand. 'OK, Dorian, lead on!' she told him.

Up went the donkey's head, ready to canter on.

Their legs ached, every muscle groaned at the effort, and night was falling. But Dorian had come to tell them that Andi was in bad trouble. They were the only ones who knew. Grimly, they followed him across fields, heading for the distant Celtic cross, over the moorside towards the Valley of the Giants.

Eight

'Are you OK?' Mandy perched on top of a stone wall and glanced back at James. Dorian stood on the road, snorting impatiently. Half an hour had gone by and they'd reached the top of the moorside. They were exhausted, and dusk had settled in a grey mist.

'Yes, hang on a sec. I've got something in my shoe.' He breathed heavily as he bent forward to see it, but Dorian wasn't going to let them waste any time. Already he had trotted ahead, his mind set on taking them to Andi. Soon he veered off to the right, down the same bridle-path as before.

'Where are we now?' James ran alongide Mandy,

using his arm to shield his face from overhanging hazel bushes.

'We're heading down towards Tindle. See, there's the lake!' Mandy pointed into the valley bottom. The smooth stretch of water gleamed silver under the full moon. 'Dorian seems to know exactly where he's going, no problem.' She ducked under more bushes and took the torch from her back pocket. Its dim yellow light lit the patch of rough grass and heather just below their feet.

'That's better!' James ran grimly on. 'Let's just hope he's got a good sense of direction.'

'Of course he has; look!'

Twenty metres ahead, Dorian stopped. He raised his head and twitched his long ears. The path split three different ways, but he chose the one that led downhill towards the water. Mandy and James followed. Their torchlight bobbed across the rough surface.

Dorian cantered ahead, his heavy hooves startling pheasants. Rabbits darted into their burrows. Dorian ploughed on.

'I reckon Andi must be somewhere down there by the water,' James told her. 'By the look of Dorian's loose saddle, she had a fall.'

'And once she was off, for some reason she couldn't get back up again. Is that what you mean?'

James nodded. 'So he came to fetch us.'

'Whoa! Good boy!' The donkey's flanks were beginning to heave. For a moment the darkness seemed to confuse him. He stopped by a wooden stile and looked all round. Then he caught the gleam of the water once more and headed on. 'Come on!' Mandy said. 'Maybe we're nearly there!'

The lake stretched up the valley; a long, thin ribbon of water. The hillside beyond rose steep and rocky. By now it was pitch black. Sure-footedly Dorian picked his way along the water's edge. He turned his head to keep Mandy and James in view, but he moved swiftly until he came to a narrow wooden bridge over a stream. Here he stood still once more and sniffed the air.

'Listen!' Mandy swung the torch up the rocky slope. 'Did you hear that?'

'No. What?'

'I thought someone called out!'

Dorian nodded and clattered off the bridge, up the slope. He was built to climb these steep, rocky surfaces. He strode with ease from one flat rock to another. Mandy and James found it more difficult. Slowly they heaved themselves upwards, sticking close to the side of the stream, past waterfalls that fell for two or three metres then bounced on to rocks. The water splashed and roared. Mandy used the torch to search for hand and footholds. The climb grew steep and difficult. 'Wait for us, Dorian!' she called.

'I thought I heard something!' James grabbed her arm. 'What was that?'

Another cry travelled down the hillside, faint and muffled. Mandy felt the hairs at the back of her neck prickle. 'Come on,' she urged. 'That must be Andi! She's calling for help.'

Dorian stood just ahead of them, on a rock which jutted over the stream. He was a silhouette against the midnight blue sky as he put back his head and brayed.

Andi must have heard him. 'Is anyone there?' she cried. 'I'm down here! I can't move! Help!'

Mandy's heart thumped, then missed a beat. The voice sounded as if it came from the depths of the earth; somewhere deep down. Now Dorian had found his bearings again. He blundered through the undergrowth until he came to a deep crack in the rock. His hooves clattered to a standstill. He stood perched at the edge of a crevice, about a metre wide, that plunged down into darkness.

'Help!'

'She's down there!' Mandy flicked the torch in the direction of the hole. It was a narrow, sheer drop. Dorian stamped and pawed the ground. 'Andi!' she yelled. 'It's me, Mandy! Can you hear me?'

'Yes!' A voice came back, sobbing with relief. 'Is Dorian there? Is he all right?'

'He's here, and he's fine. What about you?' Mandy sounded calm, but she stared at James in dismay. The torch was too weak to light up the crevice. They could see only the jagged rock-face, small ferns, tree roots and broken branches.

'I'm OK. One arm hurts. I'm cold and wet. There's water dripping down here!' Her voice shook. 'I don't think you'll be able to get me out by yourself.'

'Andi, listen. It's me, James. I'm here too. How far down did you fall?' He lay flat on his stomach and tried to peer down into the darkness. Then he pointed out a pale, blurred shape. Mandy swung the torch. Andi's blonde hair and white face stared back up at them. 'There she is! She's about four metres down on some kind of ledge!'

'Thank heavens you're here!' Andi cried.

James scrambled to his feet. 'She's right. I don't think we can get her out by ourselves. But there's a house along there. Can you see the light?'

Mandy nodded. She steadied Dorian, who pushed at her with his nose. He urged her to do something to help get Andi out.

'I'll run over there to phone an ambulance. You stay here and wait!' James was gone before she had time to think.

It was Mandy's turn to lie down on the ledge, just above Andi's resting place. 'Did you hear that? James has gone for help. It won't be long now!' She shone the torch on Andi. Her fall had been broken by a tree trunk jammed against the rock and wedged there for good. 'You were lucky!' she whispered. She heard her own voice echo. Small pebbles rattled and fell down the crevice.

'You wouldn't say that if you were down here!' Andi said. 'How long have I been here? It seems like ages!'

'OK, don't worry. We'll soon have you out!' But Mandy could see that it was impossible to reach down and pull the injured girl to safety. They would have to wait for James.

'My legs are numb and one arm's useless. Mandy, I don't know how much longer I can hang on!' Andi cried. 'I feel as if I'm slipping off!'

'No! Stay still. I'll think of something!' She leapt to her feet. 'Listen, Andi, you know there's this length of rope round Dorian's saddle? I'm going to see if I can do anything with that.'

'OK, but it's not very long,' Andi warned her. Her voice seemed to fade, as if her strength was failing. 'I brought it for emergencies. Yes, give it a try!'

Mandy took the rope and began to make a loop at one end. It had to be big enough for Andi to slip her head and shoulders through. Setting the torch on the ground, she worked quickly in its shaft of light. Soon the rope was ready. 'Andi, I'm going to hang on to this end and send the noose down to you, OK? You'll have to see if you can grab hold of it and wriggle into it!'

She held the torch now and watched as the rope snaked down into the dark space. 'Please let it be long enough!' she whispered. She craned over the edge, with Dorian close behind her. His breath was hot on her neck.

Andi reached and grabbed the loop. 'Got it!'

'Good! Now wriggle into it, if you can!'

Andi did as she was told. She was awkward and slow because her left arm hung useless. Her face showed the pain she must be feeling. 'Done it!' she gasped at last.

'Well done! Now if you topple off, at least you won't fall all the way to the bottom. I'm here to stop you!' Mandy sounded more confident than she felt. She gazed up at the track where James had run, towards the house by the dam. 'Hurry up!' she begged in a whisper, through clenched teeth. She felt her knuckles tighten over her end of the rope. Would Andi last out? Looking at Dorian, she began to pray.

The donkey seemed to understand. He'd watched the rope being lowered. He'd seen Mandy take the strain at this end. Now he had his own idea. He came close and put his head on Mandy's shoulder, nudging sideways at her face.

'Not now, Dorian. I can't let go!' At first she thought he wanted her to stroke him and tell him what a clever old thing he was. She dug her heels against a ridge in the rock and leant backwards, taking the strain. 'Are you still OK down there?' she yelled.

The answer came back, faint and unsure.

Again Dorian nuzzled Mandy's face. He jerked his neck away, then offered his nose again. His bridle jingled and the red nylon rein swung forward across her shoulder. He stood patiently waiting.

'Oh, I see!' At last Mandy got the idea. She took the rein in one hand. 'Listen, Andi! Dorian's offering to help. He's strong, isn't he? He seems to think he can pull you clear. What do you think?'

'Yes!' Andi gasped. 'Good idea! Do it, Mandy! Do it quick!'

She took the thick rope and threaded it through Dorian's halter ring. She tied it securely. He edged away from the drop, pulling the rope tight. 'Whoa!' Mandy craned forward, one hand on his shoulder. 'Ready, Andi?'

There was no reply. Mandy could see a blurred

shape slumped forward. But Andi was still conscious. She glanced up and nodded weakly.

'OK,' Mandy said softly to the old donkey. 'It's all up to you. When I give the word, pull slowly and gently. Ready?'

Dorian stood steadfast, awaiting the order.

Mandy took one last look down the gap. 'Steady, boy!' She took a deep breath. 'Now walk on!'

Dorian pulled. Pebbles dislodged and dropped with a hollow rattle. The rope strained and creaked. Andi shifted from her wedged tree trunk and hung suspended in mid-air. 'Grab a handhold!' Mandy urged. She turned back to Dorian. 'Walk on, boy!' she urged. 'Gently, gently!' Slowly he eased Andi out of the crevice.

At last the fingertips of her right hand could grab the ledge. 'I've got you!' Mandy cried. She felt the sweat start out on her brow. She saw Dorian's sides begin to heave. 'Steady, boy!' she warned. Andi's hand grasped hers. 'OK, Dorian, now one last pull!'

Andi's shoulders appeared at ground level. 'Now use your legs. Find a foothold!' Mandy said. Even with Dorian taking most of the weight, she was in danger of being pulled too close to the edge herself.

'I can't. My legs are numb!' Andi cried out, terrified. But the fresh breeze seemed to revive her. She kicked against the rock-face and found a ledge. Gradually Dorian heaved her up, centimetre by centimetre.

Mandy hooked both arms under Andi's armpits and pulled. 'Walk on, Dorian!' This was it; the final heave.

Dorian responded. Andi came clear. Mandy staggered backwards with her as she found herself on firm ground once more. Then they stood and hugged each other, leaning against Dorian, gasping with relief.

Now they would have to wait in the dark as the light of the torch was beginning to fade. Mandy put her own jacket round Andi's shoulders. She shivered with cold and shock. Moonlight showed cuts and bruises on her hands and face. She sat forward, hugging her knees, waiting for the ambulance.

It came, with a police escort, lights blazing along the lakeside, sirens screaming. Figures leapt out of the cars and ran down the slope towards them. Mandy stood waving both arms, calling loudly. Dorian rolled his eyes and skittered at the dreadful noise.

Four men trampled the undergrowth. They brought a stretcher, medical bags, ropes, lights.

'Over here!' Mandy yelled.

They ran, out of control, down the steep slope.

Dorian reared up in fright. He hated the sirens and the shadowy, hurtling shapes. Two of the men scrambled to a standstill. They shoved the donkey to one side.

'Oh, watch out!' Andi cried.

Dorian missed his footing and slipped. He crashed back towards the water, down into the waterfall, scrambling at the wet rock-face, crashing and slipping out of sight.

'Mandy, find Dorian for me!' Andi pleaded as she was carried off.

As the medical team took expert care of Andi, Mandy ran to the waterfall. She felt the spray on her face, the water splashed over her hands as she knelt to look. She thought she saw Dorian, way below by the wooden bridge, limping painfully on three legs. But perhaps it was a shadow. She heard nothing except the roar of the water. She called his name.

Then her mother and father came scrambling down the slope with James. They flung a coat round her, told her she must hurry to the ambulance. She resisted. 'Where's Dorian?' she repeated over and over.

'Never mind now, love,' Mum whispered. 'Let's get you both to hospital.' She held her by the shoulder as they climbed to the road.

'James, you've got to find Dorian!' she gasped. But she was exhausted, confused, almost collapsing with the strain of the last half hour. 'He saved Andi's life!'

They all promised to do their best. The important thing was to get the girls to hospital. Tomorrow they'd look for the donkey. Andi was the person they had to worry about first.

Nine

Andi was kept in hospital overnight. Her left arm was broken above the elbow. Her cuts and bruises weren't serious, but the doctor warned her that she would be stiff and sore. He examined Mandy and then allowed her to go home. She and James looked in on Andi's ward just before midnight.

She sat up in bed, looking pale and serious. Stephen and Silvia Greenaway were at her side. She smiled at Mandy. 'Thanks. You two were brilliant.'

Mandy blushed. She didn't see that she and James had done anything out of the ordinary. 'Will you still be able to play tennis?' she asked.

Andi nodded. 'Yes. My right arm is the one that counts, thank goodness.'

'No need to think about that just yet,' Mr Greenaway said. He looked strained, but tried to put on a brave face. 'We just want you fit and well!'

Mandy stood at the end of the clean, white bed. She felt Andi was avoiding the only question she really wanted to ask. 'Listen, Andi . . . about Dorian,' she began.

'You didn't find him, did you?' Andi leaned forward, grasping the sheet.

'No, not yet. But we'll be out there looking as soon as it gets light. Don't worry.'

Andi sighed and looked down.

'He'll be OK, you'll see. You know Dorian!' Mandy felt he could take care of himself better than anyone.

'We'll go back to the waterfall and start looking,' James promised.

'Let me know as soon as you hear anything!'

Silvia leaned over and took her daughter's hand. 'Now it's time for Adam and Emily to take these two home, and for you to get some sleep,' she said gently.

Mrs Hope agreed to run Mandy and James over

to Tindle before surgery next morning. She smiled as she dropped them off on the road by the waterfall. 'I'll call in at some of the farms on the way back,' she promised. 'I'll ask people to keep a lookout for a donkey. I expect he's just rested overnight and is heading for home this very moment!' She smiled again, then drove off, having made Mandy promise to ring Animal Ark as soon as she had any news.

James and Mandy made their way down to the scene of the previous night's accident. In the dull light of an overcast sky, the crevice looked shadowy and dangerous. It was half-hidden by bushes and ferns; easy to see how Dorian had stumbled and thrown Andi off his back. The slope was steep and the ground scattered with loose rocks. Beyond the crevice the stream fell and splashed over big ledges, throwing up white spray. The banks were bright green with slippery moss.

'OK?' Mandy asked James. She prepared to descend, close to the water's edge.

He nodded. 'We should be getting good at this by now.'

Mandy bit her tongue. She had a secret fear; a picture of Dorian vanishing over the edge of the rock into the dark water. She remembered the silence after his fall.

'Let's check for hoof-prints!' James was eager to begin. He pushed aside small, overhanging branches, then seized a long, straight stick to beat back the bushes. He found he had to cling on to roots and find safe footholds on the steep slope down.

Mandy swallowed hard before she followed him. *I hope we don't find Dorian anywhere near here!* she said to herself. She dreaded finding him badly injured, or worse, at the foot of some sheer drop.

'Not here!' James reported as he reached the wooden footbridge at the bottom of the slope. He looked back up at Mandy. 'I suppose that's a relief in a way!'

She jumped down to join him and smiled. 'Great minds think alike! Come on!'

They began to scout around on level ground, looking for fresh signs. But they found only old prints of the donkey's hooves climbing up the slope with Andi on his back. There were none at all showing Dorian heading home.

'Where are you, Dorian?' James shouted out loud. He turned to Mandy. 'He can't just vanish!'

But they spent a long morning searching the

lakeside and the fields and farms to either side of
the old bridle-path. No luck; Dorian was nowhere
to be found.

'No, sorry,' the old farmers said one after
another. 'That nice young woman vet called in
earlier this morning, asking after the old chap. I
told her I'd keep a sharp lookout.'

Mandy and James thanked them and ran on,
quick as they could.

'I've got better things to do with my time than
look out for a daft old donkey!' Dora Janeki
snapped. She was a thin, bad-tempered woman
who lived on a lonely farm next to the moorside.
'I've got shearing starting tomorrow, and fifty
sheep to round up in the top fields!' She stamped
off.

Mandy shrugged. Discouraged, she and James
made their way back home.

'No luck?' Adam Hope met them in the doorway
to the surgery. He was going down to Manor Farm
to help the Greenaways pack. He told them that
Silvia and Andi were coming to stay at Animal
Ark for a few days, once Andi got out of hospital.
'She needs somewhere to rest and get over this
business of the fall,' he explained. 'It's shaken her
up pretty badly. And of course they have to be out

of their house by tomorrow. So Mum thought it
would help if Andi could stay close by, just until
she's fit and well again.'

'Oh, good.' Mandy nodded. But she felt bitterly
disappointed after their failed search. Nothing
would give her a greater thrill than announcing
to Andi that Dorian had turned up. But where
was he? How could he disappear so completely
and without trace?

'Cheer up. Have some lunch, then it won't feel
so bad,' Dad said. He turned and went off whistling
quietly down the lane.

They dragged themselves indoors. 'Don't worry,
we'll try again this afternoon,' James promised.
'We'll keep on looking until we find him!'

'I'm glad I'm not in this by myself,' Mandy told
him. James never let her down. He was always
there. She couldn't wish for a better friend.

He blushed and shoved his hair back from his
forehead. 'I'd better ring my mum and tell her
not to expect me back home this afternoon,' he
replied, practical as ever.

Three more days went by. Stephen Greenaway's
new football team needed him to start work, so
he left Mrs Greenaway to look after Andi. When

Andi came out of hospital, her arm in plaster, she and her mother went to stay with the Hopes at Animal Ark. Every spare moment, during those long midsummer days, Mandy and James would spend combing the hillsides, returning to Tindle, searching every square metre of ground. Each time they came home disappointed.

'We're not giving up!' Mandy promised the older girl one afternoon, as they sat in Mandy's cosy bedroom surrounded by the faces of beautiful, fluffy kittens, thoroughbred Arabians and friendly golden labradors. They all stared down from her glossy posters. 'We're going to find Dorian if it's the last thing we do!'

Andi smiled. She was still pale and weak from the accident. 'The thing is, I'm sure Dorian wouldn't just go missing that night. He'd get home if he possibly could!' Her voice sounded shaky and afraid. 'You know what he's like; he can't keep his nose out of anything! He's not happy unless he's got someone to talk to!' She sighed and gazed out of the window, down the hill towards the village. 'Oh, Mandy, where do you think he's gone? What's happened to him?'

Mandy could only shake her head. But that afternoon she cycled over to James's house to talk him into another search. She wanted to go in the direction of Walton, the large town down the dale where James and Mandy both went to school. They must think again, begin to look further afield.

James agreed. 'OK, it can't do any harm. Let's ask down in the village too.' They set off together.

'I should think everyone from here to York already knows we're looking for Dorian!' Mandy said as they rode along. 'Still, we can check if you like.'

But in the McFarlanes' post office and all down the main street, they met with the same answer; 'No, sorry, love. I haven't seen him. I'll keep my ears open, though, and let you know if I do!'

Mandy sighed. 'Let's try Jude and Rowan. They know everything that's going on round here. We're heading in the right direction, in any case.' They were cycling along the flat stretch of Walton Road. Somehow Mandy felt that the travelling family would help to cheer them up, whether or not they had news of Dorian.

But once more they were out of luck. They rang the doorbell at The Riddings, and stood admiring the work that Jude had done to the garden. Perfect pink roses bloomed on neat bushes, the lawn looked smooth as a bowling green.

The door burst open. 'Come in, come in!' Marjorie Spry beamed at them as she ushered them into the hall.

The heaped piles of yellow newspapers were gone, shelves and windowsills were shiny and clean. Even the floor sparkled, and everywhere there was a smell of lavender polish.

'Wow!' James couldn't disguise his surprise. Last time he'd seen inside this place, there was dust and cobwebs everywhere.

'All thanks to Mrs Somers!' Miss Marjorie said proudly. 'Joan pretends not to like it, but I know better!'

'Is Rowan around? We'd like to speak to her, please.' Mandy thought she'd better come to the point. 'We're looking for that donkey again.'

'The one out in our conservatory?' Miss Marjorie's eyes widened.

'What, now?' For a second Mandy's heart leapt. The Spry twins were eccentric enough to be keeping Dorian quietly hidden in their conservatory.

'No, dear. Last week, wasn't it? You know!' Miss Marjorie put her bird-like head to one side and sighed. 'In any case, you're too late to speak to Mrs Somers, I'm afraid.'

'Too late?' James looked round the spruce house, through all the open doors. 'Do you mean that Jude and Rowan have gone?'

'They left us!' Miss Joan cackled from the library. She'd been eavesdropping. Now she sailed into view, head up, cradling Patch in one arm. 'Gone! Left us in peace at last!'

'Oh!' Disappointed, Mandy began to back out of the door. 'Sorry to bother you. We didn't realise.' Joan Spry must have been too much even for easy-going Jude and his family to put up with.

'No, no, dear, it's not like that!' Miss Marjorie seized her arm and dragged her back inside. 'We like them very much!'

'We don't!' Miss Joan contradicted.

'We do! Now, Joan, be quiet.' Miss Marjorie silenced her sister. 'What's more, and much to my surprise, *they* like us!'

'That's great!' James looked relieved. 'Where are they now, then?'

'We came to an arrangement. They've agreed to come to work for us for two days every week. But they said they missed the open road, and I must confess I don't blame them! All that fresh air! All that freedom!' Miss Marjorie glared at her twin sister. 'Freedom to go where one chooses!'

'So they go off for a few days, then come back here?' Mandy thought she understood.

'Yes, dear. At least for the summer. Whatever Mrs Ponsonby and Mrs Platt may have to say about it!' She flashed them a mischievous smile. 'That way we manage to keep our house and garden in good order, and they receive a wage from us. For the rest of the time they can come and go as they please. It's perfect!'

Mandy and James smiled happily. It was odd, but true. The Spry sisters and the Somers family were made for one another.

'And if you hurry up and chase after them,' Miss Joan said with a spiteful glance, 'you'll be able to catch up with them!'

'Why, which way did they go?' James asked.

Miss Joan sniffed. 'Up towards the Beacon.' She pointed airily to the Celtic cross on the moorside. 'Just before lunch. Shoo! Go along, hurry!' She waved them out of the house.

James and Mandy grinned at one another again as they grabbed their bikes and cycled off. They sped back through the village and up on to the moor road. The red van would be easy to spot. Mandy looked forward to meeting up with their friends. 'At least we can ask them to keep an eye open for Dorian,' she said. She liked to feel the wind in her hair, and the swoop of her bike as they dropped into a dip on the narrow, lonely road.

'Up there, look!' James pointed to the lookout spot at the crest of the next hill. Sure enough, the battered red van came into view, parked on the wide gravel area just along from the bridle-path. 'It looks pretty deserted though.' The doors were all shut up and there was no one around. Mandy and James pedalled hard uphill. 'Maybe they all went for a walk.'

Mandy came round a bend and jammed on her brakes. James swerved and skidded behind her. 'Watch out!' he yelled.

'Look!' she cried.

There was a procession coming down the road towards them. It walked into the sunshine out of the shade of a high, heathery bank. Jude Somers strode along at the head, with little Jason riding high on his shoulders. The boy waved his arms and sang. Rowan walked behind, holding Skye's hand. The little girl wore a bright lemon and pink T-shirt. Her legs were brown. The two lean dogs, Joey and Spider, ranged along the grass verge with their long, loping strides, sniffing out rabbits. And behind them, held on a loose rope, limping slightly on his left foreleg, but head up and going at a smart pace, was someone they couldn't fail to recognise.

He spotted them standing open-mouthed on the roadside. *About time too!* his bossy nod of the head suggested. *What on earth kept you?*

'Dorian!' Mandy and James shouted together. 'Where have you been?'

They ditched their bikes and ran to meet him. The children squealed with delight. Mandy flung her arms round Dorian's neck and buried her face in his soft brown coat.

James grinned at Jude. 'Where did you find him?'

'We didn't. He found us.' Jude wore a broad smile. 'We thought we'd see him on his way and help him home. You can see he's limping a bit.'

'Oh, Dorian, what happened? Oh, I'm so glad to see you!' Mandy hugged and hugged him. She was beside herself with happiness. 'We were afraid you were dead!'

Dorian nudged her away to arm's length and gave her a sideways looks. *Don't make a fuss!*

It was true that he was a little the worse for wear – dusty and much thinner – but it would take more than a little fall down a wet rock to finish him off. *Now let's get on, shall we?* he suggested with an impatient toss of his head.

'Here!' Rowan laughed handing Mandy the halter rope. 'He's all yours!'

Mandy felt as though she would burst with joy as Dorian took charge and limped ahead. He was in a hurry to get home at last.

Ten

Dorian limped through Welford at the head of the colourful procession of children, grown-ups, dogs and bikes. It was teatime. Ernie Bell and Walter Pickard gave them a wave and a smile from their garden gates. 'Well done. We knew you'd sort it out in the end!' they called.

Mrs Ponsonby teetered on the step outside the McFarlanes' post office. She scooped precious Pandora up into her arms and tutted loudly at the sight of the Somers family.

But Joey and Spider went over and wagged their long, thin tails at Toby. The mongrel wagged his in return. 'Oh . . . oh well, Pandora, I suppose you'd better say hello too!' Gingerly Mrs Ponsonby put the dog down. The Pekinese gave Joey and Spider a gracious welcome. 'Nice doggies!' Mrs Ponsonby proclaimed. She gave Mandy a royal wave.

Mandy smiled back and followed close on Dorian's heels. He turned swiftly into their lane and gathered speed, in spite of his limp.

Rowan laughed. 'He's in charge!' They almost had to run to keep up.

Animal Ark was in sight. 'As usual!' Mandy gasped. 'The trouble is, I'm sure he thinks he's going home!'

James threw his bike down on to the grass verge. 'Hadn't we better try to stop him?'

'Yes, there's a terrible shock in store for him at Manor Farm.'

'Have the new people moved in yet?'

Mandy nodded. 'As soon as the Greenaways moved out. We saw the furniture van go down the lane two or three days ago. We don't even know who the new owners are yet. One thing is for sure; Dorian's in for a big disappointment when he finally arrives!'

'Whoa, boy!' James ran ahead and tried to rein the donkey back so they could explain.

But Dorian had got it into his head that he was going home. He strained at the rein and forged ahead, straight past Animal Ark, heading for Lilac Cottage.

'Who said donkeys weren't stubborn?' James complained. His arms felt as if they were being pulled out of their sockets as Dorian dragged him along.

Mandy ran alongside. 'He's not stubborn. He just knows his own mind, that's all.'

Skye and Jason trotted and skipped to keep up. They clapped their hands and laughed. Jude and Rowan strode along to keep them company. 'This is something I just *have* to see!' Jude said with a grin.

'Hang on, I'd better go and warn Andi!' James said. He was red in the face from the effort of trying to control Dorian. 'She'll have to come and explain!' Quickly he slipped back up the drive to Animal Ark.

But Dorian gathered speed. He trotted past the neat hedges of Lilac Cottage, at the head of the procession. They sped on, past the small common where the Somers had once parked, down the narrow, twisting lane to Manor Farm.

'Listen, Dorian!' Mandy said, out of breath and

growing more alarmed. 'Andi doesn't live there any more! She's at our house!'

But Dorian took no notice. His head was up, his ears forward. The end was in sight.

'Oh dear!' Mandy hesitated at the gate as Dorian broke free and nipped down the long drive to Manor Farm. A glance to the rear showed her that James was catching them up with Andi, who half-laughed, half-cried as she stumbled along with her arm in its sling. Ahead, Dorian broke into a canter. He'd spotted his old paddock. His stable door stood half-open.

'Come on!' Jude insisted. 'We'd better follow him and see what we can do to help.' The procession straggled down the drive.

Dorian cantered on into the stable yard. His enormous bray echoed through the valley. *I'm back!* The new family came running out of the house. Mandy saw a boy of about ten, then a man and a woman, all standing open-mouthed in the stable yard.

Dorian stared at them with a frown. He pawed the yard. He glanced towards the stable, then trotted forward. He began to nudge the nervous looking woman to one side. He peered through the doorway into the house.

'Oh no!' Mandy groaned. 'They're going to chuck him out!' They'd arrived at the farm too late.

'No, just watch this!' Rowan pointed. She put out a hand to stop James and Andi from overtaking them and leaping in to restrain the donkey. 'I'm sure Dorian can handle this!'

Dorian backed a little way out of the doorway. He looked down his nose at the new family.

'Don't worry, I'll take care of this!' The angry father, a stout, grey-haired man still dressed in the suit he'd worn to work that day, began to stride towards Mandy's motley group.

'Oh, Mum!' the fair-haired boy protested. He approached Dorian, head on one side.

'Jack, keep away! He could turn nasty!' The mother stared anxiously at Dorian.

Dorian lowered his large head and nuzzled the boy's side. He nosed into his pockets.

'He winked! Did you see that? Dorian just winked at us!' Mandy was certain it was true.

'Shh!' Andi held her breath. 'I think he's decided that he likes them!'

'He's just being friendly, that's all. Mum, have we got a carrot?' Jack laughed at the feel of Dorian's soft nose. The woman disappeared into the house and returned holding a large carrot. 'Hold it in the flat of your hand, Mum. That's right. He won't hurt you. He's a soft old thing. There, see!' Dorian snaffled the carrot. He crunched it with evident relish, showing them his big front teeth.

'Well!' Jack's mother declared. 'He certainly knows how to get what he wants!' She stood, a smile hovering on her lips. Then she stretched out a nervous hand to say hello.

'Whose donkey is this?' the father demanded. His anger was beginning to fade, but he looked confused.

Andi stepped forward. "Hello. I'm afraid he's mine. Well, he *was* mine but now we have to find him a new home.' She choked over the words.

'You're the girl who's just moved out of here, aren't you?' The man's face lit up with recognition. 'You're Andi Greenaway, the young tennis player! My, it looks as if you've been in the wars!' He looked at her injured arm, her cuts and bruises. Then he frowned and scratched his cheek, looking round at Dorian. 'I suppose he thinks you still live here . . .'

Mandy and James stood waiting in the stable yard as everything slotted into place for the new owners of Manor Farm. Dorian glanced round at them from his position in the doorway. He bared his teeth in a smile. Jack meanwhile had flung his arms round the donkey's neck. 'Mum, we can keep him, can't we? This is his home, after all! He's come back and we can't just send him away again!'

Mandy grasped Andi by the hand. 'The cunning old thing! I bet Dorian knew what he was doing all along!'

But Jack's mum looked doubtful. 'Oh, I don't know, dear. We've already taken on an awful lot!'

Mandy couldn't bear to hear any more. 'At least he's safe!' she breathed to Andi. 'Though goodness knows where he's been these past few days!'

'I know!' Andi gabbled out an explanation about a phone call they'd had at Animal Ark just a few minutes before Dorian had led the procession down the lane. 'It was Dora Janeki. She told us she'd just had to chase an old donkey from her hay barn up on the hill. He must have been there for days, she said, and she didn't sound too pleased about it!'

'Uh-oh!' James laughed. 'Dorian would have to choose *her* barn, wouldn't he? The only person who refused to help us look in the first place!'

Andi nodded. 'Well, Mr Hope reckoned he'd

probably got as far as he could that night on his injured leg. Then he realised he would have to rest until the sprain healed. Donkeys always know when they've reached their limit. It just so happened it was Mrs Janeki's barn. And lucky in one way, because there was hay for him to eat. But then today she went in to stack some wool from shearing, and came face to face with Dorian! Like I say, she wasn't too pleased. She sent him packing.'

'Poor Dorian!' Mandy grinned. He'd met his match with Dora Janeki. She gazed across to where he stood, ears twitching, keen to join in the conversation about his future.

' . . . Only one little donkey!' Jack pleaded.

Dorian sniggered and nodded.

'Little!' His father's eyebrows shot up as he stared Dorian in the eye. 'How much hay do you think he gets through in one week? Who's going to pay for it?'

'But we can't throw him out! He's got nowhere to go!' Jack pointed out in a high, strained voice. 'This is his home!'

Dorian sighed.

The waiting was agony for Mandy. 'At least he's safe!' she repeated. 'But wouldn't it be wonderful if Dorian got his own way at last?'

As if there's any doubt! he suggested with a knowing glance.

'Oh, all right!' Jack's mum said at last. 'I suppose he is rather sweet.'

Dorian jerked his head and snorted.

'Can he stay?' Jack insisted.

'Yes, he can stay at Manor Farm!' his father said.

Andi ran forward with a delighted cry. Mandy had to stop herself from running forward too. She stayed with James and the Somers family. Dorian gently broke free from his new owners and trotted to greet Andi. *No need to worry your head about me,*

he said with a little bob of his head.

Andi's face was wreathed in smiles as she hugged him and rested her cheek against his neck.

'Now she's happy, she can go off and play tennis,' James said. 'And be a champion.'

'She can come back and visit Dorian whenever she wants!' Mandy added.

The donkey stepped forward to rattle the stable door. He knew it was time to rest. He looked round at them, paused on the doorstep of his old home. He took a nip of hay from his old haynet, and sighed as he wandered in, home at last!

Mandy grinned. 'Trust Dorian!' she said. 'He must have been born under a lucky star!'

The donkey turned and looked her straight in the eye. *Luck has nothing to do with it!* he said with a wink. And Mandy suspected that he'd planned every move!

Another Hodder Children's book

KITTENS IN THE KITCHEN

Lucy Daniels

Not everyone cares for animals as much as Mandy does. When a stray cat gives birth in Mr Williams' kitchen, he is absolutely furious. He has no sympathy for the mother, and wants nothing to do with the kittens – they have to go.

Can Mandy find homes for four newborn kittens in just one week?

BADGER IN THE BASEMENT

Lucy Daniels

James leads Mandy to a badger sett he's been watching, but they find the sett has been deliberately destroyed! Even worse, they find an orphaned badger cub near by.

Can Mandy and James find out who has done such a terrible, cruel thing? And will they find a home for the young badger?

CUB IN THE CUPBOARD

Lucy Daniels

Mandy and James are horrified when they discover a mother fox caught in a cruel trap – so is the rest of Welford! But somebody local must be responsible . . .

The two friends are determined to find the culprit. But first, who can look after the mischievous fox cub?

PIGLET IN A PLAYPEN

Lucy Daniels

Ruby the piglet is the runt of the litter and there is no place for her on Greystones Farm. But she's cheeky and adventurous, and she's won the hearts of Mandy and James – they can't accept that Ruby has to go.

Can Mandy and James turn the under-sized piglet into a prize-winning pig?

ANIMAL ARK SERIES
LUCY DANIELS

All Hodder Children's books are available at your local bookshop or newsagent, or can be ordered direct from the publisher. Just tick the titles you want and fill in the form below. Prices and availability subject to change without notice.

Hodder Children's Books, Cash Sales Department, Bookpoint, 39 Milton Park, Abingdon, OXON, OX14 4TD, UK. If you have a credit card you may order by telephone – (01235) 831700.

Please enclose a cheque or postal order made payable to Bookpoint Ltd to the value of the cover price and allow the following for postage and packing:
UK & BFPO – £1.00 for the first book, 50p for the second book, and 30p for each additional book ordered up to a maximum charge of £3.00.
OVERSEAS & EIRE – £2.00 for the first book, £1.00 for the second book, and 50p for each additional book.

Name ....

Address ....

....

....

If you would prefer to pay by credit card, please complete:
Please debit my Visa/Access/Diner's Card/American Express (delete as applicable) card no:

Signature ....

Expiry Date ....